ANTICIPATION OF EVIL

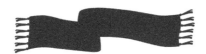

LYLA FAIRCLOTH ELLZEY

DocUmeant *Publishing*
244 5th Avenue
Suite G-200
NY, NY 10001
646-233-4366
www.DocUmeantPublishing.com

ANTICIPATION OF EVIL

Published by
DocUmeant Publishing
244 5th Ave, Suite G-200
NY, NY 10001

646-233-4366

Edited by Philip S. Marks

Cover by Roslyn N McFarland

Formatted by DocUmeant Designs, www.DocUmeantDesigns.com

Library of Congress Number: 2019937780

ISBN: 978-1-950075-00-3

"FEAR IS PAIN ARISING FROM THE ANTICIPATION OF EVIL."

—Aristotle, Greek Philosopher, 384–322 BC

Dedication

This book is dedicated to both the survivors of crimes committed against them by the amoral and the evil minded—and to the law enforcement officials who work ceaselessly towards the apprehension of same in order to gain justice for their victims.

Acknowledgments

I offer my heartfelt thanks to everyone involved with bringing this book to publication. From the workshop by Vic DiGenti where the title and topic were inspired by an exercise in which I wrote the rudiments of a story built around the word "winter", to the various members of my critique groups, some of whom saw this novel evolve from its infancy to its full-blown finale.

To my publisher, Ginger Marks of DocUmeant Publishing and my cover designer, Roslyn McFarland, also of DocUmeant Publishing, New York, NY. I thank you both and am thrilled to have had my work in the hands of such capable professionals.

To my husband, Frank Ellzey, I thank him for his encouragement and for allowing me to have the computer on with its light shining and the accompanying noises as I worked at my desk many, many times into the wee hours while he lay sleeping in our bed a mere foot or two away.

To Pat Stanford, President of Tallahassee Writers Association and award winning author, thank you for your positive endorsement of this novel.

In the near future, may we all work together to produce a second novel of which I am also inordinately proud.

Further acknowledgement is made to several publications in which other of my work appears:

1. The Seven Hills Review, Tallahassee, FL. (Several short stories and an excerpt from this novel appear in three editions of the *Review*)
2. Heartscapes Anthology, Plainfield, VT. (Short story—Romance)

3. Odet Anthology, Safety Harbor, FL. (Short story, Second Place Win in Florida Stories)
4. Baker County Writing Contest Review, CA. (Short story, First place win in Children's Lit)

Chapter One

June 22, 2013

She sat on a bar stool with her lovely long legs crossed at the knees and her tight white skirt riding up her tanned thighs. Dangling a red high-heeled sandal from the toes of one foot, she hooked the other on the rung of her bar stool. The killer watched her as she laughed up into the faces of the young students surrounding her, each eager to attract her attention and to be the man of the hour with the beautiful blonde who tossed her shoulder length curls with every movement of her head.

Stopped short by her striking resemblance to Joanie and the mannerisms which were duplicates of hers, he instantly decided he had to punish her for that. At six feet, three inches, he knew he made a handsome figure as he moved to stand near her, easing his way in among the adoring young men. Standing to her left, out of range of her peripheral vision, he waited for her to look his way. Lifting his right hand, he swept his dark hair off his forehead.

Anticipating her reaction to his hungry blue-eyed gaze, he wasn't disappointed. She smiled broadly at something one of the men said and shook her head, making her glorious mass of curls dance around her face. Lifting her left hand, which bore a platinum engagement ring with a modest sized diamond solitaire sitting atop it, she brushed aside the curls that now obscured part of her face. She glanced to her left and her eyes met his.

For an instant she faltered, the teasing talk forgotten as her smile faded and died. She must have seen something hypnotic in his steady stare, for she slid as if oiled from the barstool and turned to him. He offered her his right hand with his carefully manicured nails. She didn't hesitate as she slipped her left hand into his. Neither spoke, nor did they break eye contact, as they turned and walked away from the astonished would-be lotharios.

They walked through the bar, seemingly unaware of their surroundings, neither appearing to notice the opulent green forest décor with real fichus trees planted in large bronze urns or the patrons ordering from the bartender. They looked only at each other.

He stopped with his hand on the door and searched her face with his eyes. He had to know.

"What's your name?"

"Ginette. My friends call me Ginnie."

It was enough. He knew he had chosen the right one.

"Tell me your name."

He smiled, showing white teeth, which were even except for the slightly longer canines. "I'll tell you later, I promise."

"Ooohhh. A man with secrets. I like that," she said, bringing a broader smile to his lips.

As they walked to his car parked in a lot up the street, he continued to clasp her hand in his. Her engagement ring felt as if it were burning his fingers. He turned his face away and his smile became a grimace. She was another cheating bitch who had to pay. He knew it was his duty to see that she did.

At his apartment with its soundproofed walls, he savored the smell and taste of her in his big king bed, making love to her gently—the first time. The second time, the lovemaking became violent and the bewildered Ginnie endured a painful savaging of her body.

He restrained her with his hand on her throat as he deposited a trail of bite marks on her breasts and across her abdomen. Flipping her over, he bit her buttocks until blood was flowing.

She fought him for a while, screaming and shrieking in pain. She struck out with her hands and arms, but he simply caught her wrists in one hand and slapped her fiercely with the other. She tried kicking him with her feet. He laughed at her struggles and straddled her, his heavier weight rendering her nearly immobile. Ginnie bucked and writhed but could not dislodge him and the torture and misery continued. After a while it seemed she tuned out the horror that was happening to her as he used her body in every way his perverted mind could envision. High with glee, he wrapped his hands around her throat and pressed. He watched her as she died without a sound, as if her senses had vacated her body, with no objection save perhaps a look of reproach in her dull eyes as they dimmed further until their light was finally extinguished.

He drove away from the heavily populated area and dumped her body in the Seine.

Bagged and stuffed deep into a refuse bin, it was unlikely her clothes would ever be found in such a rural area. The bite marks didn't worry him. Nowhere in France was there an x-ray of his teeth on file. The next day he was on a plane back to the US, now a graduate of the prestigious Sorbonne.

About the same time the killer was disposing of Ginette, another tale was being told in Gainesville, Florida.

Heather Forrest was free. She'd been free of school work and studies for the last few short, sun-filled weeks. Since graduating from the University of Florida with a Master's Degree in English Education, she'd lived at home with her parents. To remain there, or in Florida at all, wasn't in her plans.

She stood in front of a wall map of the United States, closed her eyes, and turned around three times. She placed a fingertip on the map and snapped open her eyes. Her fingertip lay just south of Lake Michigan, resting atop Green Bay, Wisconsin. Heather paused a moment to absorb what it meant for her. A smile lit her face.

As she set the table for dinner, she broached the subject to her parents. "Guess what! I'm moving to Green Bay."

"No. You can't move that far away," her mother said, and turned away to take the biscuits from the oven, dismissing the subject all together.

"Mom!" Heather shrieked. "This is something I really want to do."

"You don't know one thing about how to get around in the type of winters Green Bay has," her dad argued.

She drummed her fingers on the table. Suddenly she jumped up, adrenalin pumping. "I'm not staying in Florida all my life. I want to experience something completely different. I'm going!"

Her parents didn't give their blessings, but did say she would always have their love. That would do.

She said goodbye to her friends and packed her car with her most needed possessions and checked Google for the best route. She arrived in Green Bay six days later.

Heather rented an apartment and secured a teaching job at a local high school. Mr. Aslaksen, the principal, interviewed her. He was quite professional and encouraging. She liked him.

Dancing down the hall after leaving the interview, Heather threw her fist toward the lighted ceiling in the *Rocky* arm-thrust. She was as confident as Sylvester Stallone had been in the movie. It wasn't a boxing match she had won; it was the beginning of her career. She had no doubts the next years would be exciting and would fulfill her goal of making a positive difference in the lives of her students and helping prepare them for adulthood.

December 5, 2014

Now in her second year of teaching, Heather looked into the face of her troubled Senior English student, Patti Mueller. "You will pass this test, Patti. There's no way you can possibly fail it." She looked away, trying not to show her impatience. Without realizing it, her right hand lifted to her thick reddish-brown hair and she wrapped a curl around her forefinger.

"I don't know, Miss Forrest. I just can't seem to keep all those helping verbs in my head. I know I was supposed to learn them in eighth grade, but I didn't. And I'm hopeless with adjectives and adverbs, not to mention infinitives and shit like that."

Patti gasped and quickly covered her mouth with her hand. "I'm sorry," she blurted.

Heather ignored the mild profanity. "There's a pattern to memorizing the helping verbs, Patti."

Heather withdrew her hand from her curls and picked up a sheet of paper from her desk. "Here, take this. It'll tell you the order in which to memorize them, and it'll make sense why you learn them this way." She handed the paper to Patti.

Patti looked down and squirmed in her seat. She wrinkled her nose. "Okay, I'll try. It'll be hard to find a place to study at home with my dad nosing into everything I do." She wrapped a blonde curl around her forefinger and let it go. It sprang back to nest with the others. She repeated this action as Heather watched her.

"I'm sorry, Patti. Some dads are like that." She glanced away, gathering her thoughts. She returned her gaze to Patti.

"It sounds like it bothers you. Does this mean you don't have a good relationship with your father?"

"Oh, he's not so bad when he's not drinking. I mean he doesn't beat me or anything. He just gets all up in my business."

"I understand how that goes." Heather gave the girl a sympathetic smile. "You know you can talk to me about anything that's bothering you. By the way, how did it go with your Goth friends when you told them you didn't want to hang with them anymore?"

Patti began to giggle; then it turned into a full laugh. "Sid says I've lost my mind and that I'll come back begging to be his friend. Hah! As if!"

"What about your girlfriends?"

Patti raised her chin and her merriment was replaced by a frown. "They can all kiss my butt. I'm tired of playing dress up and hanging around with just them. It's gotten really old."

Delighted, Heather grabbed one of Patti's hands between her palms and squeezed. "I'm pleased you ended those relationships, Patti. You go, girl! You find another group of friends. Someone you can study with and do fun things with."

Patti blessed her with one of her rare smiles.

"Now, try your best, Patti, and you'll do fine on the test." She checked her watch. "I've got to run, so I'll see you Monday."

She waited while Patti gathered her papers, put them in her book bag, and opened the door.

"Bye." Patti said. She waved and the door slammed shut behind her.

"Patti." Heather said under her breath as she shook her head and sighed. "I can't help but worry about you." She got up from her chair and got the papers and books from her desk she would need over the weekend and headed off to meet with her boyfriend and fellow teacher, Jeff Hoffmann.

She found Jeff in the hallway where he was saying goodbye to several of his Senior History students from his last class of the day. Jeff was a popular teacher and, like her, he often stayed late to talk with one or more of his students. Unlike her, his was usually not counseling or helping with studies. His students liked to hang around and talk sports with him. Jeff was a huge Green Bay Gamblers Ice Hockey fan and she had learned to love the sport through him. It wasn't a sport she grew up with in Florida.

"Hello, Mr. Hoffmann," she greeted him as she neared the group. She nodded and smiled to the students.

Jeff flashed a grin, his eyes twinkling behind his eyeglasses. "Miss Forrest. Good to see you."

To the students he said, "Okay you guys, I'll see you Monday. Have a good weekend. I need to speak with Miss Forrest."

The students left, heading for the exit doors, calling to each other and to Jeff to have a good weekend and to watch out for the forecasted snow.

Speaking low, Jeff said, "I wonder how long before they figure it out."

"You mean about us?"

"Right. They don't know I'm living with the prettiest, and I might add, the sexiest, teacher in this whole school."

Heather grinned. "And what will all the girls who are in love with you think when they find out? They'll hate my guts!"

Jeff laughed aloud, his voice echoing in the now empty halls.

Heather rifled through the frozen meal-size dinners filling their freezer to find something that might interest both of them. "How about chicken picatta with linguini?" she called to Jeff.

"Sounds all right to me," Jeff answered as he sorted through the mail. "Damn! There are letters still being forwarded here from my parent's old address. I bet some of them go to Fox Towers, too. I hope that stops soon. Mom doesn't need to know my business before I do."

"Right," Heather agreed, as she started water to boil for the pasta.

While they ate their dinner, Heather spoke of her day and the session afterward with Patti Mueller. "Jeff, she is so different from my other students. But, you know what? I really like her. She speaks her mind. She's so earthy. I guess that's the word I'm looking for to describe her. I do worry about her, though. There have been several times when I think she is on the brink of telling me something, and then she abruptly stops."

"What do you think it could be?"

"I truly have no idea."

"This girl spends a lot of time with you after class, doesn't she?"

"Yes, she does. But, you know, Jeff, that's all right. I hope maybe she'll open up to me soon."

"She probably will. I'd open up to you anytime. Want to see?"

"Oh, Jeff, you are such a nut! The answer is yes, I want to see. Let's leave the dishes for the night and go get in bed."

"Didn't I say you were the sexiest teacher in our school? Maybe you are the sexiest teacher in any school." He took her hand and pulled her from her chair. As they started up the stairs, Jeff was already pulling his sweater over his head. Heather chuckled and swatted his behind, then reached for the hem of her own sweater.

December 12, 2014

He watched her walk toward the frozen pond. He'd observed her every afternoon for three days, hidden as she trekked across the snow and pools of ice and, today, the cold, brittle grass of the golf course, dodging the snow dunes and patches of melting snow. Now, again with the promise of snow in the air, she hurried along, zipped into her coat, its hue a faded hunter green that should have been warmer for this cold weather, the kind that can suck the air from the lungs and freeze exposed skin. She continued walking with her head bent as the wind's icy breath sent her red and green plaid scarf tails dancing in its breeze.

Safe from view in his spot behind the small pond, he again reviewed his strategy. His heart began a snare drum beat as she stepped onto the surface of the pond, testing it with her weight. She started to slide down the slight dip of the pond on one rubber-soled boot, then the other, until she was passing him and his hiding place.

He fought to silence his ragged breaths. On silent soles, he quickly reached her, his longer legs making up for her lead. Just as he raised his hands to encircle her neck, she whipped around, staring wildly until her eyes registered recognition.

"You nearly scared me to death." Catching her breath, she smiled. "I'm glad you came today. I've been here every day waiting for you. I was starting to worry something had happened to our plan." She began to lean into him.

He let loose the grin he couldn't control. Lightning fast, like a giant snake striking, he made his move, grabbing her and turning her back into his body. Seeing her mouth drop open and her eyes widen in surprise and, yes, hurt, shot a familiar thrill throughout him. With his right hand, he grabbed her right shoulder and yanked her body back, slamming her hard against his chest. His fingers dug into her flesh through the layers of clothing.

"What are you doing?" She screamed, her arms flailing as she tried to twist away. She managed to peer over her shoulder as tears spilled from her eyes.

He heard her try to say "Stop it! Please stop!" Her words were almost unintelligible as she continued trying to twist out of his grasp.

Ecstatic that he was doing what he'd wanted from the beginning, his left hand snared the end of the scarf that dipped and swirled on her left side, sent into a spiral by a gust of wind. He braced his strong, heavy arm across her chest, immobilizing her. Tugging on the left scarf tail, and momentarily taking his arm from her chest, he pulled the tail on the right side, jerking her head straight forward. He chuckled low in his throat as she grunted and moaned, making indiscernible sounds, and tried to kick him backward with her heels.

He grappled with her heaving body until her hands dropped from her neck and her knees buckled. She slumped to the un-giving ice. He bent forward with her and eased her down. Backing off her still form, he stood up and looked down at his victim. He pulled his left foot from beneath her body and turned to leave.

He stopped abruptly and bent over her again. Throwing aside the fluttering scarf tails, he searched for the top of the coat's zipper. Grabbing the coat's hem, he yanked it down to free space to locate it. A quick unzip and the coat was opened to below her breasts. Reaching inside the scooped neck of her pullover sweater, his fingers felt the object he was searching for. A sharp tug and it was secure in his gloved hand.

Standing again, he remained almost motionless as he took another long look around to reassure himself there was still no one out and about to observe him.

The killer turned back and gazed at the body for another few moments. To him, she looked so much smaller in death than in life. He bent and positioned her so he could see her eyes. They were open and staring, the dark blue irises beginning to glaze and fade.

He laughed aloud at the thought of all the woodland creatures joining all the domestic creatures and all of them having her as a true moveable feast.

His excitement turned to jubilation. On boots that he had widened and elongated with the coverings he had placed on the soles, he walked away. No way would the police be able to trace this murder back to him. He crunched across the white blanket of snow. One last look back and he disappeared into the trees that bordered the golf course on the far side. With his spirits soaring and elated with his cleverness, he threw back his head and the giggles bursting forth from his throat became a full bellied laugh, roaring from his mouth in great gusts of sound.

Chapter Two

All they wanted was to find out if the pond was frozen.

Heather and Jeff found the entrance to the golf course blocked, so they balanced their bikes against a snow bank and crept between two of the large houses that backed up to the exclusive club and course. They picked their way across the patchy snow and ice toward the pond, laughing at their daring-do, acting like the teenagers they once were just a few years ago.

All day Heather had anticipated this outing since their discussion about it at breakfast.

They were having an unusual break in the snow and ice, especially for a December day in Green Bay. They decided Heather would take her bike to school in her car since Jeff's was already there in the gym. If the weather held, and the forecasters said it would, they would go for a bike ride on the cleared roads and sidewalks.

"I'd love to get out in the fresh air for a while. I can't believe this last snow is almost all melted. Gosh, it's almost like December in Florida," Heather said. "I'm getting excited."

"Yeah. Me, too. We might even go out to the golf course and see if the little pond is frozen enough for us to skate on it."

"Well, maybe," Heather hedged. She still wasn't comfortable with ice skating, much less on a pond where she might drop through the ice into the freezing depths.

Their plan was for Heather to wait at her car and Jeff would join her there after classes were finished. Heather had but moments ago finished stuffing herself into all the warm clothing she needed for the bike ride on this windy day, when Jeff arrived. She had on her new L.L. Bean all terrain parka with down lining. It was warm and it was red. She felt special in it. She'd never had such a coat in her life.

"Just let me get my boots on and we're off." She slid her stockinged feet into them. "I hope my toes won't get too cold without heavy socks." She slapped the Velcro strap across the stationary one. "Ready."

Straddling the bike, she pushed off as Jeff led the way onto the bike path. The wind reddened her cheeks and cooled her face, which had felt warm all day in the heat of the school room. As a southern girl, she had not yet gotten used to the high temperatures at which these northern folks set their heat. She figured there was some reverse psychology going on there somewhere. Coming from Florida, one would think she would require flames to shoot from the thermostat as she was unaccustomed to such cold weather. But, she liked it on the cooler side.

Their ride brought them to the Christa McAuliffe Park, so named for the school teacher who had died in the explosion of the Challenger space shuttle so many years before. She had not yet been born when the disaster occurred in January of 1986, putting in doubt the future of the space shuttle program. And now it had ended and she felt that Christa had given her life for nothing. But, those seconds between liftoff and the explosion must have been one hell of a ride!

She remembered for years, on the anniversary of the tragedy, the endless playing on TV of the shuttle Challenger rising off the launch pad, shooting into the air, then a spectacular growing cloud of white as it exploded, showering the skies with burning debris and smoke trails as they plummeted back to earth. It would soon be time for another anniversary. She shuddered, unable to imagine death on such a day when she felt so full of life in the cold, bracing air in which she pedaled her bike.

Jeff motioned they were stopping and she brought her bike to a halt by his. They put down their kickstands and left the bikes to go play like children on the bars and swings meant for much younger and smaller individuals.

"I'll bet you can't do this," Heather taunted as she hopped without effort onto a 2 x 4 board set on sawhorses that looked similar to the ones used by gymnasts in the Olympics for the balance beam competitions. She strode to one end of the board and executed a pirouette even with heavy winter boots. She stuck a hip out in one direction and then the other hip to the opposite side and lifted her leg toward her chest, swayed precariously, and then regained her balance. She giggled and took a few steps toward the other end and jumped off.

"Bravo," Jeff said, and then demonstrated his ability to walk a pole that stretched between another set of sawhorses and was firmly attached at each end. "Think you can do that?"

She watched him climb down and then narrowed her eyes at him. "Of course, I can, silly. Watch this." She executed the walk perfectly.

"Yeah, well I haven't had all the years of gymnastics you've had. While you were prancing around on balance beams in the southern sunshine, I was freezing my ass off skating on frozen ponds practicing for hockey games."

Jeff grabbed her waist and lifted her off the cleared rubber matting and twirled them both around in circles. "God, isn't it wonderful to be outside, free, and just having fun?" He set her down. "Oh, and speaking of being able to do gymnastics, it reminds me of playing basketball. I remember what you told me about playing in the sweltering hot gyms in the south and dripping sweat on everything."

"Yeah?"

"Well, the kids aren't dripping sweat. But when I went in to get my bike, the varsity team was on the floor practicing. There was this one kid, skinny as a beanpole, who could hit a jump shot from just about anywhere on the court. He looked about twelve years old. Anyway, I heard the senior boys call him "Mueller." I wonder if he's your Patti's brother?"

"I don't know. He could be. She said she had a younger brother."

He lowered his head to her upturned face and his warm mouth descended to hers. The kiss was long and sweet and reminded Heather they'd been too busy and tired the past few nights to make love. This kiss was a prelude of what was to come when they snuggled in their bed that night.

Jeff lifted his head and continued to look into her eyes. Hers reflected what he was feeling. He held her close in another hug and let her go. "I have an idea," he said.

"You do? What is it?"

"Speaking of frozen ponds, let's bike over to the golf course and check out that little pond I was telling you about this morning. If it is frozen, and the weather is still good tomorrow, we can come back and skate."

Heather's lips turned down, a reversal of her upturned smile.

"I know you're not comfortable yet with skating outside, but I promise you I know when it's safe to skate on a frozen pond. I've done it hundreds of times. So, let's go have a look."

She half-smiled at him and took his gloved hand in hers. "You know that scares me, but I trust you. There's no telling what we'll find. I'm hoping to find the pond is *not* frozen."

Now here they were picking their way across the patchy ice and snow of the elite golf course known as The Golf Club.

"Where's the pond?" Heather asked.

Jeff jerked his head to the left, "Over that way."

They headed in the direction Jeff indicated. Heather stopped suddenly and gasped, "Jeff, it looks like someone is lying on the pond! He must have had an accident."

"You're right, if he was shoveling snow off the surface, he may have had a heart attack."

Heather dropped Jeff's hand and started running toward the person lying on the pond. Jeff began to run as well, and his longer legs brought him to the bank's edge where his momentum took him down the soft slope. He ended up dancing to keep his balance on the edge of the frozen pond. Heather careened into him and they both went down hard and landed beside the person who lay there. Heather got to her knees over the figure and drew in a deep, shaky breath.

"Patti! Oh, my God! Jeff, it's Patti! You know, *my* Patti! The one I've been telling you about. We have to help her. Quick, Jeff!"

Heather took Patti's face between her palms. "She's so cold. Oh, Lord, let's see if I can warm her up a bit." She quickly stripped off her red parka while Jeff tried to find a pulse in the limp wrist protruding from the too short sleeve. He shook his head.

He placed his fingertips on Patti's neck under her jawline and moved them about. "I can't find a pulse here either, Heather."

"Oh no! We've got to do something. We have to save her!" Heather ripped the zipper down its remaining length and spread open the green coat. She laid her ear against Patti's chest. "I can't hear a heartbeat!" She then bent to feel for breath from Patti's nose and mouth. "I can't feel any breath, Jeff. She's not breathing!"

She grabbed the red parka from the ice where it had fallen and covered Patti's lower body before immediately straddling the prone figure and placing her hands at her breastbone. She began to count as she administered CPR. She bent forward and held Patti's nose with one hand and blew rhythmically into her mouth, desperately hoping to fill her lungs with air. Between breaths, she said, "Call 911 Jeff. Maybe they can save her."

Jeff had his cell phone in his hand and was already punching in 911.

It had taken but a few moments for the discovery and attempt to give CPR, but it seemed a lifetime as Heather continued to press both hands, one atop the other, flat against Patti's breastbone as she tried to pump life back into the cooling body. Patti's open eyes never moved.

Soon, there was the sound of wailing sirens and a police SUV pulled up to the blocked gate along with an ambulance. Heather slid off Patti and tugged up the red parka to cover Patti's chest as two police officers appeared. They'd come between the houses, as had Heather and Jeff, and an ambulance crew bearing a stretcher followed them.

"Thank God you're here," Heather called out.

One of the uniformed officers identified himself as Officer Schroeder and introduced his partner as Officer Heimerle, throwing the words over his shoulder as they rushed to the figure on the pond.

They squatted beside Patti's body and gently removed Heather's parka.

"That's mine." Heather said. "I was trying to keep her warm."

Officer Heimerle searched for a pulse, first feeling her wrist and then her neck. His face remained expressionless leaving Heather unsure what he was detecting. Heimerle continued to examine the body without moving it.

Schroeder went to Heather and Jeff and squatted where they sat huddled together on the bank. "Do you know this young woman?"

"Yes, I do," Heather said, as she wiped her eyes and cheeks. She cleared her throat. "She's a student of mine. I teach her Senior English. Or did, rather." She sniffed. "Her name is Patti Mueller." *I've got to get a grip. They need me now so I can't fall apart.*

"Okay. I'll call it in," Schroeder said to Heimerle. He looked to the entrance between the houses. "Here comes Maggie, now."

To Heather and Jeff, he said, "She's the medical examiner and forensics expert. She'll soon know what happened here."

Officer Heimerle stood. "Now that Maggie is here, we'll need to take you down to the police station so you can answer a few questions for us."

"What about our bikes?" Jeff asked.

"We'll put them in the back of the SUV and take them to the station with you," Schroeder answered.

At the Green Bay District D Headquarters, Captain Pieter Harjula prepared to address the two he considered among the best detectives anywhere.

He watched Aksel Franzen and Anja Frandsen enter his office and nodded for them to take seats in the two faux leather chairs that sat before his desk.

"Officers Heimerle and Schroeder have returned from The Golf Club where the body of a teen girl was found. Two schoolteachers discovered her while walking on the course. They questioned the couple and she was a student of the woman teacher. They are questioning them further right now."

"Any girls reported missing at any time today?" Aksel Franzen asked.

"Nope. Nothing."

"Do we have an address for the girl's family yet?"

"No. Not that, either. But we'll have it soon."

"Thanks, Captain," said Anja.

In a room down a hallway from the Captain's office, Heather and Jeff were answering questions from the two officers who brought them in.

"Yes, I knew Patti fairly well—as any teacher would know her student."

"What does that mean?" Heimerle asked.

Heather twisted a curl around her finger as she pondered her answer. She ventured, "I liked Patti. I often gave her extra time after school with lessons she needed help with. I had a session with her last Friday in my classroom after school was dismissed. I also saw her in my class Monday and Tuesday of this week. She hadn't been there for these last three days."

"Did you know of anyone who wanted to harm her? Perhaps . . ."

Heather broke in. "There isn't any hope that it was an accident? Like maybe she fell and hit her head really hard?"

"I don't know, ma'am."

"Then no. Of course not. She never confided anything like that to me. She never said anything about anyone harming her."

Officer Schroeder placed one hip on the table and leaned down to look into Heather's and Jeff's eyes. "What were you doing out there today? Strange you should be walking in the snow on the course."

Jeff explained they had left their cars at the school and were biking out to see if the little pond was frozen so they could perhaps skate on it. Schroeder nodded his head and looked to his partner. Heimerle nodded.

"All right. I think that will be all for tonight. You will likely be questioned more tomorrow, so be prepared." He stood up. "Now we'll take you to the high school to get your cars."

Detective Aksel Franzen parked the SUV at the entrance to The Golf Club and the two detectives climbed over the mounded snow. The lights the department had set up illuminated the area and it was about a fifty-yard walk to the crime scene. They trod through the icy snow and found the marked location where the body was found near the edge of the pond. The uniforms had kept the crime scene area secured.

"I've taken all the pictures I could until you had a look," Jerry, the police photographer announced. "When you're ready, I'll take the rest."

"That's good, Jerry," Anja Frandsen said. "Were you able to get decent pictures with just these lights?" She pointed to the big halogen lights run by generators which lit the scene.

"Oh yes. I got some good ones, including footprints leading away."

Aksel was squatting by the chalk drawing and now he moved to one knee, allowing him to examine it more closely.

"According to the ME, there was no bullet wound or knife wound. By the way her face looked, I'd say she was choked to death," Jerry volunteered. "I got some pictures of her face and a scarf wound around her neck."

The detectives examined the ice of the pond and the snow surrounding it. They trailed the footprints that headed toward the woods as far as the halogen lights lit them. Aksel took his large and powerful flashlight from his belt and followed them until they disappeared inside the woods.

"It looks like some kind of cover was placed on the bottoms of the shoes. The indent was heavier in the middle and quite light on the toe ends."

Anja rose from the footprints she was studying. "You're right. Let's get to the morgue."

Aksel opened the door to the morgue and led the way. Inside and bent over an exam table was Maggie Green.

"I bet it was the murdering son-of-a-bitch who knocked her up, too," she opined by way of greeting.

"You're telling me she was pregnant?"

"Yes, Detective Franzen, that's exactly what I'm saying." She did nothing to hide the anger in her voice.

"What else can you tell us, Maggie?" Anja looked down at the body.

Maggie pointed at the girl's neck. "From the bruising on the neck and the knot in her scarf, it appears the scarf was pulled tight, cutting off her breath. We're looking for someone quite strong. I don't think your average female could have pulled it that tight."

"So, you think it was a man who did it? That bit, and the pregnancy, sure sounds like a man," Anja said.

"I think that's our most likely scenario. See, the blood has settled here . . ." She swept her fingers from the middle of Patti's forehead down to her ear. Lifting Patti's hair, exposing her neck and jaw, she placed her fingertips just below the jaw. "And here." Maggie raised her eyes to first Aksel and then to Anja. "Take a look at her eyes. See the hemorrhaging in both? That asshole pulled the scarf and choked her hard enough to burst all these blood vessels. There's no doubt that the intention was to kill her, not to just frighten her."

"What more have you found?"

"Besides her being pregnant, you mean?" Maggie's face darkened and she dropped her eyes to the dead girl.

"Her body looks clean and well cared for, even though her attire would suggest she comes from a home where there's not a lot of extra money. Of course, I've not gotten too far with the overall exam, but I'll have more information for you some time tomorrow."

"Thanks, Maggie." Anja opened the door to leave.

"Detectives?"

They both stopped and looked back at Maggie.

"Get the son-of-a-bitch."

Aksel said, "We will."

"Oh, and Maggie . . ." Anja started.

Maggie looked up from her perusal of the body, appearing to be already deep into plans for her next incision. "Yes?"

Anja continued, "Let's hold back the pregnancy bit. That will be the thing we keep out of the news in case we get some hop-head strung out on drugs who wants to clear his soul by admitting to the murder. We may discern if he's telling the truth by whether or not he knows about the pregnancy."

"Good idea. It's a done deal. Now stop fooling around and go catch the bastard."

Detectives Franzen and Frandsen found the area of town in which the Muellers lived and drove down their street to get a feel for what the neighborhood was like. It had small houses with little variation in the architectural detail. Most houses and yards were decorated for Christmas.

They parked in front of the Mueller home at the curb. In front of them was a car about ten years old and in need of a paint job. A newer model, but only by a year or so, sat in the driveway and they passed it on their way to the front door. Lights were still on in the front of the house so Frandsen rang the doorbell.

"Yeah, yeah, I'm coming," a male voice called from behind the locked door. It was opened by a man wearing socks, jeans, and a red and black checked flannel shirt. "Yeah?" he repeated.

"Mr. Mueller?" Detective Frandsen asked.

"Who wants to know?"

Franzen held up his identification and Mueller squinted at it in the dim yellow light that spilled from the door. "I'm detective Aksel Franzen and this is my partner Anja Frandsen. May we come in?"

"What's this about?"

Detective Frandsen stepped forward. "Sir, we'll be glad to explain everything to you but we'd like to do it inside your home."

"Well, that makes sense, I suppose." He moved aside and they entered a small living room that served as the TV room and gathering place in this small tract home of three bedrooms, a bathroom and a kitchen/dining room combo. It did resemble every other house on the block except it had a bedraggled, carelessly decorated Christmas tree in a corner of the room, where most of the neighboring houses had gaily decorated trees situated in their windows and brightly twinkling lights strung about the outsides of their homes.

Mr. Mueller was fidgeting, picking at the gnawed index fingernail on his left hand as he watched them observe his living room. They said nothing about the Green Bay Packers afghan that lay mostly on the floor where it slid off the sagging sofa. Detective Franzen looked pointedly at the blaring TV and raised his eyebrows.

Mueller got the not so subtle hint and picked up the remote control from the floor by the afghan and turned off the TV.

In the resulting quiet Anja Frandsen asked, "May we also speak with Mrs. Mueller?"

He turned toward the hall that passed the kitchen and led to the bedrooms at the back of the house. "Elsa!" he yelled. He listened for a response. Getting none, he yelled again, "Elsaaaa!"

"What?" Her voice preceded her up the hall. She stopped abruptly when she saw the detectives standing in her living room. "What's going on? Who are you?"

Aksel Franzen took the lead. "Mr. and Mrs. Mueller, we're detectives investigating a crime." They showed their badges and waited while Mrs. Mueller compared the photos with their faces. "We've come about Patti. Do you know where she is tonight?"

The Muellers looked at each other and back at Franzen. "Why? Has something happened to her?" Dieter Mueller asked in a mildly curious tone.

Mrs. Mueller said, "Patti often stays out late. Sometimes she's with the wrong group of kids. Did they get arrested or something?"

Anja Frandsen answered, "No ma'am, she hasn't been arrested."

Aksel cut in as Mrs. Mueller opened her mouth to ask another question. "Please take a seat, won't you? We do have something to tell you."

He waited for them to sit, and after looking uneasily at each other they did, taking seats together on the worn gold and black plaid of the sagging sofa. Aksel looked at Anja, who came to stand by him in front of them.

Anja looked first at one, then the other, getting their full attention. "Mr. and Mrs. Mueller, a teen-aged girl who may be your Patti was found dead this afternoon." They looked up at her, totally uncomprehending, as if she were a space alien who had just walked into their living room. "We certainly hope it is not her, but there was no identification at the scene. We would like to accompany you to the morgue so you can see if it is Patti."

Mr. Mueller's face dropped, but his countenance immediately changed to one of indignation. "No, of course it's not her. Patti would never get herself into such a situation. It's some other kid."

Mrs. Mueller began to pick at the frayed edge of her sweater cuff, pulling the brown threads and twisting them between her fingers. "Patti stays out late and we often don't know exactly where she is. But this is impossible. It can't be Patti." She shook her head back and forth. "Uh-uh, no way."

"That's good. We are hoping it's not Patti. But we do need to make sure." Anja started to put her arm around Mrs. Mueller's shoulders.

Mrs. Mueller moved away and said, "I've got to ask Freddie. He'll know where she is tonight,"

"Who's Freddie?" Axle asked.

"Our son. He's Patti's younger brother," Mr. Mueller said. "Freddie!" he yelled. "The police are here. Come tell us where Patti is."

A younger teen boy burst into the room. "What? What's the matter? Where's Patti?"

Aksel said, "We were hoping you could tell us that."

"I don't know where Patti is. But, what's the problem? Has something bad happened?"

"We're not certain it is her, but a teen girl was found dead this afternoon and we're trying to identify her. Some of the leads pointed to Patti."

"No! It's not her. Patti can take care of herself. I know it's not her."

"Okay, then," Anja prompted. "Let's go to the morgue and rule Patti out. We can all go in the police SUV. It gets around pretty well at night on these frozen roads."

As everyone started for the door, she added, "You might want to get your coats."

They all donned their outerwear and hurried to the SUV, seemingly anxious to get to the morgue and find out it was not Patti's body they would be viewing.

Maggie Greene was waiting for them with a sheet pulled up to cover the girl's face. She wasn't anywhere near finished with the autopsy, so the sheet was there because it would be terrible for her parents to see what was being done to their daughter's body in the effort to get to the truth of her death. Maggie pulled the sheet down and away from Patti's face and tucked it under her chin. Around her lower hairline and jaw, lividity was dark purple where the blood had settled and was in sharp contrast to the bloodless lips.

Freddie ran to the table and was the first to see her. "Oh my God, it *is* Patti," he bleated. He turned to his mom, perhaps seeking comfort, but Elsa had her arms crossed over her chest as if to ward off a direct blow to her heart. She was the next to look.

"Who would do this to my daughter?" Mrs. Mueller wailed and began to cry.

"By God, I'll round up the son of a bitch and kill his ass!" Mr. Mueller blustered.

"It can't be. It just can't be!" Freddie repeated, and again sought his mother.

"Not now, Freddie. Patti needs me now." Mrs. Mueller gently touched Patti's face and traced the outline of her lips before she tucked some stray wisps of blonde hair behind her ear. "Yes, this is my daughter. This is Patti."

Dieter stared down at his daughter's body as if trying to memorize every detail. "I'll get the bastard who did this to you, Patti. I swear." And then so quietly that they weren't entirely sure he'd spoken, he confirmed, "Yes. That's my girl. That's Patti, all right."

Maggie was all business with Aksel and Anja. "All right detectives. She's been identified as Patti Mueller by her mother, her father, and her brother. Now fill out the paperwork and be sure to get it signed before you leave them tonight."

She turned to the Muellers. "I'm sorry for your loss." Maggie's eyes and voice told them she meant it.

All was eerily quiet on the drive back to the Muellers' home. Anja had, by the light of an LED flashlight, finished the necessary paperwork by the time they got to the Mueller's house. Aksel flooded the car with the golden glow of the overhead light and Anja passed the Muellers the sheet of paper that required their signatures as the parties who identified the body at the morgue. All three Muellers signed and then rather unsteadily exited the car and headed into their home . . . their refuge. Their house would be changed forever by the evil that found Patti this day and claimed her for its own.

After their return to headquarters, the detectives went in search of Captain Harjula to make their report. They found him standing with his hands clasped behind his back and looking up at the large plaque that the local Friends of Police had presented to him and District D. He earnestly looked at the wording as if trying to imprint it on his brain. Anja and Aksel stood behind him and read the words also. It was a lofty sentiment. One they saw every day. Today, however, the words seemed to have special meaning for all three officers.

"We, the men and women of the Green Bay Police Department are dedicated to providing service through a partnership with the community that builds trust, reduces crime, creates a safe environment, and enhances the quality of life in our neighborhood."

The captain turned to them and threw a hand up to indicate the plaque's wording.

"Look. Those are our goals. We're sworn to uphold them just as we do our oath. I hope we can do that in this case." He heaved a deep sigh and wearily said, "Let me hear it."

They finished their report and placed on the captain's desk the written one that Anja had created during the drive home to the Muellers' from the morgue and the subsequent drive back to the station. Captain Harjula thanked them and looked up at the big schoolhouse clock on his wall.

"Twelve-oh-five. Time for you two to go home and get some rest. Start out with the school teachers in the morning. See if you can maybe jog Miss Forrest's memory. Maybe you can get her to think of something in the girl's behavior that seemed off somehow. She may have caught a glimpse of something that might be a lead. Okay, go home!"

The detectives left the building, heading for their vehicles. The air was crisp and cold and the sky was dark and clear.

Inside Aksel's bachelor apartment, he removed his gun belt. Entering his bedroom, he hung it from a metal rack which was attached to the wall above the small bedside lamp. It was easy to get to on those mornings he found it difficult to make himself move from the comfort of his bed.

He pulled off his heavy coat, the lighter weight jacket beneath it, then his shirt, and threw them in the direction of the side chair he kept in his bedroom for that purpose. Next, off came the heavy boots, the socks and the trousers. He sniffed the socks. *Nope. Not one more day's wear left in them.* The shirt and trousers told much the same story. *I've got to find some time this weekend to take my clothes to the cleaners.* Also, he needed to find time to do all the laundry. His sheets could stand to be washed as well as his bath towels.

Aksel batted things around in the cupboard until he found a can of chili—extra spicy and guaranteed to give him heartburn. He opened it with the electric can opener, dumped the contents into a bowl and set it in the microwave. *Yum! Another nourishing dinner tonight. Or is it morning? Yes, it is morning, I think.*

He ate the chili while sprawled on his sofa with the TV tuned to the weather channel. He alternated shoveling spoons full of chili into his mouth with long swigs from the deep blood red wine in the bottle of inexpensive Cabernet Sauvignon he held in his left hand. Fortunately for the already stained denim fabric of his sofa, he drained the bottle without incident and scraped out any remaining bits of chili that adhered to the sides of the bowl and then licked the spoon.

Thinking he would get up at any moment and go to bed, Aksel fell asleep sitting up with his head resting on the back of the sofa. Sometime nearing dawn, he realized he was chilled. Instead of getting into his bed under warm covers, he stretched out on the sofa in his underwear and pulled the brown and tan afghan from the back of the sofa to cover with. The afghan his wife Barbara had made for him long ago. Back before their divorce.

In her pretty apartment with thick carpeting on the floors and decorated in the warm darker shades of teals and burgundies, Anja slipped out of her clothes and boots, hung up what was called for, and put the rest in her basket for soiled laundry. A warm, relaxing shower followed with a quick blow dry of her short, dark bob, and then she slid into soft pajamas and a cozy pink robe she'd madly splurged on when the temperatures started to drop below freezing. Anja added sock slippers to keep her feet warm while she heated a tasty frozen dinner of tilapia with capers in lemon sauce. She moisturized her face, paying particular attention to the fine lines around her eyes, etched deeper now due to the piercing winds of winter.

She turned on the TV to check the weather while she ate her fish dinner and sipped her cup of Earl Gray. Yes, more snow was on the way. The TV picture vanished with a click of the remote and she rose from her chair in her small dining area. A quick wash and rinse of her dishes followed by a liberal brushing of her teeth, and she was ready to end her day.

As she did every night, she checked her apartment door to make sure it was locked securely. That was the last thing to be done before she could sleep.

She padded in the soft glow thrown by the tea-pot-shaped night light to her bedroom and took off the fluffy robe. Slipping into her bed, she was transported to fragrant fields of lavender. Before sleep took her, Anja's last thought was of Patti Mueller and her killer. *I wonder what tomorrow will bring. Will he kill again?*

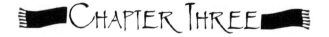

Chapter Three

December 13, 2014

Aksel Franzen woke to the theme song of the old TV series *Dragnet* coming from his cell phone. It sang and danced across the coffee table where he'd carelessly placed it last night.

"Yeah?" he growled into the phone.

"Aksel, it's me," Anja said. "I'm on my way to your house. Want me to pick you up some coffee?"

"What the hell time is it?"

"Seven thirty-eight."

"In the morning?" he asked with a great deal of irritation.

"Uh-oh. Sounds like Mama Franzen's baby boy got a little too deep into the fruit of the vine last night. It's a good thing I called. I'm stopping by to get me a tall coffee. Can I bring you some?"

"Oh, you sweet, sweet angel! Yes! Bring me about a gallon of high-test, black as sin and hot as the very fires of hell. You'll be my best friend forever!"

"I thought I already was. Be ready when I get there because we've got lots of work to do today."

Heather lay in bed in the same position she fell asleep in the night before, tucked into the crook of Jeff's body. Both distressed by the events of the day, they had lain close, each offering comfort to the other. The closeness had ended with them being intimate and they remained with Heather encircled in Jeff's arms as they slept. Now, since she was plastered against him, her hair was just below his nose. She awakened with a yawn and moved her head just enough to tickle his nose, causing him to sneeze. It was explosive and nearly blew them out of bed.

"Sorry, sorry, sweetheart! I tried to hold it in, but I just couldn't. Your hair was tickling my nose."

Instead of getting angry with him, Heather giggled at the remorse etched in his face and puppy dog eyes. He began to laugh with her and, at that moment, they were carefree again, and not thinking of the afternoon before. Their merriment was ended by the chiming doorbell, which was seasonally set and now played "Here Comes Santa Claus."

Jeff leapt out of the bed, snagged his flannel draw-string lounging pants from the hook on the closet door and said, "Who in the hell is ringing our doorbell this early on a Saturday morning?" just as Heather's happy mood was shredded and she whispered, "Oh God, I'll bet that's the detectives wanting to talk to us."

Every memory of the day before flooded her senses as Jeff took the stairs, heading down two at a time, probably to give somebody a piece of his mind. He unlocked and threw open the front door as Heather dragged herself off the bed to find something to put on.

"What do . . ." he began, but was interrupted by, "Good morning, Mr. Hoffmann. I'm Detective Aksel Franzen. My partner and I are assigned to the Patti Mueller case. May Detective Frandsen and I come in and ask you and Miss Forrest a few questions?"

"Wait a minute. I thought you just said *your* name was Franson." Jeff looked at Aksel like he must've heard wrong.

"Different spelling," they said in unison.

With a puzzled frown, Jeff ushered them into the living room where both detectives remained standing after taking off their heavy coats. Jeff turned his back to them as he laid the coats on the sofa. "I hope you don't have a lot of questions. We told all we know to the police yesterday afternoon."

Heather descended the stairs. She had thrown on a light robe over a speedily donned nightgown and was, like Jeff, barefooted.

Her gaze went from one to the other. "Y'all must be the police assigned to find Patti's murderer. Why don't you take a seat over here at the kitchen table and I'll put on some coffee." Her innate Southern hospitality was firmly in place.

Anja Frandsen nodded. "Sure, that would be lovely, Miss Forrest."

She looked at Aksel and nodded in the direction of the table. They both took seats as the coffee dripped and waited to gather what information was forthcoming.

"I need to go back upstairs and put on a shirt and some shoes before we start," Jeff said.

"Bring me my slippers, please, while you're up there, honey."

"Will do." Jeff looked at the detectives for their okay. A nod from Aksel sent him on his way while Heather busied herself putting some pistachio biscotti on a plate.

"Oh, you should've seen the mess here last night when we got home," Heather blurted with a nervous giggle. "I was so upset until I just let everything hit the floor. But I simply had to pick up and put away the boots and clothing we dropped just inside the door. I didn't want to do it, but even in the state I was in last night, I couldn't go to bed and leave it there." She wound down and was rescued from her nervous babbling by Jeff, who was back in no more than a couple of minutes.

He handed Heather her slippers and took a seat at the table. Soon he was up again and pouring the steaming coffee into four mugs while Heather put milk and sugar on the table. All but Aksel added milk and sugar to their mugs. He took a sip of his strong black brew then set it down to watch Heather slip her feet into her fuzzy slippers. She sat down at the table and took a sip from her coffee cup.

"Thanks for the coffee and cookies, Miss Forrest," Aksel began, "and now we need to know what you can tell us about Patti Mueller. I understand she was your student?"

Heather sniffed and reached for a tissue on the counter. Aksel moved the box closer to her and she pulled one free and honked in it like a Christmas goose. She blushed, her face turning deep pink at the unladylike sound. She laughed. Jeff laughed. Both detectives smiled.

"Yes. Well, Patti was in my Senior English class. We were working on grammar to learn the proper skills and for brushing up on those mostly forgotten. They need a refresher in grammar for writing those essays when applying for college. Patti was not an honor student. She had to study hard to maintain an average grade, so sometimes she would stay late after school for some special work with me."

Aksel looked at her sharply. "You didn't mind her taking up your time?"

"No, not at all. On the contrary, I enjoyed being with a student who had reached out to me for help."

"What kind of help did she want?"

"I thought it was just lessons that she wanted help with at first. Using grammar correctly, and the reasons why, is often hard to grasp for even the college freshman. However, as we got to feel comfortable with each other and she began to trust me, other reasons came out."

"And what would those be?"

"After the first few days, maybe three, she began to drop hints about her family life not being so great, how she was stupid, and her brother was her parents' favorite—things like that."

So, she used you as a counselor of sorts?"

"I'm not sure it was that so much as it was her need to talk to somebody who would listen to her. Maybe, because I'm younger than her other teachers, and also younger than the school guidance counselor, maybe she thought I'd understand more about what she so obviously wanted to talk about." "Did she talk about anything other than her home life?" Aksel cut in as Heather was saying "I can't think of anything specific that was alarming, but she did say that her dad drank too much, and they never had any money for anything, especially for her."

Aksel looked into his cup and saw it was still two-thirds full. "I simply cannot take another swallow." Realizing he'd said it aloud and in response to Heather's questioning look, he said, "No, no—it's good. I've simply had too much coffee today already. Let me ask a question instead. Did you get any vibe that there was more she wanted to confide?"

Heather looked at Jeff as if looking for inspiration. He shrugged as if he could be of no help. She concentrated on the question.

"Yes, there could've been more. She seemed to loosen up a little more every time we talked. I think she may have started to say something a couple of times but changed her mind." Heather closed her eyes and a tear rolled down each cheek. "I didn't push her. I'm sorry."

"Don't be. You couldn't know," Jeff said heatedly.

The detectives rose and gathered their overcoats.

Detective Franzen paused and turned back to Heather. "Could I maybe use your bathroom before we go?"

"Sure," Heather said, pointing to a closed door off a small hallway.

Closing the door behind him, Aksel hurriedly rifled through the contents of the vanity's drawers. Toothpaste, extra toothbrushes, lipsticks and lip balms. Careful to return everything to its original position, he then checked the medicine cabinet. He found ibuprofen and acetaminophen, but no prescription drugs. Toilet brush and extra toilet paper were under the sink. He pushed the toilet handle and was rewarded with a loud flush to cover any possible sound from closing the magnetic medicine cabinet door. Turning on the faucet, he zipped his hands under the cold water. Wringing his hands to dry them, he returned to the living room where the other three were discussing the weather.

At the questioning looks, he explained, "I didn't want to soil your pretty hand towels by drying on them."

"My goodness," Heather responded, "that would've been fine. I have to wash them occasionally, anyway."

"Well, thank you, Miss Forrest. And you, too, Mr. Hoffmann. You've been most helpful." He looked at his partner and, as one, the two detectives walked toward the door.

"We'll let you know if we need to speak with you again," he added. His voice was muffled as he slung his heavy coat around his shoulders.

Detective Anja Frandsen slipped into her coat. "Thank you both for your time, and for the coffee."

Aksel fought to keep the smile off his face as they got out the door. Heading toward their car, he mimicked in a girlish voice, "And for the coffee!" He kicked aside a lump of snow that had fallen into the street, watching as it sailed to rest atop the snow banks plowed to the side of the road. Looking sideways at Anja, he snorted, "I can't believe you even mentioned the word coffee. Where's the closest McDonald's so I can go pee before I explode?"

"Didn't you just pee?"

"No, I was checking out the drugs and things in their medicine cabinet."

Anja rolled her eyes.

After the detectives left, Jeff told Heather, "You've got to get your mind off this for a while, sweetheart. Why don't we go to a game or maybe go ice skating this morning? Well, maybe not ice skating."

At the hurt look on Heather's face, Jeff apologized for being so insensitive by even mentioning ice skating. "I didn't mean ice skating on the pond, Heather."

"I'm sure you didn't, Jeff. Just forget it. Maybe we'll go to a game. And perhaps after that we could have dinner somewhere.

"I know what we'll do. Let's have dinner with my mom and dad. The news that we found a dead girl's body, who happens to be one of your students, is going to be all over the local news. We better go ahead and call and tell them we'll tell all in exchange for a meal tonight."

His attempt at levity fell a little flat, but it brought a slight smile to Heather's lips, even if it was a tad bit disapproving.

"God, it's great to see you smile again!" Jeff exclaimed around the upward curve of his own lips.

Sitting in the spectator seats at the Resch Center where the Green Bay Gamblers played their home games, Heather felt some of the tension in her body begin to dissipate like the famous Wisconsin milk, fresh from the cow, draining through a strainer.

"Go, go, go!" she yelled as the player with the puck moved it down the ice, weaving this way and that through the mighty efforts of the opposition to steal it. The skater threw an elbow to the helmet of the opposing player and never missed a beat as he kept the puck in front of him, ever progressing, protecting it with his hockey stick and his big, thickly padded body.

Ever competitive and quite a sports fan, Heather's interest in the game kept the fear she carried at bay. It was like an ever-present photograph of Patti's body was seared into her brain.

"Yay, Gamblers," she yelled, as the puck rocketed past the bulky legs of the goal tender, hit the net, and dropped to the ice. Too late he swiped at it. Score one for the Gamblers.

They left the Hockey game crowing over the big win. Naturally, the Gamblers were Jeff's favorite ice hockey team. The team was also Heather's favorite by default since she had never seen a hockey game, except for the televised Winter Olympic Games, before she came to Green Bay. She had enjoyed her very first ice hockey game right here in the Resch Center on the first date she had with Jeff.

She thought back to the day they met. He had teased her about her southern accent throughout the day and before she departed the premises that afternoon Jeff asked her for a date. She was not playing coy. Not with this good-looking young man. She accepted his invitation and went to her first ice hockey game.

From the start, she really liked the handsome young high school teacher with the Harry Potter eyeglasses that he had, later in the day, donned because he had to remove a contact lens. And the rest is what history is made of. They were in love. They were living together. What would be next for their future?

Heather's privileged upbringing was different from what Jeff experienced in his blue-collar working family. The home in which he grew up was on the other side of the Fox River near the warehouses and business areas that at one time lined the edge of Lake Michigan and the Fox River. His dad was a warehouse supervisor and his mom was a school cafeteria manager. They didn't have an excess of money, but they had hopes for their only child. His dad's hope was for his son to get a college education and be something more than a warehouse manager, even though he was not ashamed of the hard work he had to do to clothe and feed his family. He also sought advice from the company's human resources personnel and began to invest $50.00 per month. He added larger amounts to his investments over the years and it paid off well.

Gone now were the old warehouses and business that once dotted the landscape. Georgia Pacific, the exception, is still there in the old Broadway district and has been producing paper products since the 1920s. It was the growth of industry that led to the area's decline. As factories grew, so did taverns and bars. So did the crime rate. For over sixty years it was a neglected part of Green Bay. That began to change in 1995 when On Broadway, Inc. started making the populace aware that something could be done.

During Jeff's formative years, his dad continued to work and save money. From 1998 to 2002, the city got behind the efforts of OBI, as it came to be called, and the area was cleaned up and new business came in. Existing building owners began to refurbish. Today the 54303 zip code is no longer a morass of derelict buildings and drunkards. Velp Avenue and North Military Road saw much growth in buildings erected and businesses filling them.

Upon retirement for both John and Eva Hoffmann, they had accumulated a nice sum to put toward their retirement home. They told everyone it was to be their last home here on Earth before they were called to their final home in Heaven.

The couple had moved into an over fifty-five retirement community earlier than they had planned, since both were still healthy and active. However, a developer offered them an exorbitant price for their little house. They truly had no choice but to accept since the developers planned to raze the existing houses, clean up the area, and build a new development of expensive homes. Eva and John Hoffmann were ecstatic about their move to the Fox River Towers where they were still on the west side of town and near the river. It had five stories of contemporary apartments plus an indoor swimming pool and a gym. They were living the life!

Eva was delighted to have her meals cooked and served to her after a long career of cooking for and serving untold numbers of students. John was pleased to be able to sit and watch TV whenever the mood struck him without having to order this, fill out that, sign the other, or ream out some schmuck who got drunk the night before and could only half-ass do his job. Eva and John were happy. And this day they were extra happy because their only child, and the joy of their lives, was coming for dinner.

Chapter Four

The murderer lay awake in his large four-poster bed well into the morning hours of December 13 and thought back to the events in his life that had played out to get him to the point he was now. *Damn my parents for the cold, unloving sacks of shit they were during my childhood. No! I won't think about them now. I'm just going to revel in my memory of killing that stupid, childish Patti.* He eventually went to sleep and began to dream.

The killer later awakened tangled in his covers. His elated feeling over killing Patti brought his memories to his first kill when he was a younger man. In acting it out while asleep, his thrashing movements had entangled his bedclothes and he lay with cold sweat soaking his pajamas.

He remembered when he was sixteen. He was alone most of the time as his parents were often away on business. He badly wanted to live in his own apartment and to be master of his own domain. He vowed to speak to his parents the next time they came home.

The time came and he made his move. "Mother, I'd like to speak with you and Father."

"It'll have to wait until dinner. He's busy now. I am as well. Excuse me." She gave her son a dismissive nod. "I have things to do."

That night at dinner as the three sat picking at the paltry meal his mother had prepared, he spoke to both parents. "Mother, Father," he looked at each one in turn, "I want to move to an apartment of my own. You're seldom here and I'd prefer to live where I can at least see people once in a while and have someone to talk with after school."

Expecting at least some argument, he was both surprised and delighted when neither objected.

"Find a place and bring me a lease to sign before I leave next week. I'll pay a year's rent in advance and you can move in immediately. Is there anything else?"

Wanting to jump up and down with joy, he stifled the urge and replied, "No, Father. That's all I need. Thank you."

"Thank you, too, Mother." And that was it. He secured the apartment and moved in the same day his parents left again, this time on a trip to Istanbul. He did not miss them.

Needing the outlet, he continued to report to school every day, where he saw people and interacted with them. He became a chameleon, adept at changing himself to be whom and what he needed to be under any given circumstance. Quite intelligent, he had a hunger for learning and was a voracious reader. He was on the fast track for college, taking many college courses in twelfth grade. It was at the start of the second semester in one of these advanced placement classes that he met Joanie.

"Hi," she said. "I'm Joanie." She bumped his hip with hers, and unleashing a dynamite grin, she exclaimed, "Come on, big guy, loosen up. We need to study together to get through this course, so I pick you to be my partner.

I hope you know something about Advanced Trig." She hooked her arm through his and grinned up at him.

He was taken aback by her assurance. No one in his life had ever acted so self-confident or exuberant. It took him a micro-second to decide she was what he needed in his mundane life. *Wow! I could really like this girl.* Joanie was far from mundane, as he was about to discover.

Recovering quickly from his initial surprise, he fired back a jaunty response. With one eyebrow raised, he tipped his head back, and regally looking down his nose at the intriguing girl with the wild blonde hair and the laughing eyes and mouth, he said, "Who could possibly deny you anything, you marvelous creature!"

They both burst out laughing. Joanie slipped her arms around his waist. "Who are you, anyway?" she asked.

I've never felt so in touch with another person in my life. Looking down into her eyes he was lost. He gave her a name and asked. "Would you like to go get some lunch with me?"

After that day, one was rarely seen without the other, and indeed, they did study together. They discovered they were in all the same college track courses. Although they begged to be allowed to live together at his place, Joanie's parents drew the line and would not budge from their position, so they spent every moment they could in some activity that they shared.

Joanie was so ethereal she almost seemed to float above the floor when walking, as if she were a fairy princess with her beautiful blonde curls bouncing upon her shoulders and down her back. Mesmerized, he couldn't believe after all his years of being lonely and unloved he had been so lucky as to have everything he ever hoped for tied up in the one shiny gift package that was Joanie.

With the sexual knowledge and experience he had gained from a series of housekeepers, he was ready to introduce Joanie to the pleasures of sex. Believing he loved her more than life, he waited two months before he attempted it so as not to offend or frighten her. He succeeded one evening when they were listening to love songs on his tape player. While wrapped around each other on the coffee colored leather sofa his parents had furnished him, he made his first move.

His voice thick with emotion and desire, he whispered into the ear which lobe he had moments before swirled with his tongue, causing Joanie to gasp aloud, "I love you, Joanie. So much. And I want to show you how much."

He slipped his hand under her sweater, as he had done before, and gently cupped her breast. She leaned into him ever so slightly. He then pulled her body erect and slid both hands up her back under her sweater and unhooked her bra. He pushed up her sweater and let her breasts fall free into his hands.

"Beautiful," he breathed. His lips came down to capture one pink nipple, tugging it softly into his mouth. He did the same with the other, circling it with his tongue, harder and stronger, until Joanie was moaning.

"I've wanted you from the moment I saw you," he said, lifting his head and looking intently into the blue depths of her eyes. "Now, let me make love to you, Joanie. Oh, I do love you so much."

Joanie made a protesting noise, which he cut off with his mouth and talented tongue. "No, don't worry. I have protection. I've wanted this for so long, Joanie. Let's make love together. We'll join our bodies and be like we're one person. Oh, Joanie, I love you more than anything in this world and I want us to be just one. We can do that."

Soon Joanie stopped making her ineffectual negative noises and gave him her mouth and her body. Using many of the gentler techniques he'd learned in his years of sexual abuse, he bound Joanie to him. And so it went for the balance of their senior year in high school and the first year at the university they insisted upon entering together.

When registering for classes, he chose a curriculum composed of Education and Administration courses. Only a few of their classes were to be the same as Joanie chose an Elementary Education course of study.

They were required to live in separate dorms on campus, but that did nothing to keep them apart. They found ways and places to assuage the all-consuming need of their bodies.

After the first year in the dorms, the school allowed the sophomores to live off campus. He quickly secured a small, but nicely appointed apartment near the campus. Parents were not there to stop them, and wielded little influence, so Joanie moved in with him. All was bliss for that second year. Happiness reigned at home. Love was king in their house. They both continued to do well in their respective course of studies. It was all good.

In their third year at the university, he began to notice a slow, but definite, change in Joanie. They began to argue, something they'd never done before. Something he would have declared impossible before it began.

"Where were you?" he asked, worried the first few times Joanie didn't meet him as planned or was not home when expected. Her airy replies, accompanied by a toss of her head which set that mass of glorious curls in motion to cascade over her arms and shoulders, were a sure way to melt his heart. It worked. For a while.

"What kept you so long at the store?" This was accompanied with an audible grinding of his teeth.

"Oh, you know; the usual." She flashed her delightful smile that until today had lit up his world.

He raised his voice and frowned. "No, I don't know. What is the usual?"

"Oh, don't get angry with me! So I was gone a little longer than you wanted me to be. So what? They were very busy at the grocery store. There were not enough cashiers and the check-out lines were miles long." She poked her bottom lip out, pouting prettily at him. "So, don't be mad at me. Okay?"

"Come here," he ordered.

She put the bags she still carried onto the floor and stood before him, smiling seductively and raising her arms to place around his neck.

He reached to stop her arms. "Get undressed."

"What? Now?" The smile slid from her lips and she looked confused as she frowned and narrowed her eyes at him.

He smiled a feral grin. "Yes, now." He held her eyes with his as she pulled her sweater over her head and down her arms, and then dropped it on the sofa. She reached behind her and unhooked her bra and let it slide down her arms to drop on the floor. Unzipping her jeans, she stood on one foot and then the other to slide them off her legs. She looked up again into his face.

"Now the panties," he directed.

Joanie stood naked before him. With a groan, he stripped his off his clothes and roughly drew her into his arms, savaging her mouth with his while grinding his hips into hers. He backed her to the sofa, and for the first time, he punished her with the rough sex he had learned when he was fourteen and well versed in the sexual games of his housekeeper.

Acting surprised, but attempting to please him, Joanie gamely tried to match his actions until the pain grew too great for enjoyment. Then she cried, silently shaking, with tears rolling out of her eyes and down her temples to wet her beautiful curls.

After the charade of love-making ended, he sat up on the sofa and put his head in his hands. Joanie sat up and touched his face, turning his head so he was looking at her. "What happened to us?" she asked in a broken voice.

"You make me crazy, Joanie."

"I'm sorry. I'll try to pay more attention to the time from now on. I promise not to be late again." She sniffed back her tears, rose, picked up her clothes and went to take a shower. As he watched her go, he speculated on what he would do now.

He followed her. At a safe distance, of course. He tailed her when she said she was going to the library. When she said she was going shoe shopping. To the grocery store. To class. And, as if it were pre-destined, he saw her meet up with another student. At the library. On her way to class. Riding with him in his car. Having lunch in the cafeteria with him.

It made no difference to him that these were times when he was supposed to be unavailable, having classes or obligations of his own. He looked at it first one way and then the other. First—he *was* unavailable, so she might just be innocently passing time while she waited to be with him. *OR* she knew he wouldn't be anywhere around to see her with someone else. And she was cheating on him. His thoughts returned to the days of no love from his parents when he was lonely and alone. He thought those days had ended with Joanie. But they were back; the evidence before him as Joanie threw back her head and unleashed that infectious laugh which was joined by the fellow with her.

Red flashed before his eyes and he knew what he had to do.

While the detectives were interviewing Heather Forrest and Jeffrey Hoffmann that Saturday morning, the killer continued to think of his life with Joanie and how he had snuffed it out. He couldn't think of anything else. He recalled making the chicken stew that was to be Joanie's punishment for cheating on him. He was in the kitchen when Joanie came through the door of their apartment.

"Boy! Something smells good. What is it?" Joanie sniffed appreciatively as she laid her book bag in his leather recliner in the living room and headed to the kitchen from where the delectable aroma was coming. There he stood, a red polka-dotted dish towel tied around his waist and a large spoon in his hand.

"It's got a fancy French name. Coq Au Vin, I believe it's called. Basically, chicken stew. But I made it a little different. Instead of wine, I put in champagne."

"Champagne!" Joanie echoed. "Wow! What's the special occasion that we have champagne in our chicken stew?"

He looked at her a long time, as if trying to memorize every detail of her lovely face. "You," he said simply. "You are my special occasion. I wanted to make something special for you tonight, so I went online and found this recipe. I hope you like it."

She came to him and put her arms around his waist, drawing him tight against her. She laid her head against his chest. "I can feel your heart beating. It's pretty fast. That must mean you love me a lot." She drew back and looked up into his face, laughing low in her throat.

"Kiss me. Show me how much you love me."

He obeyed, dropping his mouth to hers and kissing her warmly and deeply, and as gently as his raging insides would allow. *Just wait, Joanie. Just you wait.*

While they ate the delicious champagne chicken, he continued to devour her with his eyes, eating little while Joanie consumed a large portion. The chicken was made with the dark meat, the legs and thighs, and as Joanie finished the pieces of meat, she laid the large bones on the side of her plate.

There was plenty of champagne left over from what was used in the recipe and they'd each had a glass with dinner. Now that dinner was finished, he said with a leering smile, "Let's go sit on the sofa and make out. And take our champagne with us. Here, let me top off our glasses." He poured the rest of the sparkling bubbly into their glasses and motioned with his for Joanie to take a seat on the sofa.

Joanie turned and sat where he'd indicated. She smoothed her hair back from her face and looked at him with her face open and trusting, waiting for him to join her. He turned his back so she wouldn't see him pick up the largest of the chicken thigh bones, its ends crushed and jagged, and slide it up the cuff of his shirtsleeve.

He sat beside her and drew her into his arms. His mouth covered hers and he could taste the champagne lingering in her mouth. "Drink it, Joanie. Drink it all. We sure don't want to waste this champagne. It's special."

Joanie obediently sipped from her glass. He tilted his head back, mimicking turning up the glass with his hand and drinking it all. She obeyed.

"Here. Want mine?" he asked, offering her his almost full flute.

"Sure," she giggled. "Why not?" She tipped his glass up and slugged it down. "There," she slurred. "I drank it all."

"Yes, you did, you sweet girl," he said low with approval. "You're my good girl, aren't you, Joanie?" *Yeah, if only you were.*

"Yes," she whispered, her head now beginning to droop as contentment, relaxation, and sleepiness set in.

"Kiss me," he whispered, tilting her chin up. He continued to hold it with his hand.

Joanie promptly parted her lips for another deep kiss, eyes closed and ready.

In one swift move, he wrenched her jaws open and jammed the chicken bone down deep into her throat. Too late he realized he'd pushed it farther than he'd intended.

Joanie immediately jerked upright, arms flailing, champagne glass knocked to the floor. Eyes bulging, she emitted horrible small noises as she desperately tried to get air into her lungs through her rapidly swelling throat. She reached for him, her eyes wild and frightened, puzzled, as if she couldn't believe what was happening. He drew back and watched her, evading her grasping hands. She then tried to put her hand in her mouth to remove the bone, but he caught both her hands in his, and held them still as her struggles slowed. Her eyes were locked on his as she died.

He stood and looked down at Joanie's body. His body sagged and he fell to his knees beside the sofa. He gathered the limp body into his arms, holding her close to his heart as he began to cry. Great heaving sobs burst forth, wrenched from his throat, and hot tears streamed down his face, wetting her blouse as he buried his face against her still warm body.

"Joanie," he wailed. "Oh, Joanie, why did you make me do it?" Another ragged sob erupted from deep inside him. "I had to do it, Joanie. You betrayed me! I loved you more than I thought it possible to love anyone. You were the only person I ever loved."

Hot tears dripped from his chin and nose. As if wrenched from the depths of his soul, he shuddered out the words, "You were the only person to ever love me!"

He drew a hitching breath and laid her body back on the sofa. "And then you cheated." He ran his hand over her face and down her body, touching her one last time, while sobbing afresh and uncontrollably.

When his crying was spent, he got up to call 911. He had to stick to his plan so the police would believe his story of a drunk Joanie choking on a chicken bone. He looked again at the body on his coffee colored sofa. "I loved you, Joanie," he whispered, now dry-eyed. *I'll never love anyone or anything again. I'll never allow myself to be hurt. Ever.*

Now so many years later, up and in his bathrobe and slippers, the killer peered into his well-stocked refrigerator. Eggs. *Yes, I'll make scrambled eggs.* He perused the large fruit bowl atop its pedestal and decided to have banana and pear slices with the eggs. He snared a bright yellow banana. Reaching for the pears, he knocked one to the pristine, white-tiled floor. At the peak of ripeness, the pear split upon contact and its juicy sweetness spread into the grout between the squares of tile. He snatched a paper towel and bent to wipe up the mess. Something about it brought again his memories of Joanie and the day she died. Rooted to the spot, he stood while the events of that terrible day played out in his memory.

The medical examiner found the bone in her throat. Fortunately for her killer, Joanie's throat muscles, in spasm, had pushed the chicken bone back up toward her mouth. He declared it death by asphyxiation due to a foreign object blocking her airway. No foul play involved.

The next day he went online and found a small town where he was unknown and, sight unseen, rented an apartment. He arranged with an independent furniture mover, a twenty-year-old with a gutted van as old as he, to take his few belongings, including the coffee colored sofa, far away from sunny southern California to the cold and rainy Pacific Northwest, a distinct change from everything he'd known before.

It was there in his apartment in the quaint little arts and crafts town of Snohomish, Washington, where he worked in an antique store, that his parents' attorney contacted him with the news that both had died in a horrendous pile-up on Interstate 5 in California. They sustained fatal injuries and were dead upon being pulled from their car. The good news was they had invested well for years and also had a substantial savings account of several million dollars. The savings account had from the beginning been their safety net in case they had to disappear, spies that they were. The money was guaranteed to be available within twenty-four hours as long as it remained in that bank.

The attorney handling the funeral arrangements also arranged for the withdrawal from the bank. He arrived back in southern California the next day. The following day he sat impassively in the chapel of the funeral home while a pastor, whom the attorney contacted, droned on reading bible verses. He had no information about the deceased pair whose ashes were in the urns sitting on a table at the front of the chapel. He and the attorney were the only mourners. It was inconsequential that the family could possibly have been Jewish. He, himself, did not know. Religion of any kind had never been discussed in their home.

After leaving the funeral home and the thoroughly depressing memorial service, he headed to the bank

"I'm here to withdraw all the funds in my family's account." With those words, he became a multi-millionaire.

Chapter Five

After his parents' funeral, the killer returned to his small apartment in Washington and prepared it for a long absence. He made arrangements to pay the rent and electricity online with automatic withdrawal. This was to be his safe place, somewhere to which he could return to his few belongings, if the need ever arose.

He visited an attorney and had his name legally changed. Most things of importance started with the chronological order of the alphabet, and he wanted to always be at the beginning. Perhaps not the very first person to be called on in class or to be visited by the Publishers Clearing House team, or he would have chosen a name starting with double A. He looked up the names that did and was quite taken with Aaby. It looked to him like a mixture of Abby and Baby. No, he was satisfied with his choice. One A would suffice.

At the largest and most solvent bank in town, he deposited a large portion of his inheritance, preferring to carry on his body a million dollars in the largest bills. Exiting the bank, he randomly chose a financial advisor whose sign he saw across the street. It was a nationally recognized giant in the financial and investment world. Arrangements were made and the advisor pledged to invest and re-invest to insure his portfolio would grow and earn dividends under his watchful guidance. Leaving there with a secure feeling about the future of his fortune, he stopped at a travel agency.

The young woman manning the phones and the business looked happy to see a customer. "I hope you're in the market for travel. We've got lots of good deals going on right now." He gave her a rusty smile, stretching his lips over his teeth. He hadn't even attempted a smile since the night Joanie died.

"Yes, I am definitely in the market for travel. Show me what you've got."

He left the travel office with airline tickets to France. Returning to his apartment, he picked up his packed bags, turned everything off, and locked the door. He didn't look back.

Continuing to be a loner, he preferred the astounding sites he saw in traveling the world and the amazing objects d'art he purchased to the chatter of the air-headed girls who boldly eyed him because of his good looks and his air of mystery. They enraged him and he knew he had to stay away from them. He wanted to wrap his strong hands around their slender necks and squeeze the life from their bodies. He couldn't take risks for fear Joanie's death might somehow rise up and bite him in the ass. He still thought of her often. And the more he thought of killing her the more he wanted to kill again.

He occasionally took some blonde to a hotel, never his residence or where he stayed on his travels. There he would have rough sex with her and thoroughly degrade her.

"Get out, you stupid bitch. Don't ever try to contact me again. Go! Now!" was his habitual order as soon as the sex and rough play were finished. The unfortunate girls left sobbing, their bodies hurting from his teeth, hands, and punishing penis.

He had to exercise great restraint to stop short of killing them. It became an obsessive thought and his fantasies and craziness grew.

Returning to Paris often during his first two years of travel, he discovered he loved the city and prepared to stay for a while. After taking specialized tests and meeting all the requirements, he applied to and was welcomed into the Humanities and Social Science curriculum at La Sorbonne, this course of study being one of four still housed and taught within the original walls of the old Sorbonne. He learned about the wonders of the world and wanted to see them in person. He made it happen.

On his first summer break, he traveled to Egypt, where he saw the Great Pyramids of Giza and the neighboring Sphinx, the magnificent Temple of Luxor, and in the Valley of the Kings he visited the tombs of the pharaohs, including that of King Tut.

The next summer he spent in Russia, visiting the incredible blue, white, and gold Katherine's Palace in St. Petersburg and the Kremlin in Moscow whose Red Square boasted perhaps the most beautiful place of worship in the world—the opulent St. Basil's Cathedral with its colorful onion domes. He continued to travel at every break and summer vacation. In each place he traveled, he found some exquisite and expensive item to purchase. Owning such pieces of art gave him almost the exact thrill as extinguishing life.

He always returned to La Sorbonne and carried on with his studies, while he spurned all attempts made by others to draw him into a relationship. He'd killed once and he knew he'd do it again. But not yet.

In four years, he graduated from La Sorbonne with a bachelor's degree in Humanities. He decided he'd seen most of the world, and he needed to do something with himself that would challenge his self-control and keep him on the hunt that he now had time for.

Years now separated him from Joanie's death. There would never be a connection between his first and his next kill, so he decided it was time to give in to his urges.

The killer shook his head as if awakening. He still stood by the fruit bowl with the soiled paper towel in his hand. *I've got to stop thinking about this. I have things to do today.*

Reaching into a white-fronted cabinet, he retrieved the PAM spray. He got a non-stick frying pan out of the cupboard, turned the gas stove's burner on medium low, and sprayed the pan's bottom with the spray. Cracking two eggs against the side of a bowl, he relieved them of their shells, whisked them, and added them to the bowl with a bit of cream and a couple of grinds from the salt and pepper mills. He tried again with a different pear, slicing it and arranging it on his plate. The fluffy eggs were next. *I have to make myself stop thinking about Joanie. I need to eat my breakfast.* He ate his breakfast all right, and he did stop thinking about Joanie, but he couldn't stop his thoughts from returning to Paris and the things he'd done there—and afterward.

Back in his small apartment in Snohomish, Washington, he'd developed a rudimentary plan. In the next few days he developed it fully. After arranging to have his belongings—and the almost priceless antiquities and objects d'arts sent to a monitored, climate-controlled storage facility in Green Bay, Wisconsin—he flew to Green Bay and set about purchasing a home. It didn't take long to find a lovely home on Nicolet Drive which afforded him all the views for which he could ever hope. Lake Michigan glistened outside his huge lake-facing windows.

Not that his interest lay in views. He paid almost two million dollars for it, realizing he could've paid much more for a different home. *But why?* He had his movers drop his shipment there instead of in the storage unit.

Soon he enrolled just down the road from his home in a Master of Education Course of study at the University of Wisconsin and took all the necessary courses in school management as well as the education courses. He wanted to be a principal in a school in the area.

His plan was to eliminate a girl or two while he proved himself to be an exceptional principal. He would take care of his business there and then move on to teach education courses at the university. He'd leave at least one deserving girl's body at each school.

It sometimes gave him a headache to think about what he was sacrificing in order for his plan to succeed.

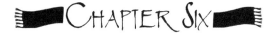

Chapter Six

The two detectives stood on the front steps of the Muellers' home. It was dark inside so Aksel rapped hard on the wooden door that bore no Christmas decoration, and rang the doorbell for added urgency.

Elsa Mueller answered the door in her robe and slippers.

"We have a few more questions we need to ask the family about Patti's everyday schedule. We need to know what she was doing on the golf course yesterday afternoon."

"May we come in, Mrs. Mueller?" Detective Frandsen shot a glance at her partner. It said, "Be nice."

As if mute, Mrs. Mueller backed into the living room and the detectives followed.

"Are your husband and son home? We need to ask them some questions as well," Anja continued.

Aksel thought Elsa Mueller appeared to be dazed as she nodded and headed down the hall to get her son and husband. He looked around the doll-sized living and dining area. There was no sign of activity, no smell of breakfast food, nothing to indicate those living in this house had begun their day. It was, after all, only a little after nine in the morning after the tragic and sorrowful night this family had endured.

"I'll make some coffee," Mrs. Mueller said when she returned with her husband and son.

Mr. Mueller looked pretty rough to Aksel. His beard grew significantly over night and his eyes looked, as Aksel's father used to say when someone had been on a bender, "like two piss holes in the snow."

Freddie's hair rose in spikes all over his head. It made him look like a punk rocker. His body was thin enough to look like he had the drug-induced emaciation so many members of the punk rock genre possessed.

"None for me thanks." Aksel shook his head.

"We've had too much coffee already," Anja explained. "But go ahead and make it for your family."

Aksel spoke again. "Can you tell us why you weren't concerned about Patti being out 'til ten o'clock on a Friday night? Whatever you can tell us about Patti's habits, where she usually went, and especially about being at the golf course pond on a Friday afternoon, will help us get to the bottom of our investigation, and it can help us catch her killer." *These people better wake up to what was going on with their daughter. I don't care if I get tough with them.*

The three Muellers looked at each other, as if wondering where to start. Freddie was the first to break the silence. "My sister is, was, different. She was independent, I guess. She pretty much did what she wanted to do. If she wanted to go to that pond . . ." His voice cracked and he turned his head to wipe away tears.

He was so obviously trying to be an adult about this matter of dealing with his sister's death. It made Anja's heart ache for him. "Freddie, I think you must have been close to Patti."

Freddie nodded. "Yeah."

"Did she sometimes invite you to go on these, umm, let's call them "unconventional" trips she made? We know she cut classes and didn't go to school for the last three days."

"Sometimes."

"But you didn't go, did you?"

"No."

"Why not?" Aksel asked.

"Because I didn't want to get in trouble. I hope to go to college, so I didn't want to take a chance on getting caught skipping school or some of her other crazy ideas. She didn't give a rip if she got caught."

"A bit of a dare-devil, huh?"

"Well, I guess you could call it just being who she was."

Dieter Mueller angrily broke in. "Why didn't you tell us about these things, Freddie?"

"What would you have done, Dad? You gave up worrying about her a couple of years ago."

Elsa Mueller jumped into the conversation in a likely attempt to defuse a situation that had the potential to blow up. "We had to let her do her thing, whatever it was, because she was going to do it anyway. Patti was not a bad kid. She was just willful."

"Hah!" Dieter fired at Elsa.

Elsa ignored him. "We tried to punish her for disobeying when she was little. For instance, if she had been told not to get into the packages of raisins, she would go ahead and get a package. Just one small box. Because she wanted it. I would tell her to put it back and she'd refuse. She'd just stand there shaking, clutching the box of raisins to her chest with both hands, and even though she knew she was going to get a spanking, she wouldn't give them up."

With eyes misty and unfocused, as she recalled the events of those not so long-ago days, Elsa stopped telling her story. She shook her head and absent mindedly twisted the ties to her robe's belt, the light blue fabric now frayed from wear.

"So," she said, as if awaking from her reverie and realizing the detectives were waiting for her to finish, "she'd take her spanking and I'd snatch the box of raisins from her hand. The point is, she did what she wanted to do. That's why we weren't overly concerned when it got to be ten o'clock and she wasn't home yet. She never got into any real trouble or did anything to involve the police."

Once more Elsa's voice faltered and she looked away from the detectives. "Until yesterday, that is."

The small family had taken seats at the kitchen table while Anja perched on the over-stuffed arm of the sofa. Aksel remained standing near the kitchen table and he now put his notepad inside his heavy jacket. He spoke to the Muellers, his gaze going from one to the next.

"Thank you for talking with us this morning. I think that will be all for now. But, if you think of anything that you think might be important, give us a call. You can always call directly to police headquarters and they'll take your message. Also, here's my card with my phone number. Detective Frandsen, perhaps you'd like to leave a card as well?"

Anja handed her business card to Elsa Mueller as Aksel handed his to Dieter. Then Anja opened her card case a second time, extracted a card and handed it to Freddie.

"You too, Freddie. Anything at all, please call."

Freddie, acting very much the man of the family, started to rise from his mismatched kitchen chair to see them to the door.

"No, don't get up. Stay there and talk together. You may hit on something. We'll let ourselves out and we'll be in touch when we know more," Anja said and nodded goodbye.

“Oh, Jeff, I hope the evening goes well. I don’t want to rehash everything that’s happened over and over again.”

Jeff nodded and pressed the doorbell to the pretty high-rise apartment. Eva answered the ring and gave her son a reproving look. “Jeffrey, you know you don’t need to ring the doorbell. Just use your key. This is your home!”

Jeff graced his mom with an indulgent smile and leaned down to kiss her cheek. “You know this isn’t my home, Mom. I’ve never lived here.”

“Oh, you know what I mean.” Eva glanced at Heather to see her reaction. A slight rise at the right corner of her mouth passed for a smile.

“Well, come on in and we’ll eat. Dinner is ready. It’s your favorite, Jeffrey. Wurst with sauerkraut and potatoes.”

“Thanks, Mom.” Jeff ushered Heather into the dining room, the window of which looked out on the cold, dark night that had swiftly set in on their drive there.

His dad rose from his recliner and held out his hand to Jeff. They shook hands and then he turned to Heather. “Nice to see you again, Heather.”

“It’s good to see you, sir.” She turned to Mrs. Hoffmann. “And thank you so much for the dinner invitation. It’ll be good to eat someone’s cooking besides Jeff’s and mine.”

Mrs. Hoffmann sniffed. “Well, he’s always liked my cooking.” She looked expectantly at her son. “Haven’t you, Jeff?”

“Sure thing, Mom,” Jeff said, with a sideways wink at Heather.

They had just enough time to pass the food and serve their plates before the questions started. Jeff and Heather repeated in detail everything that they had seen and done that was related to the Patti Mueller murder.

"Oh, how horrible that must have been for you, Jeffrey!" Eva cried.

"Yeah, it was pretty bad for both of us, but more so for Heather since she knew the girl."

Tears welled up in Heather's eyes, as much from Eva's insensitivity as from her grief over Patti's death.

"The dinner was lovely, Mrs. Hoffmann, and the dessert was delicious." She sniffed back more tears that threatened to overflow. "However, we're both very tired and I know I need to go to bed and get some rest. I hope you two won't mind terribly if we cut our visit short tonight." Her mind was a whirl of thoughts. *I'm so scared I could scream. I don't want to be here where you make me feel worse than I already feel. I need Jeff for just myself. I don't want to share him with you. I need him to hold me while we talk about this. I'm so afraid the person who killed Patti will come after us. He probably thinks we found something. Or the police did, and we might be of some help to them. Oh God, I'm scared!*

Jeff was quick to add, "Heather's so right. We're both running on fumes and badly need to get some rest and sleep. Perhaps next time we won't have been through something so traumatic and we'll stay longer."

"I understand, son," his dad said.

"Well, if you must leave so early," his mom said, adding a sniff for emphasis, "then I suppose you'll have to go." This time the reproving look was turned on Heather.

As they left the elevator and walked to their car parked beneath the building, Heather mused, "I don't know why your mom doesn't like me. Your dad seems to think I'm okay."

"You know there is no woman my mom approves of. Don't let it worry you. She'll come around sooner or later."

"Yeah, when pigs fly," Heather muttered.

As he drove home, Jeff reached for Heather's hand and held it in his big palm. He brought it to his mouth and kissed the back.

"I know you're scared and worried about the investigation and how much we're going to be involved in it. But remember, I'm Superman—I even have the Clark Kent eyeglasses—and whatever tomorrow and the following days bring, I want you to know I will do my damnedest to see that you aren't in danger from the maniac that killed Patti. We'll get through this, sweetheart. One way or another, we'll be all right."

"I so hope you're right, Jeff. It's scary and macabre to think somebody's out there who could do something like this." She took his hand and turned it around and brought it to her lips. "I liked that sweet kiss on my hand so much that I'm giving one back to you." She placed her lips against his knuckles close to the University of Wisconsin ring he proudly wore on his right hand. Her lips lingered as she raised her eyes to Jeff's profile.

Looking straight ahead at the falling snow, she said soft and low, "Thank you for loving me, Jeff. I feel so much safer being with you." She raised her voice, "But, I really can't even explain this feeling of fear I have inside me. It's like I'm walking around a corner into the unknown, and yet I know something horrible is waiting for me there, ready to pounce on me and d-devour me. I'm really scared, Jeff."

His hand still in hers, he squeezed tightly. "I've got you, Heather."

Chapter Seven

December 15, 2014

Patti's killer woke to the softly playing alarm on his clock radio. He listened to the airy, gentle strains of Debussy's "Afternoon of the Faun," savoring the lilting notes from the French horn. He then rose, attended to his bathroom needs and his shower and toilette. From his closet he chose one of the laundered, starched and pressed white shirts. He always wore a crisp white shirt and today he would pair it with a maroon cable-knit, V-neck pullover sweater. The temperatures would be quite cold today.

He consumed a fortifying breakfast of mixed fresh fruit; the luscious strawberries and bananas liberated from a homeland filled with sunshine far away from Green Bay's often bitter cold. Next, he had an English muffin spread with real butter and the bounty of orange blossom honey from Florida's orange groves. All this was accompanied by a tall glass of skim milk. *None of that nasty coffee for me, thank you very much!* To him, drinking coffee was tantamount to drinking battery acid. Both would destroy the lining of the stomach and would kill you. "No siree, it's not for me," he said, and then laughed aloud at his clever rhyme.

Rising from his seat at the kitchen table, he carried his dishes to the sink where he rinsed and stacked them in the stainless-steel drainer on the counter top by the sink. He wiped down everything and left his kitchen spotlessly clean. Shrugging into his heavy London Fog knee-length coat, he entered the garage to get his car. Soon, he joined the other Green Bay professionals on their way to work on this Monday morning with Christmas fast approaching.

Quite subdued, Heather Forrest attempted to teach her English classes on that Monday following Patti's death. All her students wanted to do was talk about her discovering Patti's dead body on the frozen ice of the pond at The Golf Club—and to speculate on who might have been her killer. After trying and failing to capture the attention of her first period class with the lesson plan she had ready, she gave up her attempt to teach the grammar lessons she had stayed up late into the night before to prepare. *Obviously, Patti's murder is going to be the topic of the day.* She put her lesson plans inside her desk and shut the drawer. She looked at her students' expectant faces, took a deep breath and let it out slowly.

"What you heard on the news is correct," Heather told her excited class. "Mr. Hoffmann is a friend and we decided to take a bike ride after school on Friday. We went to The Golf Club to see if the little pond was frozen enough to hold our weight so we could skate on it over the week-end." She paused and looked around the classroom. The students were as quiet and attentive as she'd ever seen them. "And that's where we found the body."

She almost ducked at the barrage of questions rapidly fired at her.

"Patti's body?"

"How'd you know who it was?"

"What did she look like?"

"Did the police arrest you and Mr. Hoffmann?"

"Is Mr. Hoffmann your boyfriend?"

Heather blushed at this last question. "Yes," she said with a smile. As the day progressed, she answered again and again all the questions as truthfully as she could. She pulled the memories from the recesses of her mind where she had compartmentalized them. It was difficult to talk about, but she owed her students this much. Most had, after all, known Patti longer than she.

Heather found it was much the same in Jeff's classes. He told Heather he was unsurprised by his students' interest in the murder. By now, everyone in Green Bay who watches the news on TV or reads it in the newspapers was aware that Heather and Jeff had found the body of one of her students. It was a certainty that his students knew about it just as hers had.

When they got together in her classroom at the end of the day, Jeff told Heather, "The first student through the door immediately came to my desk where I was reviewing what I hoped would be my lesson plans for the day. Then they all gathered around and asked questions."

He threw his hands out with palms up and rattled off several of the things the kids wanted to know. "Wow! What was it like seeing that dead girl? Did you actually touch her? Were you a suspect? Do they have any leads yet? Do you have any idea who did do it?" Jeff shook his head and said, "Really, Heather, I was almost bowled over. I put my lesson plans away, told them all to sit down, and then I answered their questions. They wanted to hear our story about finding Patti's body and the police's questions.

And you can probably guess which question was asked the most. I finally had to answer it."

Heather said, "Yeah, I'll bet I can. They wanted to know if I was your girlfriend."

"That's it."

"Yes. It was the same with me. I got asked a couple of times during each class if you were my boyfriend."

"So, all of your classes were like that? All of my students were upset and wanted to know everything."

"Absolutely," Heather said, taking a deep breath. She exhaled as she said, "I've had a monstrous headache all day that got worse class after class. I'm sure looking forward to going home and relaxing. I hope we can sleep tonight."

December 16, 2014

During the funeral service at the King of Kings Lutheran Church, the Mueller family sat weeping silently; even Dieter had to swab his face with a handful of the tissues provided in each pew. The church was filled except for the front row, right side, where the three lone figures huddled.

Detectives Franzen and Frandsen were there, watching like hawks for any untoward behavior that might lead them to a suspect. Heather Forrest and Jeff Hoffmann were there, as were other teachers who had taught Patti. Quite a number of students were in attendance, sitting with the teachers who had allowed them to leave school early, or with their parents who each most likely thanked God it was someone else's child lying dead in the light oak colored casket.

Funeral home staffers dislike dealing with funerals in the winter months in Green Bay because the ground is often frozen. They were lucky that the milder weather of last week had held on through the weekend, and even into

Tuesday afternoon. The predicted snow had held off. Even though the ground was partially frozen, it was possible to dig into it. Thus, the preparations for the grave, while not optimum, had been managed, and now the burial was taking place. A large group of mourners from the church service had opted to brave the cold for the burial.

The high school principal stepped from the front side of the group and approached the Muellers as they turned away from the casket that awaited everyone's leave-taking before being lowered into the cold earth. He extended his gloved hand to Dieter.

"Mr. and Mrs. Mueller, I'm Principal Addison. I just wanted to tell you that Patti was truly a lovely girl and she will be deeply missed by all of us at our school. You have our sincere sympathy and we share in your loss."

Although dazed, almost as if in a stupor and perhaps due to some medication, Elsa Mueller murmured, "Thank you, sir. You're most kind."

"I need to speak to Patti's parents, too," Heather said to Jeff, nodding her head in the direction of the principal, who was taking his time as he took his leave of the Muellers.

"Sure, sweetheart. I'll come with you." They walked to the other side of Patti's grave and approached the Muellers.

"Mr. and Mrs. Mueller," Heather began, but was stopped by Elsa Mueller.

"I know who you are," Elsa said. "You found my Patti."

Freddie thrust his cold-reddened hand forward first for Heather and then for Jeff to shake. "I'm Freddie, Patti's brother. It's good of you to come. Patti would've liked that."

"Thank you, Freddie," Jeff said. "I remember seeing you at school."

"Patti was a really sweet girl and I am privileged to have been her teacher," Heather got out, as her tears threatened again. "I'm so very sorry for her death and for Jeff and me to have found her like that. If only we had gotten there sooner, maybe with us nearby this wouldn't have happened."

"There's no telling," Principal Addison said, finally turning away, "It might have made a difference."

Dieter watched him go and then spoke for the first time. He lifted his red-rimmed eyes to Heather. "No need to apologize. If the killer meant to kill her, he would have done it somehow." Bitterly, he added, "No matter what."

Others of the community offered the family their condolences, murmuring in low voices, and then left in groups, dodging both graves and patchy snow that had lain on the ground long enough to turn into mushy crystals of ice.

Detectives Franzen and Frandsen stood together on the other side of Patti's coffin and observed each interchange with her parents and brother. They watched for facial expressions, falsity of sentiments and sympathy, and any suspicious body language. It was a fact; killers often gloated in the certainty they were getting away with their crimes and simply had to be around as many aspects of the victim's final disposition as possible—including funeral services and burials. They noted each person and filed what information they could into their memory banks to check out as soon as they were back at the station.

Catching the eyes of Dieter and Elsa, they both nodded an acknowledgement and headed for their issued SUV, freshly weatherized and well equipped to handle Green Bay's notorious winters. Both detectives were deep in thought as they left the mourners, many of whom were

Patti's age and much too young to be dealing with the murder of a classmate. Would one of these kids be the murderer's next victim?

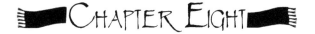

Chapter Eight

December 19, 2014

As she entered the faculty meeting on the last Friday afternoon before the Christmas break, Heather was more than ready to go home and not return until after the new year began. The students were dismissed early since the expected snowstorm had materialized earlier in the day. The snow was getting heavier and already several inches covered the ground. Now the staff was gathered for any last-minute information and to go over school closing policies for January when, traditionally, there was much more snow than in December.

Heather was eager to see if the policies had changed since last winter, when she first experienced, as they called the school closings in Green Bay, "snow days." So, she was quite surprised by Principal Addison's opening remarks. They weren't about school policies at all. They were about Patti.

"It's a tragedy that we lost such a lovely young girl last Friday. I would imagine that by now you are all aware that our own Patti Mueller was killed and her body left lying on the little frozen pond at The Golf Club. In fact, it was her English teacher, Heather Forrest, who discovered her body and brought it to the attention of the police." He swept his arm in an arc to indicate Heather where she sat near the end of the large rectangle that had been assembled from eight-foot tables set end-to-end and across.

Heather returned the looks she was given from all around the tables while the principal continued, "It's a darned good thing Miss Forrest happened to visit The Golf Club that afternoon. Had she not, there's no telling how long that beautiful little girl would have lain there exposed to the elements. A coat and a scarf provide a poor defense against the wild animals that come in from the woods, during any kind of warming spell, seeking food in cold weather. It's rare to see wild animals in the winter here because they've gone to earth or perhaps migrated to warmer climes. But in this stretch of warmer weather, they're probably out there."

He glanced the length of the tables, taking in the open faces of his staff who were all intently listening to him. His gaze returned to Heather. "Why, her body could have been destroyed before being found."

Across the table from Heather, a female teacher from Home Economics gasped and said, "How awful!"

A male teacher from the Math Department directed to Heather, "It's a damned good thing you found her. Even if she was dead, that would have been horrible."

Principal Addison asked, "Do you have anything you'd like to add, Miss Forrest?"

Heather shook her head. "I'd rather not talk about it, please."

"Pretty traumatic, huh?" the principal continued.

With eyes downcast so she didn't have to look anyone in the face, Heather quickly nodded several times. *What's the matter with him? Why doesn't he just drop it?*

He was silent for an uncomfortably long time, and then Principal Addison continued, "Well, then, let me go over the regulations regarding school closings." He droned on about the regulations, but Heather absorbed not one word. Her mind was in turmoil as she relived once again the events of the Friday one week before. She was relieved when the school secretary passed out copies of the guidelines. *I fervently hope I'll find the time and the inclination to familiarize myself with them before school resumes in January.*

As the conference room emptied there were the usual calls of "Merry Christmas!" and "See you next year!" and "Stop by during the holidays, won't you?" among the teachers and other staff members. Most made the effort to speak to Heather as they gathered their things and left. She answered with a wan smile and no one lingered by her chair for long. She remained seated by herself while the others filed out trailing coats and scarves. They would be donned in the spacious hallway before braving the wind and falling snow found between the heavy school doors and the staff parking lot where their cold cars awaited them.

Coats and scarves! Suddenly a disturbing thought struck Heather. She looked at Principal Addison. What was it he'd said about Patti and her coat and scarf? Oh yes—that they weren't enough to protect her body from predators. What a strange thing to say! She quickly pushed back her chair, rose from the table, and joined the group in the hall. With her own scarf and coat on, she headed for her car.

The last thing she saw as she pushed open the front hall door and was hit by the wind's force was Principal

Addison leaning casually against the corner of the hallway and watching her.

It was late on that Friday afternoon before Christmas and both teachers had taught their last lessons of 2014. Heather sat on the sofa and twirled her hair around a finger. "Jeff, I've been thinking."

"Yeah? About what?"

"I think I really need to go home for Christmas. I don't mean to be a baby about this, but it's magical the way Mom can perk me up."

Heather looked at Jeff through the screen of shiny red-brown hair that obscured most of her face as she dropped her gaze to the mail accumulated in her lap. It was mostly Christmas cards and flyers advertising the best deals on Christmas items.

Through her fall of hair, she checked his reaction. Seeing nothing but a thoughtful expression in the slight frown between his eyes, she continued in an excited rush, "And I would love for you to go with me. I could show you what Florida is like in the winter. We could get away and forget about this for a little while."

Jeff puffed out his lips, looking reflective. Heather was sure he was weighing the merits of going with her to Florida against what would be a costly last-minute plane fare on the Saturday before Christmas on Thursday. She knew he would be considering the what-ifs and the potential problem of flying the next day because the airport and many incoming flights would be full of Tampa Bay Buccaneer fans arriving for the Packers and Buccaneer game on Sunday.

"I don't know, sweetheart. You know I'd love to go with you. Nevertheless, I know it would be very expensive and probably you should take this time alone with your family to try and heal in a completely different environment."

"Oh, Jeff, are you sure? I'll miss you like crazy if you don't go!"

Jeff moved to stand in front of Heather. "Well, at least it'll make somebody happy. My mom can have me all day for Christmas. She'll be in her element, cooking and force-feeding me from the time I arrive until I have to leave in order to save my waistline—and my sanity."

Heather rose from her seat on the sofa, torn envelopes, unopened cards, and sales flyers falling unnoticed to the floor, and threaded her arms around Jeff's waist, holding him tightly against her as his arms encompassed her. She looked up at him. "I love you so much, Jeff. You are such a good person."

"And I love you, Heather." He showed that love by capturing her mouth with his in a deep kiss that had them both breathless when their lips separated. Jeff gave Heather that special look that he saved for only her.

She swatted his bottom and flashed him a knowing grin. "Later. Right now I'd better make my plane reservations."

December 20, 2014

Heather called her mom who was in her airy kitchen baking her daughter's favorite, her delicious oatmeal-raisin cookies. Ann Forrest hung up the phone. Heather had just told her she was flying down to spend Christmas with them. She had previously told her mother about finding Patti's body and how it upset her badly and Ann had shared everything with Heather's father, Jack. Ann told her then that she needed to be coddled and to come home whenever she could. Now, she was to arrive the next afternoon at the small Gainesville Airport. Ann hurried to tell Jack the news and ended with, "So we have to pick her up at the airport and then our family can have a Christmas like we used to have before Heather left us for the frozen north."

Chapter Nine

December 21, 2014

Heather wriggled in her seat, fidgeting in anticipation of seeing her parents. She sighed with relief when the plane landed with a soft thud and taxied to the terminal. Inside, she looked for her mom's familiar up-done dark brown curls and her dad's thinning red hair. She almost panicked when she didn't immediately see them. Oh, there they were, hurrying down the hall to meet her, her dad lagging behind her mom. She held out her arms and hugged her mom and then her dad. *God, I'm afraid I might cry at any moment.*

"I've so looked forward to being here. It's really cold in Green Bay and here you two are wearing short sleeves and no jackets."

"Well, yeah," Jack said, "It's seventy-five degrees."

As they drove home from the small airport, Heather looked around at the cars with back seats practically filled to their roofs with packages and shopping bags. On Thirteenth Street, Heather watched University of Florida students wearing Gator T-shirts and shorts pedal by on bikes, carelessly weaving in and out between the slow-moving cars.

"It's so strange to look out and see green grass and people wearing shorts instead of shivering in the ice and snow."

Jack craned his neck around to the right. It allowed him to see Heather in the seat behind Ann. "Do you and Jeff have a gun at home, Heather?"

"What? A gun? Why, of course not. Why are you asking me that?" Her eyes went to the rear-view mirror to catch her father's.

"Because, by God, I want my daughter to be able to protect herself from homicidal idiots. Who's to say the crazy ass who killed your student won't be looking for *you*, or come shoot up the school?"

"Your father's right, Heather," Ann said. "Think about all the cases in the news about high school students, even middle school, too, shooting their teachers and classmates. We want you to do what you can to be safe."

"But I don't have the faintest idea how to shoot a gun. I don't think Jeff knows, either."

"Then we'll sign you up for some shooting lessons while you're here. There's a great place out on Archer Road that'll have you a sharpshooter in no time," Jack said.

"Actually, it's closer to Bronson," Ann argued.

"Wherever," Jack snapped, his worry seeming to get the better of him, "she still needs to do it."

"Dad," Heather protested, "I came home to get away from thinking about that stuff. Please don't push me."

"We'll talk about this some more, Heather. But, if anything else happens when you go back, I'm going up there and bring your butt home," Jack vowed with a steely look at his daughter in the rearview mirror.

I'm not arguing with him. If I don't say anything, maybe he won't.

Ann broke the uncomfortable silence. "I made oatmeal raisin cookies for you. We'll have some with icy cold milk for an afternoon snack."

"Oh, that's great, Mom. I can't wait."

At her parents' home, Heather went straight to her old room. Would it be changed much? Did her mom turn it into a sewing room? She was pleased to find it was as she'd left it, except the clothes she'd discarded this past summer when she was home were no longer on her bed.

She wanted to take a nap and then have milk and cookies, but first she needed to call Jeff. He answered on the third ring.

"Hey, sweetheart, I've been waiting for your call. How was your flight? Everything go okay? How're your parents? I miss you!"

Heather had to laugh at his rapid-fire words. *He sounds like a man who is lonely for his mate.*

"Hey, honey. Yeah, the flight was totally uneventful, and Mom and Dad were waiting for me at the terminal. They're fine and everything is good. But they do have some concerns about our safety. Yours and mine."

"Really? What did they say?"

"My dad thinks I should take shooting lessons and that we should get a gun."

"Well, he might be on to something there. I'd feel better knowing you could shoot, and actually hit someone, if you needed to."

"Can you shoot, Jeff?"

"Sure. I bagged a six-point buck when I was twelve."

"Good to know you can protect me if need be. You're my big bad hero." She lowered her voice to a husky purr. "So . . . you miss me, huh? How much?"

"More than you would ever believe."

"Hold that thought and we'll do something about it when I get back," she promised. The sexy teasing left her voice and she sobered to say, "I love you and I miss you, too, Jeff." A pause, then, "You're sure everything is all right there?"

"Sure, sweetheart. Everything's cool here—no pun intended."

"Ha-ha. You're a riot. By the way, it is so nice and warm here. You'd love it."

"Next time, I promise. I'd love to share some of that sunny warmth with you."

"Yeah," Heather replied with a touch of wistfulness. "Next time for sure. Good night, Jeff. I love you."

"I love you, too. Good night, Heather."

Heather sat up with her mom late into the evening discussing old times as well as her horror at finding Patti's body. She poured her heart out and Ann offered love and support, and the suggestion that Heather and Jeff move to Gainesville. Barring that, she said they should be sure to take every precaution to stay safe. Heather conceded, knowing her parents worried about her now more than ever. *Okay, I'll take the damned shooting lessons.*

December 22, 2014

To appease her parents, Heather agreed to go to the shooting range and fire a few rounds that morning. Jack made the arrangements and they were at the range by midmorning. She was accurate to a modest degree with the pistol, but totally threw in the towel with the shotgun. Both shotguns.

"Place the butt of the stock against your shoulder, sight down the middle of the double barrel, and sqeeeeeze one of the two triggers," the instructor, a retired police officer, told her.

She followed his instructions to the "T". The recoil almost knocked her on her butt.

"Here, try this single barrel," he offered. "It won't be as bad. I just wanted to see how you'd do with the double barrel."

She took the shotgun, wedged it against her shoulder, and fired. She hit the target, ripping its upper right corner off. Firing it almost ripped her arm off.

"That's it. I quit," she fumed, rubbing her shoulder. "I won't be able to move my arm for a week."

"That's about right," the instructor agreed.

"Mom, something's niggling at me. There's a spot there in the back of my mind that's telling me I know something. If I could only figure out what it is. I can't remember if it's something Patti said to me in passing, or confided to me, or something I saw or heard. But it's driving me crazy."

Heather and Ann lay in lounge chairs on the back patio while Jack rehung the Christmas lights that sagged along the eaves of the roof. They sipped hot coffee and ate a variety of Christmas cookies from a red tin with Santa's face on its side beaming through his white mustache and beard. The coolness of the evening had set in and they were wearing jeans and light sweaters now.

"There you go. It's driving you crazy," Ann said. "Don't you think seeing a counselor would help you? Get all the fear out front and examine it and see if you can find a way to get past it. I don't mean for you to be passive about this. I truly want you to consider all the ways to make yourself safe. By the way, what have the police told you? Do they know anything yet?"

"I don't know, Mom. They haven't said, at least not to me." Heather paused and watched her dad step down the ladder. He stood back and looked at his handiwork. The lights glowed brightly against the darkening sky.

Heather turned back to Ann. "I know I need to find out what's back there in my head. I feel like it's something really important."

"Maybe it'll come to you, honey. I do know, however, that you will make yourself sick if that's all you can think about. It'll eat you up from the inside."

A huge grin suddenly spread across her face. "I'll tell you what will take your mind off it."

Heather leveled a questioning look at her. "What?"

"Let's stop eating cookies and go inside and finish the oyster stew. We'll have dinner and then go to bed because we need our rest. You and I have to get out of this house and brave the crowds at the mall. We still haven't got your father a gift from you."

She dropped her voice to a near whisper as she watched her husband enter the house. "And I haven't got his extra special "for his eyes only" gift yet. You know we girls have to keep our men interested!" Ann wiggled her eyebrows as she said this, and Heather couldn't stop the laughter at the thought of just what that particular gift might be.

Amid fits and starts of giggles, Heather got out, "I can't believe you just said that, Mom! My mother! And, oh, my God! My dad!"

"What? You think we're too old for sex?"

"I'm not going there, Mom!"

"Damn right!" Ann said, as she rose and pulled her daughter from the lounge chair and pointed her toward the kitchen door. "Set the table while I get the stew made. It'll only take a few minutes. And after . . ." she waited for Heather to look at her. "And after, we'll go to bed. You will sleep well. I mean it, no worrying. Then we'll be ready in the morning for a fantastic shopping trip."

Heather went to her room still smiling from the family conversation over dinner. Alone, her thoughts turned to Jeff. *I hope he's doing okay and nothing else has happened.* Reaching for her travel bag that served as a purse, she dug in the side pocket, pushing aside pens and lipstick and lip balm until she came up with her cell phone. She punched in Jeff's cell number and listened for the rings. Just as worry took hold on the fifth ring, Jeff answered.

"Hi, sweetheart. Glad you called. Talking with you will be a welcome break from Christmas cards."

"Christmas cards?"

"Yeah. It looks like all the girls in my classes mailed me Christmas cards. Must be because I'm such a wonderful teacher."

"And modest, too."

"But of course. So . . . what's up? What did you do today?"

Heather told him the gist of the conversation she'd had with her mom and that they were going shopping in the morning, since it was the last opportunity before Christmas arrived.

"Two things," Jeff said. "Number one: I don't think I'm quite ready just yet to move to Florida. And number two: I've got to go shopping tomorrow, as well. Oh, and I called the folks today and accepted their Christmas dinner invitation. Mom said she'd make my favorite pumpkin pie." He chuckled. "I'd love to tell her I positively hate pumpkin pie."

"Jeff, you can't do that!"

"But I can't stand the stuff, Heather. I guess I'll have to suck it up one more time and eat some of it." He sounded resigned.

"That sounds good. At least the shopping part does." Heather emitted a huge yawn. "Well, I'm off to bed now. I know we're both tired, I expect you're on your way to bed, too. We'll have a longer talk tomorrow."

"Okay. Goodnight, now. Sweet dreams. And make sure they are about me. I love you."

"And I love you too. Good night, Jeff."

Heather undressed, donned a light weight gown, and crawled into the familiar bed she'd slept in for years. She didn't go to sleep right away. She thought of her confirmation classes at Good Shepherd Lutheran Church and the values she was taught there. Pastor Robert wouldn't be happy with her living with Jeff out of wedlock. *But I love him. I want to live with him. I want to marry him. He just has to ask me, and we need to make plans. Oh, I don't know what to do.*

Her thoughts returned to Jeff at home in Green Bay where he was dealing with whatever the investigation into Patti's murder was turning up. *I hope the detectives will have no reason to bother Jeff while I'm away* was her last thought as she drifted into sleep.

On that Monday morning in Green Bay, Patti's killer sat hunched in his home desk chair, absently flipping a ball point pen back and forth between his index and middle fingers. He needed to sign and address about four dozen Christmas cards that were expected to be received from him. A man in his position had responsibilities and duties and all-around niceties to perform and he couldn't put it off any longer. This was Monday and Christmas was Thursday. As it was, he couldn't get them into the mail until the next day, therefore it was chancy that they could be delivered before Christmas. *Well, hell! I've had far too much to do at work and other things to think about. Can I help it if the damned cards are late?*

One thing that was bugging him badly was the couple who had found sweet little Patti's body. He narrowed his eyes and pursed his lips while he formed a plan. It was always good to have a plan. *Perhaps a warning might be in order. A warning for them to keep their noses out of my business.*

With a plan in mind, he went back to writing a clichéd ditty on each card, working late into the night, and signing each one with a flourish. Finished with that, he got busy devising the steps needed to make his plan work. *I'll show them I am not to be trifled with. God, it's great to be brilliant!*

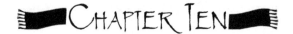

Chapter Ten

December 24, 2014

Jeff and Heather talked every night, which helped ease the pain of being apart on their very first Christmas as a couple. So, here Jeff was, alone on this Christmas Eve, but he still enjoyed the Christmas music playing in each bright as daylight store. He walked into first one and then another, crunching along the shoveled sidewalks that bore a light crust of icy snow in the quaint downtown shopping area. Everything was joyful and Jeff couldn't help getting caught up in the happiness of the shoppers around him.

A guilty conscience brought him out amidst the last-minute shoppers and the sightseers on Christmas Eve. He needed to buy a gift for both his mom and his dad since he would be participating in the family gift opening the next morning. The new tabletop convection oven he and Heather had gone in together on was a gift from the two of them to both of his parents. It wasn't enough. *I have to find something very personal from just me to each of them.*

He entered the bright lights and colorful decorations of a small gift shop. Its windows were filled with green garlands, different kinds of decorated Christmas trees, and fake snow. Carved wooden snowmen wearing their gaily painted scarves, hats and gloves caught his attention and fired his imagination. *Maybe a scarf and a pair of gloves for Mom?*

On his way to Women's Accessories, he stopped at the perfume counter in the trendy boutique, thinking his mom might like a nice perfume. She'd never been one to wear scents, but he bet if he gave it to her, she'd love it. He asked a clerk for something light and smelled of flowers.

"I have no idea where to start. Is that combination too much to hope for?" He used his best "little boy needs help" look.

"Right here, Mr. Hoffmann. Try this."

Jeff whipped around and looked over into the face of one of his students; her glorious red hair was tucked under an elf's cap.

"Sorry, Nicole, I didn't recognize you with your hair hidden under that cap." He took the proffered bottle from her hand. "So, you recommend this one, huh?"

He gave an apologetic shrug to the first clerk, an older woman with an elaborate upswept hair style and a heavily made-up face. She winked at Jeff and smiled in response.

"Yes sir," Nicole said. "It's my mom's personal favorite. She's worn it for years. Whenever I smell it on someone, it immediately reminds me of my mother."

"Red Door. Well, the bottle *is* red, and it's shaped like a door, so that's a good start." He laughed at his witticism and Nicole smiled as if she were the adult.

Nicole took the bottle and picked up a little strip of white paper from the counter. She spritzed a bit on the paper, waved it in the air, and said, "Smell this. You're going to like it."

Jeff did as directed. “Oooh, that’s really nice. My mom will love this. I’ll take it. Could you gift wrap it for me, Nicole?”

She looked around to see who was watching. The only people nearby at this time were two older teen boys fingering the merchandise in the sale bin, their backs turned to them.

She whispered to Jeff, “We’re really not supposed to gift wrap at the counters or stations. However, I hate for you to stand in that long line over there . . .” She nodded her head toward the far-right corner of the room where a line snaked its way in serpentine movement across the back of the store. “. . . wait just a minute and I’ll put it in a little gift bag with some tissue paper. Will that work?”

“Absolutely. Thanks, Nicole.” He grinned and added, “And now can you give me some advice for a gift for my dad?”

She responded at once. “Does he like football?”

“Sure. He’s a huge Packers fan.”

“Great. There’s a store in the next block that sells all kinds of sports stuff. I’m sure you can find something there.”

“Remind me to give you an “A” on your next paper,” Jeff teased. “Not that you wouldn’t make an “A” anyway!”

Nicole laughed and sent him on his way with a wave of her hand.

He took his purchase and headed for the door. *I’m going to take Nicole’s advice and visit the store in the next block that carries Green Bay Packers stuff.*

Absorbed in the festivities around him, Jeff barely noticed as two young men in hoodies under their heavy coats slipped out the door behind him, passed him with long strides, and headed up the sidewalk in front of him. He didn’t see them disappear into the narrow alley that separated the two buildings and was used for deliveries.

Snow scraped from the sidewalks was now piled a foot or more at its entrance.

As Jeff stepped into the space between the buildings, he was grabbed by a powerful arm and another circled his neck. He could feel the pressure of something sharp pressed against his neck, right above the zipper. His blood went cold. *Oh my God; I'm going to die!*

The knife wielder whispered in his ear, "Forget about anything you know, or think you know, about the Patti Mueller case. No playing private investigator or messing with any of it. You don't know anything, and that's the way it's gonna stay. Make one wrong move and I'll be back," the raspy voice threatened.

Jeff was so relieved that he was getting out of this alive until he was unprepared for the blow that landed just above his left knee delivered by a third attacker who had joined the fray.

"God Almighty! Shit!" Jeff yelled as he went down with his knees buckling beneath him. He landed hard on the injured knee which felt as if it was going to burst through his long johns and jeans. Before he could say more or think beyond the here and now, an SUV skidded to a halt on the ice and snow and the two attackers picked him up, and with no finesse or worry about the state of his leg injury, they threw him into the open space in the back where the row of seats had been removed. One ski-masked attacker quickly snatched Jeff's woolen scarf and yanked it up over his eyes in a make-shift blindfold.

Don't touch it!" The raspy voice was back. "Don't move a muscle! Now listen to me carefully. This is a warning for you and Miss Goody Two Shoes. If you even think you have something to tell the police, you'd better stow it. You talk and you and your girlfriend will get the same thing Patti Mueller did."

The car made a series of turns and traveled for a few minutes before it abruptly slowed and stopped. The back door opened and Jeff was dragged from the car through the deepening snow and dumped onto something hard. He pulled the scarf from his eyes and saw that he was lying on the steps to his apartment.

As the SUV drove away, the raspy voice yelled, "Just a little Christmas gift for your girlfriend. Tell her she could be next!"

With his leg and knee throbbing like a son-of-a-bitch, Jeff didn't think to look for a license plate number, not that he could have seen it in the night with only a lamp's feeble glow to light things. He fumbled with unlocking the door and hobbled inside. *I know I need to get to a doctor but first I have to call the police.* He fished in his wallet for the detectives' cards and came up with Aksel Franzen's. He placed the call.

It was Christmas Eve and although he wanted more than anything to go home, relax with an Irish coffee made with lots of the Irish, Captain Harjula was still at the headquarters questioning his detectives and wondering aloud to them why they hadn't discovered more information pertaining to the Mueller case. "It's been a week and a half. Where do we stand with information gathered?"

Aksel Franzen spoke first. "We've been canvasing the homes by The Golf Course, but no one seems to have seen anything that day that was in any way out of the ordinary."

"Well, go back and ask them if they saw anything *out* of the ordinary on any *other* day. Maybe somebody saw something, even if it didn't register at the time. Also, we'll get Officers Heimerle and Schroeder back out there to canvas the houses on the other side of the street. Am I mistaken in thinking those houses are smaller than those bordering The Golf Club?" Captain Harjula's right eyebrow traveled toward his hairline as he asked the question.

Having seen that particular action many times, the detectives knew that he already knew the answer to the question. "That's right, sir," Aksel confirmed.

"I would think that perhaps someone there saw something unusual on the golf course. They can look between those larger houses, can they not?"

Again Aksel answered, "Yes, sir."

"Then let's get to it," the captain directed.

"Yes, sir, we'll do that," Anja said. "We're also continuing to have regular talks directly with the Muellers and with the two schoolteachers who found her body. We've talked to neighbors of the Muellers who all pretty much say the same thing. Nice family, but the dad drinks too much, and they don't seem to have much money and, while the brother acts responsible and disciplined, Patti tended to be less so and, in fact, tended to go and do as she pleased."

"Yes," Aksel picked up the thread, "and since she did do as she pleased, no one noticed anything that was any different than usual. However, Anja and I are leaning toward her knowing her killer. We need to find out who she was spending time with."

"And who the father of her baby is," added Anja.

"Oh yes. We definitely need to find who the father is," said Harjula. "Since we've gotten DNA from the fetus from Maggie Green, we have that smoking gun. Hell, what we *need* is samples from any man or boy that she's spent time with in the last few months!"

Harjula looked down at the floor, placed his hands on his hips and rocked backwards. "Oh, my aching back."

Bending forward again, he could see the expressions on his detectives' faces. He laughed long and hard, slapping his thigh in merriment.

"I said that's what we *need,* not that we'd *do* it!" he spluttered.

"Oh, thank God!" Anja said. "I couldn't figure how we could do that."

Aksel's cell phone played *Dragnet.* "Something's definitely up. I gotta take this. It's from Jeff Hoffmann." He listened for a moment. "Don't move. We'll be right there."

Aksel thumbed off the cell phone and looked to Captain Harjula. "We've got something now, Captain. Jeff Hoffmann has been attacked."

At the hospital, while waiting for his leg to be x-rayed, Jeff accepted an oxycodone for pain and thanked the detectives for bringing him to the ER. *It's time to tell them exactly what happened.*

"Okay. Here's the how it all played out. I was buying some perfume as a gift for my mother to open tomorrow morning. I told you Heather went to Florida to be with her parents, right?" He looked at both detectives for confirmation, his face drawn in pain.

"Yes, you did," Aksel responded.

Jeff nodded. "And so I'm going to spend Christmas day with my folks." He stopped and stretched out his leg. Immediately he closed his eyes and groaned with pain as his knee throbbed.

He opened his eyes. "One of my students, Nicole Peterson, was the clerk helping me choose a fragrance my mom might like."

Anja asked, "Did you buy the perfume?"

"Yes."

"Is that the only thing you bought?"

"Yes. I was on my way to the sports store in the next block to get my dad something with the Packers' logo. They jumped me as I was crossing the alley. I don't know what happened to the perfume."

"What else do you remember?" Aksel wrote in his notebook.

"I didn't see anything or anybody in that store, or the previous ones I went in, that looked suspicious. But they had to have been following me and anticipated I'd continue with my shopping along the street. I know they were waiting for me in the alley."

"How many were there?" Anja asked.

"Four, I think. Three attacked me and then there was the driver of the SUV, unless one of them was driving it. Their whole intent was to warn Heather and me not to talk to the police. I got roughed up to make sure she got the message, too. I hate to even tell her about this and ruin her time with her parents."

"Then don't." Anja laid a hand on his shoulder. "Let her enjoy her time with her family. We'll start checking this out and you can talk to her about this when she gets home."

A young nurse approached them who looked to Jeff to be no older than his students.

"Okay, Mr. Hoffmann. Let's get that X-ray."

After the X-ray, Jeff was seen by a doctor on call. The doctor told Jeff, "The whole area of the injury is a hematoma resulting in a nasty bruise. The tissue above the knee was quite damaged by the force of the blow. Perhaps a board or a baseball bat was used." The doctor shook his head in apparent disgust.

"Your knee is badly swollen, and you'll need to keep it cold with the ice-packs the nurse will provide. You do know how to use them?" He looked up from his reports and shot Jeff a questioning look.

"Yes, I sometimes work with the athletes at my school. I know all about icing an injury."

"Fine, then. Don't put your weight on it for forty-eight hours and you must use crutches to move about." He offered a feeble grin and added, "Merry Christmas." He gathered his papers and left the room to see the next pressing case needing to be attended to in the emergency room on this long Christmas Eve night.

The detectives took Jeff home and accompanied him inside to make sure he was safe. Discovering nobody inside and nothing out of the ordinary, they left Jeff to hobble upstairs and get in bed. He did, pain gliding up his thigh toward his hip and riding the hill of his knee and skiing down his shin.

He thought he would never fall asleep, but another dose of the oxycodone dulled the throb to a niggling ache. Turning from his back to his right side with the injured left leg resting atop his right leg, he was soon gently snoring.

After taking Jeff home, Franzen and Frandsen stopped by the alley in which Jeff was attacked. Sure enough, a sodden blue paper bag with handles lay atop the trodden snow, now frosted with new flakes. Anja picked up the bag and looked inside. "Yep, it's the Red Door perfume."

She put the bottle to her nose and sniffed. "This really does smell nice. I suppose the cap loosened when Jeff dropped it. Or," she grinned at Aksel, "it just smells so good until it escapes the bottle."

"You like it?"

"Yeah, I do. It beats any of the sweet, fruity things named after the girl singers that are all the rage now."

"Well, you can't have that one since it's evidence, but I know where we can get you another one. Come with me."

Aksel took her by the arm and marched the twenty or so feet to the boutique. The door was locked but lights were still on inside. He banged on the door and when a young woman peered through the glass, he showed his badge.

They asked for Nicole Peterson to get her version of the events. Nicole came from the store room where she was sorting through the glistening perfume bottles with which she would replenish the stock inside her counter. She told them she had seen the two young men or, most likely, older teens, hanging around. They'd stayed back and hadn't approached Mr. Hoffmann.

"Do you think Mr. Hoffmann saw them?" Anja glanced at the perfume bottles.

"I don't think so. But I'm sure they followed him outside. I think they wanted to talk to him, probably about grades, but just didn't want to do it inside where others could hear. I've heard that failing students are always trying to get the teachers to change their grades."

"Thank you, Miss Peterson," Aksel said. "Now I have a request of you, if you don't mind. It's not too late for you to make a sale now, is it?"

With a smile, Nicole said, "Certainly not. Especially for a police officer. What can I get for you?" She eased behind the perfume counter.

"I'd like to see a bottle of your Red Door perfume."

Nicole nodded and produced a mid-size bottle of perfume and a blue gift bag. "Is this size what you're looking for?"

It was the same size Jeff had bought for his mom. "That's perfect."

The credit card transaction was made, Aksel signed it, and he turned to Anja. "Here, Partner. Merry Christmas."

"Aksel! Thank you, but I can't accept this."

"You thought I was joking, didn't you?" He laughed aloud at her embarrassed look.

"Since when can't an officer of the law accept a Christmas gift from her partner? Now take it before I change my mind."

She took the pretty blue bag, thanked Nicole for her help, and turned and hurried to the door. Aksel followed.

In the car, Anja said, "Okay, I don't have a gift for you but, since I'd really rather not spend Christmas Eve by myself and I'm starving, why don't you come home with me and I'll make you some dinner?"

"I was just waiting for you to ask."

In her apartment, Anja took two crystal wine flutes from her china cabinet and got a crisp pinot grigio from the refrigerator. She set them in front of Aksel, who was sitting with one haunch on a barstool at the counter, one long leg stretched out in front of him. "You do the honors while I start dinner."

Following her tradition on Christmas Eve, Anja started pulling ingredients from the fridge. First came a pint of small select oysters, fresh and in their juice. Next came a quart of half and half and a quart of heavy cream. Then came a stick of butter. From the shelf by the stove she picked a container of white pepper and a salt shaker.

As he handed her a glass of the refreshing white wine, Aksel remarked, "Looks like we're having oyster stew."

"Yeah, you betcha, by golly. Gotta have oyster stew on Christmas Eve. I'm glad you're here to share it with me, Aksel."

"Thanks for asking me."

Anja quickly assembled the stew, heating the oysters in their juice just till the edges curled and then adding the other ingredients. While the stew heated, she tossed together a green salad with frilly lettuce Aksel had never seen before and slid a half loaf of already prepared garlic bread into the oven to toast.

Accepting a top-up of the delicious wine, Anja set silverware and plates on the coffee table that faced the fireplace in the small, vibrantly accessorized living room. She turned a switch, and with a small whoosh, the gas fire leapt to life behind its decorative screen that depicted a filigreed pewter peacock.

Soon she was ladling the rich, creamy stew into bowls big enough to assuage her appetite, and maybe even Aksel's.

"Would you open another bottle of wine, please, and bring it with you? That way we won't run out while we're eating." She giggled like a young girl and flushed bright pink. She ducked her head so as not to look at Aksel. "I'm putting the salad and bread out and then I'll bring in our stew."

Aksel chuckled and got the wine from the refrigerator. He deftly used the wine bottle opener he'd left on the counter. He brought the bottle to the coffee table and set it down beside their steaming bowls of stew. Then the two detectives sat down together behind the long coffee table. They stretched their legs out beneath it, their sock-covered toes reaching toward the warming fire that flickered and flared merrily as they ate and drank together, neither one having any other place to be on the cold, snowy, Christmas Eve night.

It was unlike the coming days when they would be searching for a killer.

Chapter Eleven

December 25, 2014

Jeff slept fitfully and was relieved when he could finally get out of bed Christmas morning. He had been in too much pain and his brain felt filled with gauze the night of the attack, so he called neither his parents nor Heather to tell them what happened. He'd hated to call Heather the night before, since the unwelcome news would be very upsetting to her. Instead, he had texted a quick message saying he'd been out shopping until late. And since it then was extremely late, he'd call her in the morning. He ended with "I love you, Heather."

Her texted answer was, "That's fine. Hope you were lucky in finding gifts for your parents. And me! Love you and will talk with you in the morning. Merry Christmas!"

He pondered what to do. Should I tell her? Perhaps I can simply call and say Merry Christmas and tell Heather I love and miss her, engage in a little chit chat, and put off until this evening the details of my injury. Or maybe just wait until she gets home. That might be better. Damn! I just don't know.

His mind was going in circles. He shook his head, hoping to clear it. Bad mistake. His headache started crawling from the back of his head over the top, settling behind his eyes.

As for his parents, he decided last night he would call his dad and ask him to come get him so he could spend a good portion of the day with them. He'd tell his dad, of course. Maybe together they could come up with what to tell his mom. Having a plan in mind made him feel somewhat better, and he'd gingerly got into his bed. And, amazingly, he'd slept.

Now, using the crutches, he hobbled to the bathroom to freshen up and to take another dose of the painkiller. Just getting out of bed, and then his leg dangling, was all it took to set his thigh and knee to throbbing.

After brushing his teeth and swiping at his whiskers with the electric shaver, Jeff began to get dressed. Pulling Jeans up over his knee was a game of torture. As he donned layers of warm clothing, he looked at the unmade bed and determined it would still be there when he got in it that night.

He called his parent's number, hoping his dad would answer. Luck was with him. He told his dad that he would explain later why he needed him to come get him. While he waited, he placed the call to Heather.

"Merry Christmas, sweetheart."

"And a very Merry Christmas to you, Jeff! Boy, have I missed you. I'm having a wonderful time, but I wish you were here."

"I've missed you too, Heather. I wish we were together. Either here or there. Makes no difference. But since we're not, I guess we'll both make the best of our day and enjoy being with our folks."

"I know, honey. Try to have a good time today. And do like I'm doing and think positive. Next year we'll have all this mess behind us, and we will be together."

"That sure sounds good. But now I've gotta go eat Eva's pumpkin pie and keep peace in the family." Even though Heather couldn't see him, he rolled his eyes just thinking about the pumpkin pie.

"Good boy. And Jeff? I'm sorry we didn't get a chance to go shopping because I don't have a gift there for you to open."

"That's true, but I don't have one for you, either. We'll have our own private Christmas celebration when you return day after tomorrow. Sound okay to you?"

"Yes. It sounds perfect. Please give your parents my love and best wishes."

"And you do the same. I'll call you again this evening and we'll compare our days. Bye, for now." Jeff ended the call and figuratively patted himself on the back for being sharp enough to wait to tell her their ordeal was not over. Not by a long shot.

What he didn't know was it seemed to Heather that she was a million miles away from Jeff. She tapped off her cell phone and, deep in thought, stood holding it against her cheek. Something just didn't feel right. She couldn't put her finger on it, but Jeff was off somehow. She decided to think about it for the next couple of days and confront him when she returned home.

Jeff explained to his father what had transpired the night before as they drove through the snowy streets back to the retirement condominium. His dad paid close attention to his driving as the snow made it difficult to see what was coming around the next bend or corner. He also listened intently to what Jeff was telling him. He was no man's fool and, as usual, he had a theory.

"You know that the man who spoke with the scratchy, or raspy, or whatever the hell it was voice, was disguising it. Now I wonder why? I bet you a plugged nickel that he did it because he thought you'd recognize his voice, thereby recognizing him. This whole thing pisses me off big time, and I'm telling you, he was probably scared you'd know him."

"You might be right, Dad," Jeff sighed, rubbing his forehead. "But, I'm so frustrated! I can't imagine how I would know the killer. Hell, I didn't even know the girl, so how could I possibly know the bastard who killed her?" *This is a whole new can of worms.*

"Well, there certainly was some reason why he and his goons gave you an almost broken leg as a warning."

"You're right." Jeff had a whole new direction to go with his wondering. Now, however, he had to concentrate on this Christmas day with his parents. *But, there's no way I can contend with Mom's questions and motherly hovering.*

"Dad, let's not tell Mom what really happened. You know it will worry her sick and she'll be babying me all day. Why don't we tell her that while I was out last night shopping for your presents from me, that I slipped on the ice and took a bad fall on my knee? That will explain my going to the hospital. Oh, and it will also explain why I don't have any presents for you two to open this morning."

"Son, the presents aren't important."

"Like hell they're not! If I hadn't really wanted to get something for each of you, I wouldn't have been out last night, and this wouldn't have happened. Not in any way am I blaming you two, Dad, but I already had Mom's present and was walking to the next block to get yours when they jumped me. So, yes, presents for my mom and dad are important."

"I understand, Jeff. I know that you're tired and in pain and that simple things can easily irritate you." John narrowed his eyes and seemed to Jeff to be thinking. Soon he said, "I'll try to keep a rein on your mother so she doesn't pester you too much."

"Thanks, Dad. I appreciate it."

"Merry Christmas, Mom," Jeff called as he entered the foyer of the condo, trying to stay upright on the slick floor with the crutches under his arms.

"Something smells delicious!" He smelled turkey and the sweet potato casserole that he'd always loved.

Eva Hoffmann rounded the corner from the kitchen and stopped dead at the sight of Jeff on crutches. "What on earth . . ."

Interrupting her, Jeff started rattling off his fabricated story about slipping on the ice.

His mother broke in with, "My word, Jeff, that's such a shame." She helped him to sit on the sofa, placed a throw pillow on the coffee table and instructed him to put his foot on it and to keep it elevated.

Jeff finished his story. By the look on her face, he wasn't certain his mom bought it.

Eva pursed her lips and was looking very thoughtful. "I thought it was a law that the merchants had to keep the ice off the sidewalks. Hmmmm . . ." She turned away, heading back to the kitchen.

Over her shoulder she said, "Okay, Jeff, sweetie, you sit right there and keep your leg still. I'll get you a cup of coffee and a piece of strudel." Brightening, she stopped, clapped her hands together and said with a big smile, "And then we'll open presents."

Jeff remembered Christmas mornings in his childhood when his mom tried to make the inexpensive and sometimes meager gifts seem like a full bounty. She said St. Nick's bag was very, very heavy with all the toys and books and games inside that he shared with all the little boys and girls and he only had so many. Just enough to go around and he made sure every boy and girl got something.

Bless her. She was a good mother, and still is. I'm pleased she seems delighted with the table-top convection oven Heather and I gave to them.

His dad had asked, "What's a convection oven?" When it was explained to him, he said, "Another modern marvel."

From his parents Jeff and Heather received a decent set of pots and pans. Jeff was overjoyed. Their mismatched pots and pans were remnants of cast-off pieces from both sets of parents that they'd each carried from place to place with them since college days.

"Wow! These are perfect. You couldn't possibly have given us something we needed more. Heather is going to go crazy when she sees these. Thank you. Thank you. Thank you both so much."

His mom handed him two more gifts, one larger than the other. Inside his larger box was a heavy wool sweater in earthen tones of tans and browns. Eva accepted his thanks with a smile and told him the smaller box for Heather contained a sweater as well.

"That's great, Mom. Coming from Florida, Heather doesn't have nearly enough warm clothes for a Green Bay winter."

He finished the story he and his dad agreed to tell her by promising to get her another bottle of perfume to replace the one he dropped when he fell on the slippery ice. He promised his dad that when he was walking comfortably, he would get his gift from the sports memorabilia store at the same time.

The day went well and passed more quickly than he'd thought possible. After pushing the pumpkin pie around his plate and taking a couple of bites, he announced he simply couldn't eat another morsel. With hurt feelings no longer an issue, it was time to go.

"Will you do the honors again, Dad, and drive me home?"

"You bet, Son. We'll leave your mom here to clean up the remains of this feast," John teased, bestowing a smile on Eva.

"A woman's work is never done," Eva stated mournfully. "I cook for hours, cleaning up as I go, and then we eat and it's all over in just a few minutes, except the final cleanup, that is."

"Ahh, poor Mom . . ." Jeff began.

"Oh, just go on and get out of here," Eva said, as she threw a dishtowel at her men.

Driving through the mostly empty streets to Jeff's apartment, John asked him to fill him in when they found the culprits who ambushed him.

"I just hope the police find them soon and we can put all this behind us," Jeff said, as he opened the car door and began to limp from the curb to his door. He stopped and awkwardly turned to his dad, who sat watching him with the car idling, sending out gusts of vapor into the cold air.

"What is it?" John called to Jeff, who balanced on his crutches.

Jeff looked down and a frown grew upon his brow. "I just thought of something, Dad."

Suddenly, Jeff wailed, "Ohhh-uhhh." One moment he'd been standing there thinking. He moved his crutches to turn to his dad in his car, causing them to skid on the ice, and the next moment he was on the ground beside the front steps.

"Dammit!" he hollered. "Shit! That hurt my knee."

John scrambled from the car and rushed to help his son get up. "Are you all right, Jeff?"

Jeff braced against the front door while his father gathered the scattered crutches. He looked into his dad's face.

"I don't think I will *ever* be okay, Dad." He looked far away, gazing at nothing. He then turned back to John. "When I find the sons-of-bitches who did this, and I *will* find them, I am going to kill every last one of them."

John believed him.

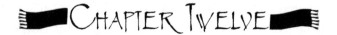

Chapter Twelve

December 27, 2014

The killer sat in his library in a leather wingback chair the color of black coffee with a hint of oxblood mixed in. Currently he was staring holes into the three teens who slouched with their hands thrust into their coat pockets on the matching sofa across the elegantly appointed room. They huddled with woolen cap-covered heads drooping to avoid his gaze. Patti's murderer considered them low and distasteful. *Not one of them would have any idea that this lovely room in which they sullenly sit was decorated with turn of the nineteenth century antiques.*

He was quite proud of his home, especially this library with its old-world décor of heavy, flowered drapes framing the big picture window and thick, wool rugs on the glossy wood floors. The wingback's coffee and oxblood color was repeated in the medallions of roses spread across the rug on a muted gold background. The library's richly paneled walls supported two ornate wooden bookcases where first editions and almost priceless antique books marched like soldiers the length of the cases. *Idiots!*

But I had to have someone attend to that nosy Jeff Hoffmann, didn't I? Even if they didn't succeed in breaking his leg, they still must have done some major damage, especially considering how loudly he yelled. He almost giggled aloud at the thought of the big guy going down when the kid struck his knee with the baseball bat.

Abruptly, his mood changed. *Dammit, it should have broken his knee!*

He had no real idea or evidence that Jeff Hoffmann suspected he was Patti's killer. Or if his pretty girlfriend, Heather Forrest, had any inkling it was he. However, a warning was always good. Particularly one that was so deliciously painful.

The idea of pain brought him back to Patti, the stupid little bitch. Sexy, beautiful even, but stupid. How stupid could she be when she even dared to hope that someone like him could love someone like her? He remembered seeing her the first time. She'd walked past him as if he wasn't there. He'd turned to watch her walk away from him with her womanly figure and lush mouth and knew instantly he must have her. She was eighteen years old and ripe for his picking. So, pick her, he did. He'd devised a plan to gain her trust. The ignorant little tramp had fallen for it.

They'd met the first time in his office. He set up an appointment for her to see him. He read her records thoroughly and with great glee discovered she had an unstable home life. That was his starting place; win her trust and get her to feel comfortable with him. They would continue their special appointments together and over time she would begin to trust him. And then he could gently guide her into confiding in him. Once that happened, he would have her under his control. That's what he would work toward, and in the end, all the acting nice and caring and being both sympathetic and empathetic would pay off big time.

Oh, he would delight in the chicanery he would use to get her where he wanted her. And, due to her inferior intelligence, he knew it would all work out the way he wanted. The way he used his greater intelligence to get what he wanted amazed and fulfilled him. He was meant to use the superior intellect that he possessed to get the things in life he wanted. Patti he wanted; Patti he planned to get; Patti he'd gotten!

"If I suspect, or have any idea at all, that you three have been discussing this in the presence of another, I promise you will pay for it, Better yet, don't let a word of this escape your lips. Don't talk about it, period."

None of the boys responded or even bothered to look at him. He could feel his blood begin to heat and rush through his veins. The vein in his temple throbbed painfully. By God, he'd show them who was boss around here and just who deserved their respect.

"Rocky, what do you think your parole officer would say if he were to find out you've been getting inebriated on a regular basis and keeping company with your old automobile theft buddies? Oh, please do pardon me." His voice dripped sarcasm. "I'll put it in words you can understand. What would he say about you often being drunk and hanging around with your chop-shop cronies? Maybe joining in on their robberies?"

Rocky jumped up from his slouched position on the sofa.

"No! Don't talk to my parole officer. What you're saying is a lie! I haven't done anything wrong since juvie. If you tell him something like that, I won't go back to juvie this time. I'd go to regular prison with all them perverts who like to stick it to all us new guys."

He yanked his watch cap off and wadded and re-wadded it in his hands. “I promise not to say anything to anybody. Just don’t talk to him, please.”

Ah, now I’ve got him where I want him.

“Joe? Are you going to remain silent or must I take action against you and the Nygaard family? You’ve got a lovely little sister. It would be horrible if she were to meet the same fate as poor Patti.”

Joe ground his teeth together, but affirmed in a meek voice, “No Sir. I won’t say anything.” He swallowed hard and added, “Please don’t mess with my sister.”

“Stay quiet and things will turn out fine. That goes for all three of you. Now, get out of my sight!”

Later that day as she waited to board her plane at the Gainesville, Florida, airport, Heather hugged Ann tightly, reluctant to let her go. Her dad had remained home watching yet another football game. His beloved University of Florida Gators had not been galvanized enough this season to do well. She knew he hoped they’d do better in the Toilet Bowl, or whatever bowl game in which they were invited to participate. She knew, too, he didn’t hold out much hope, and while sad about that, he would watch almost any team play. Gainesville was a football crazed town and she had grown up with a football crazy father.

Heather thought fondly of the several pairs of shorts she had worn during this visit home. She’d put them in the washing machine along with other items of soiled clothing and started the washer before she left for the airport. She knew her mom would practically scrub the entire room with a Brillo pad to make sure it was pristine clean for her next homecoming.

She'd donned a pair of heavy tan corduroy slacks she'd had the foresight to pack for the trip home and a new bold Christmas-red pull-over sweater. Her parents gave it to her, among other presents, for, as they said, that awful weather up north. Now, she'd be lucky if she didn't have heat exhaustion on the way to the airport for the flight back to Green Bay.

Having agreed to meet at the baggage carousel at the airport in Green Bay, Heather rounded the corner into the corridor leading to Baggage Claim. She dug in her purse for her moisturizing lip balm and applied it hurriedly so her lips would be moist for the kiss she would undoubtedly get from Jeff. Dropping the balm back into a pocket of her purse, she looked for the carousel with the baggage from her flight and was astonished to see Jeff propped up on crutches as he waited for her.

She stared straight ahead with mouth open and smile frozen. "Oh, my God, Jeff! What happened to you?"

Jeff limped into Heather and put an arm around her, holding her close. She put both arms around his neck and held him tight. "Jeff, you're hurt. Tell me about it."

"I had a little accident but didn't want to worry you. I'll be fine in a few days." Their lips came together in a kiss filled with love and longing.

"You have to tell me how it happened and what the doctors say," Heather demanded as she drew back to see his face.

"Oh, believe me, I will. Let's get home and out of this weather and traffic."

"God, that sounds wonderful. You wait right here while I grab my bag."

At headquarters, Captain Harjula was being briefed by the two policemen who answered the call the day Patti was killed. The two detectives working the case were also giving him a verbal report on their progress with the investigation into the Mueller case.

"We went to every house across the street from the big houses that back up to the golf course. It took some time, but I think we got lucky . . ." Officer Schroeder was saying when he was interrupted by his partner.

"Oh man, did we get lucky! We thought it would be someone from directly across the street that saw something, but it wasn't!"

"Right," his partner quickly continued. "It was the lady who lived in the last house at the end of the street who actually saw something that could be of use."

Before he could go into further detail, Heimerle volunteered, "She walks her dog every afternoon at the same time and she says that twice she saw someone out by the pond . . ."

"But it was too far away to tell if it was a man or a woman . . ." Schroeder was saying.

Heimerle added, "Or a big kid."

The captain's head and those of the detectives swung back and forth between the two officers as they relayed their story, like spectators at a tennis match. The captain again looked from one to the other and said, "One at a time, please."

Both were quiet for a few seconds and then Heimerle divulged what they knew in a concise form. "Sorry, Captain. This lady who walks her dog every afternoon at three o'clock said she'd seen someone by the pond twice and she thought it was the Wednesday and Thursday before the body was discovered on Friday. She couldn't be sure if it was an adult, but the body size indicated that it probably was. She also couldn't think of any reason for the person to be there. No upkeep is being done to The Golf Club course at this time of year." He looked from the captain to the detectives and ended with, "I don't have any idea where to go from here."

"Nor do I," Captain Harjula admitted, "but you two did a good job with this. The detectives here will be working toward finding out how this information fits into the big picture. But for now, you're dismissed." He watched the officers leave the room and then turned to the detectives.

"What is the latest on the school teachers?".

"Heather Forrest is due back today." Frandsen checked her watch. "She should've just arrived at the airport. Hoffmann said he would wait until they were at home to tell her about the attack. I suppose we'll head on over there in a little while and see if either one has an idea about who did it to him."

In the two days since his dad had driven him on Christmas day, Jeff had improved to the point that he had driven to the airport to get Heather and now he joked with her to keep her from suspecting the truth of his accident. In his best Groucho Marx accent, with imaginary cigar held between his fingers and with which he accented his story, he told her, "Yep, just call me Wiley Coyote, ma'am. I got that TNT dropped on me and I look a bit frizzed."

He took his eyes off the road to look at Heather. She wore a puzzled look as if she was trying to make sense of his story.

Jeff continued his tale, hoping she would believe him.

"It was a true Wiley E. Coyote move when I slipped on the ice. I bet I did cartwheels for fifty feet before I fell on my knee. And let me tell you, sister, I was frazzled, but my knee wasn't broken." He tapped his thumb and forefinger together several times as if tapping ashes from his cigar and gave Heather a goofy grin.

Heather appeared to accept his story but, other than smiling at him and rolling her eyes at his lame attempt at Groucho Marx, she kept the conversation light, talking instead about how warm it had been in Florida and how much she had enjoyed being with her parents. She hopped out to get her luggage as soon as they stopped at the curb.

Inside their home, Heather pulled off her outer layers and wrapped herself around Jeff, engaging in a slow kiss during which she held him close as if he might fly away. Letting him go, she encouraged him to rest, making sure he was comfortably settled on the sofa with his leg propped upon a pillow on the coffee table. Only then did she take her bags upstairs to the bedroom to put away their contents and to give herself a few minutes alone to think.

She remembered their phone conversations, which seemed to have been a little forced, and it seemed Jeff was a bit too hearty about the mundane things he talked of. Now she was thinking this accident had happened and he was either trying to cover it up or, at the very least, he was trying not to mention it for fear of worrying her. *And why should it worry me? He slipped and fell hard on the ice, damaging his leg in the process. But he was all right. Why not tell me? Unless it wasn't an accident. Oh, my Lord, what if it wasn't an accident? What if the person who killed Patti did this to him?*

"Oh, don't be ridiculous!" she said aloud as she put the few items she had not washed before leaving Florida into the laundry hamper inside their bedroom closet. Finished with the task of emptying her bags and putting all of the items in their respective places, Heather determinedly headed down the stairs to confront Jeff about his accident. *I fervently hope my suspicions are incorrect and that*

Jeff won't be angry with me for suggesting he's withheld the truth.

"Jeff, darling," she started, as she stepped from the last stair step to the polished hardwood floor, cold now to her socked, but shoeless, feet. She was saved from the confrontation by the doorbell's ring.

"Stay where you are, honey. I'll get the door." She opened it and was only mildly surprised to see the detective duo standing on the steps. Before they could say a word, Heather invited them in out of the cold. It was not snowing, but the temperature hovered around zero degrees and she didn't want to talk for even a minute outside the warmth of the apartment—no matter why they had come.

"How was your Christmas?" Anja Frandsen asked, as she tugged her arm free of her coat sleeve.

"Oh, I loved being with my parents, but I missed Jeff dreadfully," Heather said immediately, giving Jeff a saucy, suggestive look and a wide smile. Jeff returned both accompanied by a wink.

Dragging his eyes away from Heather and addressing Anja, he patted his belly. "I had a good day with my mom and dad. Ate way too much, though. I even ate my mom's pumpkin pie, which I hate." Jeff chuckled at that. Again, he looked fondly at Heather. "But I sure wish Heather had been here. I missed her, too."

Aksel grinned. "It's terrific that you both were with family and had good Christmases. We had the usual cop's Christmas. Work, work, work."

Anja darted a glance at Aksel. Heather's eyes followed the glance and she thought she might have seen a warm glimmer in Anja's eyes when she looked at him. *Ah-ha, something's going on there.* "Won't you take a seat?" Heather pointed to the two chairs that matched the sofa.

Aksel, instead, perched on the arm of the sofa and told them the reason he and Anja had stopped by. They were checking on Jeff and wondered if he remembered anything that might be of help in apprehending the perpetrators who damaged his knee.

"Yes, Jeff, perhaps you would like to shed some light on what really happened to your knee." Heather's voice was mild as she moved to stand beside Jeff and laid her hand on his shoulder. "It must have been quite an ordeal for you." She silently congratulated herself for keeping her cool and for not provoking an unsavory scene which would only serve to make everyone uncomfortable.

The two detectives looked at each other and then at Heather. Their eyes swung back to Jeff.

Jeff said with a grimace, "I truly didn't mean to hide anything from you, sweetheart. I was simply waiting for the best time to go into the whole story." He looked at the three expectant faces and launched into the events of his shopping trip on Christmas Eve and the resulting injury and abduction. When he was finished, he reached his hand out with palm upraised in a question to the detectives. "That sound about right to you?"

"That's exactly what you told us that night," Aksel confirmed.

"I also remembered something else," Jeff said, as he played the best card dealt him so far. "I'm pretty sure I recognized the voice of one of the three younger guys. I'd bet big bucks it belongs to one of my students. He's a very troubled young man and comes from a relatively poor family. If he was paid to attack me, I could see him doing it for the money."

"Name?" Anja asked.

"Joe Nygaard."

"That's good. Anything else? Think hard. Anything at all could be of help."

"Trust me, I think hard about it all the time," Jeff said.

Aksel stood and briskly rubbed his hands together before pulling his gloves from his coat pocket. "Well, we better get going." He pulled on the gloves. "Just wanted to see how you were recovering from the attack and if you remembered anything else. We'll follow up on the Joe Nygaard tip."

As Heather walked the detectives to the door, Jeff added, "I'll be sure to tell you if something else surfaces."

Heather locked the door behind the detectives and returned to put her arms around Jeff's waist as he awkwardly rose from the sofa. She laid her head against his chest and stood silently, holding him for a couple of minutes, reveling at having him safe in her arms.

Her warring emotions battled for supremacy. She continued to hold him, with her head against his chest, showing him her love.

Unable to, and if she admitted the truth, not *wanting* to contain it any longer, her anger blasted to the surface, as well. Throwing her head back and glaring at him, she ordered, "Don't you ever withhold something like this from me again, Jeff. I *need* to know if you're in danger or if you've been harmed, dammit!"

"I'm so sorry, sweetheart. I thought I was doing the right thing. Don't be mad at me, please." He bent and laid a line of kisses along the soft underside of her jaw.

She dropped her head and sighed. "This has to be connected with Patti's murder, but I don't see how at this point. Oh, God, what'll happen next?"

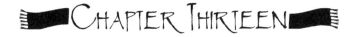

Chapter Thirteen

The Killer
December 29, 2014

The killer delighted in looking back and remembering how he had made his moves on Patti. He thought of it again and again, and each time the thrill of arousal ran through his body. She was so vulnerable, so needy, and responded to his overtures with hesitation at first, but soon she responded with an ardor that could be expected from one considerably beyond her years and experience.

Patti, there for a pre-arranged appointment at their first meeting, knocked on his door right on time. His excitement leapt to the forefront and he had to tell himself to slow down and not to frighten her. It was imperative that he gain, and keep, her trust if his plan was to work. With a burst of certainty, he knew it would. Exhilarated, he called, "Come in," and busied himself with papers on his desk so that she stood awaiting his direction.

Addison looked up at Patti from his desk chair. "Hello Patti. Take a seat on the sofa, won't you? Just let me finish up here." *Good; not too eager.*

She sat on one end of the sofa, looking sullen with her lush lips pouting prettily. He knew she had no idea why she was there. But he knew why. He was confident she would be his conquest, and soon. *Oh, and when that day comes...* He shook his head, breaking his reverie. *I can't think about that now. I must attend to the moment because she's sitting right here in front of me.*

He rose from his desk and went to sit beside her on the sofa. Not too close, but much closer to her than to the other end with its expanse of caramel colored leather.

"So, Patti, tell me a little bit about yourself."

"Why?" she demanded.

He realized he would have to be sensitive and charming because she was hostile and distrusting. "Because I care about you."

"Why?" she said again, turning to look at him, suspicion radiating from her tense body, the set of her shoulders, the jut of her jaw.

Oh, those lips. I've got to possess that luscious mouth.

He reached for her hand with his palm up, silently asking her permission to take it, looking into her eyes, searching their blue depths and willing her to soften and let him hold it in his.

"Trust me, Patti. I'm here for you. I want you to know that you can tell me anything. You can talk to me about whatever you'd like. Anything at all."

He leaned closer, securing her nail-bitten fingers in his. He lightly held her hand, his heart racing, beating madly in his chest. Glad he was wearing a tie so she couldn't see the heart beat in his neck, he was also acutely aware of the galloping pulse in his wrists.

As he said, "Patti, I wanted to have you here today so we could establish a rapport together." He kept his hands palm down, holding her fingers curled in his. "Do you know what I mean?"

She shook her head, looking more interested and less defensive.

"It means we trust each other. It's important that my students trust me, if I'm going to be able to help them through this school year." He smiled at her with loving fondness reflected in his eyes. An answering small smile played around Patti's lips. "It means we genuinely like each other, too," he continued.

He gazed into her wide eyes which looked like she was still trying to take in all his actions and what they might mean. "Do you agree that we can trust each other?"

Patti replied quietly, "Yeah, I guess." She lifted one shoulder in a shrug.

"And that we genuinely like each other?" He paused a beat, then said in a seductively low and earnest tone, "Because I surely do like you, Patti."

"Why do you think you like me? You don't even know me." The suspicious Patti was back again.

Whoa, she may be tougher to get to than I'd planned for. I've got to make her believe me. "Patti, do you remember the first day of school when I spoke in the assembly about my goal as your principal?"

"Yeah. So?"

"Do you remember me saying I wanted to be a friend to my students?"

"Yeah."

"Well, Patti, I meant that. That's why you're here today. I want to help my troubled students. I want to find out why your grades are not up to par with your intelligence. There are things going on in your life that I may be able to help you with." He reached for her hands again, taking them gently into his own. "Trust me, Patti. Let me be your friend. Let me help you."

"Okay," Patti said, her voice barely above a whisper, while she searched his face with her eyes, as if daring to hope he might be the real deal.

"What do you want me to do?"

Inwardly Addison groaned. *If only you knew.* "We'll meet regularly here in my office and you can tell me what you'd like to share with me. As our trust of each other continues to grow, we will become closer friends and we'll be able to work out some of the problems that are keeping you from being a model student. All right?"

"Maybe." A tiny smile again played around the corner of Patti's mouth. "Yeah, I guess."

Addison wanted to hug her; he was so delighted with her response. He chuckled aloud, elated by how well this first meeting had turned out. "Great! We'll do this again soon. I know you need to get back to class now."

He stood and offered her a hand in getting up from the sofa. Just touching her and the anticipation of what was to come made him a little weak in the knees. He swayed almost unnoticeably before regaining his stance. *Good, Patti doesn't seem to have seen it.*

"Make an appointment with my secretary for our next visit." He placed his hand on her back and ushered her to his door. He watched her turn to go to his secretary's desk, across and down the hall a bit from his office, to make the appointment.

"Bye, Patti," he said, with a lilt in his voice.

She came to him at her next appointment, again arriving at precisely the scheduled time. After that second visit, he asked her to come shortly after three o'clock after the office staff had left for the day.

He instructed the staff that they were stay no later than three. "You have lives after you leave here. Husbands and children need you more than I do in these after school hours."

"Oh, you've got to be the best boss on earth," Angela Rauhala, one of the office workers, gushed.

While Addison thought she resembled a cow and had no interest in her whatsoever, he flashed a brilliant smile. "Only because I have such sweet people like you as my staff. You work hard and deserve to go home exactly at three."

It was now in effect. All office workers, as well as his secretary, gathered their purses and personal items and were on their way home precisely at three every afternoon.

By the fourth visit, he thought Patti not only trusted him but had begun to relax in his presence. She spoke of her home life, divulging the problems with her parents that they likely would have been distressed to learn someone outside the core four of them was privy to.

They now sat close together on the caramel leather sofa. Often Patti was brought to tears as she related to him how her father began drinking as soon as he stepped inside their home after work. Or how there was never enough money to go around for the things the family needed, much less for the things they might simply like to have.

"I want to have some new dresses and wedge shoes like all the rich girls are wearing this year." She looked down at her too tight blouse which gaped a bit at the bosom. "And I'd like some clothes that *fit*. Not too tight like this old blouse."

She's sexy as hell in that too tight blouse that shows more than a hint of cleavage. He made himself not go down that road of thoughts. He simply could not move as fast as he would like.

"What else would you like to have, Patti?" he asked in a low, conspiring tone. "You know I'll be glad to help you get some of the things you want." He took her hand in both of his, his eyes beseeching her to please let him do this for her. "After all, we're good friends, and hey, what are friends for, huh?"

Patti lifted her trembling chin and eyes that were suddenly teary. "You'd do that for me?"

"In a heartbeat. Tell you what. I'll have a surprise for you when you come next time." He took his handkerchief from his back pocket and began to gently blot the tears from her face. "There. Just as beautiful as ever."

That brought a grin to her full-lipped mouth and he almost lost control, wanting to mash his mouth into hers, seeking her response as he showed her what a thoroughly passionate kiss could be. *Later. I just have to be patient and I can have all of her.*

When Patti stepped through the door a couple of days later, Addison rose from his desk and picked up an object from the desktop which he then hid behind his back. He'd talked to her about the value of money and the reasons why she should save her allowance and her baby-sitting money and how to spend it wisely. She was also to be helpful to others and to accept their tip offerings for work well done. These things she could do until she could secure a paying job after school and on weekends. Good money management would allow her to have some of the things she wanted, even if her parents couldn't get them for her.

So, now it was time to give her a gift from him. He met her in the center of the room and offered her a big grin. She responded with her own wide smile, looking happy, and perhaps eager with anticipation.

He brought his hand around between them, his thumb brushing against her tee-shirt just below her breasts. The blue and yellow shirt bore a silkscreened baby chicken and proudly proclaimed that she was a happening chick. He chuckled and rubbed his thumb back and forth across the lower writing on the front, which just happened to be on the soft underside of her high, full breasts.

Patti sucked in a short breath and sighed a ragged exhale. Addison's grin remained in place and his eyes gleamed brighter as he opened his hand. Patti dropped her eyes from his face to see what he held. A midnight blue jewelry box nestled in the cup of his palm.

She looked up at him. Her face radiated what he thought to be a mixture of hope, doubt, and wonder. "For me?"

"Yes, you! It's just for you. Take it. Open it. See if you like it as much as I enjoyed shopping for it to give to you."

When she hesitated, he flipped open the lid of the little jewelry box and watched her face. There on a white satin bed lay a fine silver chain. Sitting on the prominent raised circle right in the middle of the box was what appeared to be a diamond ring.

"Ohhhh, it's beautiful!" Patti gasped, eyes shining.

The ring had a silver band with two diamonds almost one-quarter carat each. When jewelry shopping, he'd remembered the story Patti had told him about a girlfriend who had a promise ring with a single small diamond as its setting. Given to her by her high school boyfriend, it meant they would wait for each other and get married one day. Patti's diamonds were bigger than those of her friend Rachel. Her ring was more beautiful, the diamonds separated by a raised filigreed heart.

Patti couldn't take her eyes off it. She lifted the chain, laughing at its fluid motion as it glided through her fingers, like the mercury from a broken thermometer, and pooled in her left hand.

"Do you like it, Patti?" By God, she'd better like it!

"Oh, yes!" she breathed on a sigh. "Thank you so much. No one's ever done anything for me like this. Oh, my God, it's gorgeous!"

"Now, you do understand what the chain is for, don't you?"

Patti replied hesitantly, "To put the ring on?"

"Absolutely. Unfortunately, you won't be able to wear the ring on your finger because it's our secret and we mustn't let anyone else see it. *We* know it's all right for me to give you a gift that shows I care about you, but it's likely that others won't think so."

He laid his hand on her shoulder and she leaned into it. "So, let's slip the ring onto the chain, or necklace, if you prefer to call it that." He lifted the chain from her fingers, picked up its flowing, serpentine-like length and plucked the diamond ring from its mount in the blue box and slid it, glowing brightly, onto the glimmering chain.

Addison held the chain and ring in his left hand, and pressing closer to her, he turned her just so.

"Now, move your hair to the side," he directed. Patti, trembling, lifted her hair and he threaded the chain around her neck and fastened the clasp.

Turning her so she was again facing him, he put both hands at arm length on her shoulders and gazed at the way the chain and ring fell below her collarbone. The ring was low enough to hang inside her shirts and sweaters.

"It's beautiful on you, Patti," he said in a hoarse whisper. "And you are beautiful." His breathing was a bit ragged and he fought to control it. "In fact, you are the most beautiful thing I've ever seen." Placing his fingers on her chin, he gently lifted it so he could see her eyes.

Patti looked at him with eyes big with wonder, gratitude, trust, and yes, there was love in her eyes, too.

"Thank you," she replied, her voice soft and broken.

As if his emotions had gotten the better of him, and actually they almost had, he slowly gathered her into his arms and dropped his mouth to hers.

As he hoped, her full lips parted beneath his and he slipped his tongue into the Juicy Fruit recesses of her mouth. He deepened the kiss and was over-joyed when she returned it, her tongue dancing with his. Forcing himself to stop, he lifted his head and looked at her upturned face, now completely open and giving. Inwardly his heart soared and his blood rushed so that his arousal was evident as he pressed against her. But not today. *I must stop now!*

"Wow!" he said shakily on a long blown out breath. "No one's ever made me feel this way before, Patti." He pretended to gather his thoughts, his eyes searching the room, apparently thinking deeply. "I think our session is over for today, you'd better go. You're making me crazy."

He backed away, putting several inches between them and returned his gaze to her. Silently, he looked at her for several long seconds. Taking the ring and silver chain in his right hand, he pulled open the neck of her tee-shirt with his left and hid the chain out of sight, the ring falling as the chain snaked downward in a sensuous flow.

Try as he might, he simply could not resist brushing her breasts with his fingers as he sought the chain hanging between them. "It'll be safe right there, Patti."

Bending and touching his forehead to hers, he whispered, "I'll see you in a couple of days, so just remember to keep our ring hidden inside your shirts out of sight. And don't tell anybody. Okay?"

Patti's breath was coming quickly as well, but she promised, "No, of course not. I'd never tell anyone about you. They'd make me stop seeing you and I don't want that. You're the only one who understands me."

"Exactly." He gave her another quick little hug in which she clung to him longer than he expected. *Yes! I've got her! She is mine. Next time will be even better.*

She slowly turned away from him, adjusting the neck of her tee-shirt and feeling for the ring with her fingers. She reached the door and placed her hand on the knob. As she opened it to leave him, she still held the eye contact they'd established at the end of their hug.

He winked and swept his eyes down her body, breaking their locked eyes, and whispered, "Wear a dress next time."

With her link to him broken, Patti nodded and slipped out the door, closing it on his still smiling face.

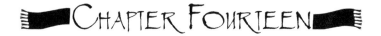

Chapter Fourteen

Patti

September 2, 2014

On the first day of the new school year, the group gathered to the left of the entrance doors was comprised of assorted misfits. They were called troublemakers by the school officials. The ones the teachers kept their eyes on, and the ones most likely to be sent to the principal's office for infractions of the school's rules. Patti Mueller stood among them, huddled close, lest someone mistake her for one of the "teacher's pets" types who stood openly staring at the group's black clothing, garish make-up, and abundant tattoos.

"Would you look at that," one of the Pollyannas said, pointing to Patti defiantly taking a drag from a cigarette being passed around the group.

"What's it to you?" Patti fired back. "I'm surprised you can even see me with your nose stuck up some teacher's butt." The whole group of misfits burst out laughing while the teacher's pet flushed bright red.

The loud ringing of the school bell signaled everyone inside the building where they were directed to the auditorium by teachers stationed along the entry hall. The misfits looked at each other, shrugged their shoulders to show their indifference, and sauntered in to take their seats.

As a twelfth grader, Patti was among the elite, the so-called upper-classmen, who were almost god-like in their exalted status. They were hero-worshipped by the younger grades. Special seating was reserved for them across the back several rows of the three sections of seats. Patti threaded her way into a back row, followed by several of her group, and sat lounging in her chair, awaiting the start of the assembly.

Several faculty members she knew from her previous years in this school climbed the side steps to the stage and took their seats. A man Patti had never seen before emerged from the wings off stage and moved to stand behind the podium. He tapped the microphone, which made a loud but muffled, whup-whup. The auditorium grew marginally quieter.

"Thank you, students, for being so attentive this morning on your first day of the school year. My name is James Addison and I am your new principal." He waited for the rustling and buzzing of voices to settle down before he continued.

"Mr. Aslaksen has accepted a position with a high school elsewhere in the state. So, now I am privileged to work with this great staff of teachers and the best student body in all of Wisconsin." He started clapping and leaned forward to the microphone to say, "Give yourselves a big hand. I know this will be a year to remember for all of us."

Patti rolled her eyes and yawned in utter boredom.

"What a dick," said her buddy, Quentin, loud enough for the kids around to hear. Their group laughed and slouched farther into their seats, a demonstration of complete indifference. The rest of the seniors clapped along with the principal.

After the room became almost quiet again, Mr. Addison leaned on one side of the podium and lowered his voice, as if he were speaking in turn to each student there.

"I have something to tell you I want you to remember. I'm here for you. A good way to remember that is the word principal. You know there are two meanings to the word. The first, and spelled p-r-i-n-c-i-p-l-e, means several things, but for my purpose today, we'll use one meaning. That meaning is ideals; not ideas, but ideals, things you care about. Things you'll fight to keep." He stopped and looked around the auditorium, making eye contact with those students who were not engaged in tearing strips of paper and chewing them down into small, slimy balls, and other such misconduct.

"The second meaning is just what I am. A school principal. The way you tell them apart is the spelling. The first, you will remember, ends in p-l-e. *This* meaning, and let me tell you I am mighty proud of it, is spelled p-r-i-n-c-i-p-a-l, with p-a-l on the end. And what does p-a-l spell? Pal, of course. And I want to be that for each of you. I want to be your pal."

His statement was met with hoots of laughter and cat calls accompanying the spitballs sailing through the air, many reaching targets in the Pollyanna groups.

"He's a complete dork," Patti stage-whispered to Quentin. "Is he for real?"

Again his eyes swept the amassed students. He ignored the rude interruptions by the various groups of unruly students. Patti saw his eyes sweep over her and on down the row, looking at as many students as possible on an almost one to one basis.

"Anytime you need to spell principal, just think of me as your friend, your pal, and the spelling will come to you.

Just like you may always come to me. I know I'm going to enjoy being a pal to all my students. Remember that."

A few snickers came from the audience. Principal Addison acted as if it hadn't happened.

His eyes swept the auditorium again. "I'll be seeing you around. In the halls. In the classrooms. And in my office." He paused and looked down the row of staff members and said, "I'll now turn the assembly over to Mrs. Braaten, your assistant principal."

He turned to the empty seat on the end and sat. Spitballs and laser jet lights still flew all around the auditorium—except for the section where the honor students and other intelligent students serious about their studies and going to college sat. They alternated between looking at the speakers on stage and sneaking disapproving glances at Patti's black attired group.

Patti watched the principal take his seat. *I swear that man looked right at me.* She flipped her hair with her right hand and said low, under her breath, "Yeah, right, you'll be my pal."

Patti's day had begun that morning like most others. Her dad was red-eyed and staggering a bit, the result of his drinking himself practically unconscious the night before. His breath was foul as he told her he loved his little girl and tried to aim a kiss at her cheek, which she expertly dodged. Her mom covered for him, as usual. "He works so hard to provide for us. He needs a little drink to calm his nerves before bed each night."

Liars. *He does a mighty poor job of providing for us.* She looked down at her feet. Flat sandals from last year, instead of the spiffy new wedges all the other girls would be wearing.

Her brother, Freddie, had tried to cheer her up by reminding her that as a senior she would be king of the roost and this year would prove easier than the last.

"Perk up, Patti. It's an exciting day. I'm a sophomore this year and I have a good chance of making the varsity basketball team."

"Get out! You really think so?"

"Yeah, I do. Wish me luck because I'll have an awesome year if I do make the team."

"Well, good for you, Freddie." And she meant it. *Freddie is the only good thing about this family. I wonder sometimes if Mom and Dad adopted him at birth.*

After the assembly was over and the students were dismissed to the remainder of their first period classes, Patti read the information on the letter she'd received a week before the start of school. She discovered she was in Senior English her last period of the day. She liked English better than any of her past classes, but that wasn't saying much. She really didn't like any classes. She went through the day ignoring her teachers and the stares of any new kids around her. At last, it was time for her English class.

She found her classroom and ambled through the door. The teacher was young and pretty. She was glad she wasn't like that skinny geography teacher she'd had last year. *That woman was scary!*

"Good afternoon, everybody," the teacher said. She stood from her chair and came around in front of her desk, smiling at all the students as they entered the classroom. "There is no assigned seating, so take a seat anywhere you'd like."

At any other time, Patti would have found a seat in the back of the room however, something told her to sit in one of the front row seats. She obeyed the call and sat dead center in front of the teacher's desk. *What is the matter with me? I've never done that before. Maybe Freddie was right, this will be a good year.* When all had found seats, the teacher spoke again.

"Hello, again, everyone. This is Senior English and I'm your teacher, Heather Forrest." She paused and picked up a piece of chalk and wrote her name on the blackboard. "Some of you may know me from last year, which was my first year teaching here." She grinned, an impish look taking over her face. "In fact, it was my first year teaching anywhere." The students laughed with her.

"You may call me Miss Forrest. If you don't use my name, yes ma'am and no ma'am are acceptable. We say this in the south and I kind of like it. It shows respect." She made eye contact with several of the students to show she was serious, and then a smile tugged the corners of her mouth. Continuing, she advised, "If this is not where you're supposed to be, I'll be sad to lose you, but you must leave now and find your correct class."

She glanced all around the classroom and found no one was leaving.

"Good. I didn't want any of you to leave, anyway." She emitted an infectious laugh and soon Patti found she was laughing along with everyone else. *Now, that feels good.*

The teacher leaned against her desk. "Let me tell you a little about myself and about this class we'll be in together for the next nine months. First, as I'm sure you've already guessed by my accent, I'm from the south, and specifically Florida. I grew up in Gainesville and graduated from the University of Florida. My father is a professor there."

Again, she looked around at the students and lowered her voice as if conspiring with them, "Are any of you football fans?" Every boy and most girls raised their hands.

She continued, "Good. I thought so." She dropped her voice to an almost whisper, "Are any of you Gator fans?" This time only two hands were raised, both hesitantly.

A smile lit her face once more. "It's okay to be a fan of a team out of your area. Heck, I've been a Packers fan all my life. Now, let's move on from football."

Her remark was met with good natured groaning from the class.

Still smiling, the teacher said, "We do have classwork to consider. This year we will look at reading, even venturing into some British writers, and writing, where you will do research papers and presentations. So, expect a refresher in grammar, which will help you determine if what you're reading is written well *and* will help you with your own creative writing. I ask that you come to class prepared to discuss and share. I'd hate to listen to just myself talk for an entire period."

Patti surprised herself again by actually listening to this teacher. She hoped she'd be different from all the rest. *Maybe she won't be a liar.*

In the next couple of weeks, Patti continued the pattern of behavior she had adopted last year. It provided a hard shell around her to protect her from the comments of others about her heavy mascara, her dyed black hair, and her old clothes. However, although she looked the same, her behavior changed when she entered the door of Miss Forrest's English classroom. She did no other homework but that assigned for this class. She discovered she enjoyed reading. It took her to another world so she could escape hers. She felt confident enough to raise her hand to both ask and answer questions.

So, when Miss Forrest announced she'd be pleased to stay after school ended one day a week to help anyone with their studies, she was quick to sign up. But it went further than just studies. Before she knew it, Patti was telling her teacher about how unhappy she was at home, about how there was never any money to buy anything special, and about her dad's drinking problem.

"I don't have any real answers for you, Patti," Miss Forrest said, "but I will be here to listen and let you get it off your chest. It does irreparable damage to our psyches to carry around a burden of unhappiness by ourselves. Sharing it always helps. And sometimes just talking about it helps us to discover answers." She had put her arm around Patti's shoulder and leaned close to her.

"Don't despair, Patti," she said, as Patti, angry, knuckled away tears that formed out of nowhere.

"Dammit. I don't *cry*!" Patti muttered low. "I don't know what's the matter with me."

Miss Forrest said, "Everybody has a reason to cry at some time, Patti."

She is so cool.

"Shit! What do they think I've done now?" Patti exclaimed when she got the notice to go to Principal Addison's office at the start of the last period of the day. One of the over-achieving teacher's pets delivered it to her during lunch in the cafeteria. It was sealed in an envelope, thank God, so the butt kisser hadn't read it. *I'd hate to think I'd have to spend any free time I might have working as a go-fer girl for the school secretaries. I can think of better things to do.*

She jammed the note into her backpack and with lunch ruined, she carried her tray to the deposit window, viciously scraped the almost complete meal of chicken nuggets and French fries into the garbage can. She flung the tray onto the counter. With her lips in a tight line, she stormed out of the cafeteria.

One of the guys in the group she hung with caught her arm and stopped her. "Yo, Patti. What's the almighty rush, girl?"

"I've gotta go to the principal's office, and I have no idea why," she spat out. "Some dickhead made up some lie about me, I'm sure. I wish everybody would just leave me alone. You too, Sid." She withdrew her arm from his grasp and continued down the hall, wishing for any other destination.

From his office around the corner from the school's main office, Principal Addison heard an angry voice ask, "What does he want to see me for?"

His secretary responded, "I'm not sure. I'll let him know you're here, Patti." She hit a button on her phone and relayed the message. Patti couldn't hear what he said, but the secretary put down the receiver. "You may go to Mr. Addison's office now, Patti. It's just around the corner." The secretary watched her go. It wasn't the first time Patti Mueller had been called to the principal's office.

Patti knocked once on the door frame and stalked through the open door to the principal's office, expecting it to be like it had been the last time she was there. She had but a moment to take in the changes before the principal was literally in her face. And boy, was he playing Mr. Nice Guy! When he said he wanted to be friends and for them to like each other, she amazed herself by agreeing with him. She thought he was full of shit when he first started that friendship crap, but she soon began to think he really meant it. *He isn't so bad, after all.*

She left and happily made her next appointment, which his secretary already had in her computer. *Wow, he acts like he really does want to talk to me.* Being the Patti who was used to disappointments, she decided to wait and see what happened at the next appointment.

Patti was mesmerized by all the amazing things he had in his office. She asked about them and found he was happy to explain what they were, what they meant, and where he'd gotten them.

"But it can't be a real egg all decorated up like that!" she said, staring in disbelief at the replica of one of the original Russian Faberge eggs.

"No, of course not. It's made of real jewels and is formed with precious metals into the shape of an egg. The Russian Czars in the mid-1800s had a leading jeweler, Mr. Faberge, make them as presents for their wives. He actually made about fifty of them."

"Oh, no way . . ."

"Yes, it's true. This one is not one of the original fifty. It was made by another leading Russian jeweler who learned the technique. It's quite old and very valuable, so we are very careful with it. Right?"

"I can't touch it?"

"I'd rather you didn't."

Detecting a harsh note in the tone of his voice, Patti immediately promised, "Oh, I'd never do anything to harm any of your pretty things."

"That's my good girl." Addison gave her a one-armed hug from the side.

"And that statue? What's that all about?" Patti pointed from the sofa, where they now sat side by side, to the bust of Caesar positioned near the window.

"That's a bust of Julius Caesar. He was the emperor of the Roman Empire that at one time ruled most of the known world. That was before Jesus Christ was born. Do you know how long ago that was, Patti?"

"Well, it'd have to be over two thousand years then, since it's been over two thousand years since Jesus was born."

"Wonderful. That's right." He gave Patti another one-armed hug and laid the side of his head against hers.

She answered by slipping her arm around his waist and squeezing him back. *I love it when he asks me questions and I know the answers. He always hugs me and acts like he's proud of me for knowing.*

In no time, they became so close until they hugged a lot. She was pretty sure he more than just liked her because she could feel his desire when he pressed close to her. And the first time he kissed her? Wow! She couldn't believe it. It was wonderful. His mouth tasted so good and since he French kissed her, she did it back to him. She *wanted* to kiss him like that. And then he asked her to wear a dress next time. Just thinking about why he asked her to do that had her stomach in knots. She really wanted to...what? *Just what do I really want to do?*

"Oh, I don't know," Patti moaned, wrestling with her emotions. "He acts like he really does like me. I'm pretty sure he wants to screw me. But that's crazy. He's a grown man and I'm just a teenager. I've managed to keep the boys out of my pants this far. I don't think I'm ready to do it with him either, no matter that he can kiss like crazy." *Oh well, I'll wear a dress next time and we'll see what happens.*

Now she was slipping in the outside door to his office after three o'clock two or three times a week. The first time she wore a dress, he held her against him with one arm across the back of her waist and his other hand in her hair, cradling the back of her head, and kissed her, his tongue exploring her mouth. She returned the kiss with ardor. After that she always wore a dress or a skirt and blouse.

During her visits in the following two weeks, he became more aggressive in kissing and touching her, and she became bolder in permitting it. The next week he slid his hands from her breasts to her back, slipped them under her sweater and unhooked her bra. She loved the sensations his mouth on her breasts brought her.

Finally, a week later, the day came when he slipped one hand under her skirt and felt her through her panties. She allowed it. On her next visit, his hand left the "V" between her legs and slipped her panties down. She let him pull them down to pool at her ankles and stepped out of them with only a small hesitation. *Oh God, what am I doing? But, I really, really want him to do it. I want him to be my first.*

Taking Patti by the hand, her principal led her to the sofa where he helped her lie down. He pulled the skirt of her dress up to expose her. When he put his hand on her, he exhaled a ragged breath.

"Oh, my God, Patti," he groaned. "You're beautiful. You're not a girl anymore. You're a very desirable woman." His fingers worked magic and she gasped and shuddered, loving everything he was doing to her.

He withdrew his hand. "I have to stop right now, Patti. You must go." He retrieved her panties and helped her put her legs in them and pull them up.

"You don't want me?" Patti asked in a small, choked voice.

"Oh, God no, that isn't right. I want you too much. Even though you look like a woman, kiss like a woman, you're still too young, Patti. We can't do this yet."

"All right. I guess not," she mumbled. Her head drooped, fearful she had displeased him.

"When do you want to see me again?" She'd fastened onto his word "yet" and that gave her hope it would happen. *I'm crazy in love with this man and so want to make him happy. If he makes me his, that'll prove he loves me.*

"Next Tuesday will be fine. Wear a special dress for me again." He drew her close and dropped a kiss on her parted lips before opening the door to the unused parking area so she wouldn't be seen as she left.

October 20, 2014

Patti arrived in Addison's office wearing a kicky short skirt that fell several inches above her knees. Her blouse was low cut and revealed a bit more of her breasts than the school dress code allowed. She looked lovely and, for the first time, she realized it. She felt sexy and desirable. Standing in front of Addison, dipping her head and looking up at him through her cascading hair, which she had returned to its original dark blonde, she loved the look of what had to be pure love on his face.

He reached for her and dropped his mouth to hers. Guiding her backwards to the caramel colored sofa, he lay her down upon it and undressed her, taking his time with her virginal white panties.

Patti lay back against the sofa pillows, eagerly awaiting each of his moves and breathing hard with excitement. She watched him rise and rapidly divest himself of his clothing, laying them across his desk chair. He kicked off his loafers and stripped off his trousers. When all that was left was his boxers, Patti lay mesmerized as his hands went to the waistband. Her body thrummed at what she knew was going to happen.

Addison knelt upon the sofa and gazed at her. His mouth went to hers and he kissed her deeply, holding it, as he began to teach her the art of sex.

Oh, I do love this man. I'll do anything for him.

Patti found it easy to sneak into his office after school. She waited in the parking lot outside the principal's office, assuming the guise of waiting for her mom to pick her up. Usually no one was around since the office staff were the only ones who parked there.

Parents picking up their children, however, drove past the lot to get to where their precious cargo waited. It appeared to be mostly the wealthy students who were picked up by their mothers, all driving huge Lincolns, Cadillacs, or some other expensive SUV. Thus, few people paid any attention to the girl in the faded green coat. Most didn't see her at all.

She shuddered each time she thought of how close she came to being caught. When Sid, who renamed himself after the deceased punk rocker, Sid Vicious, and dressed as he once did, happened by and found her with her hand on the outside door knob of the principal's office, she panicked in surprise and fear.

Busted! Oh, my God! What can I say now?

"What're you doing, Patti?" he'd asked.

"Um, uh, I'm waiting for, uh, my mom to come get me and, um, and I have to go to the bathroom."

Sid had smiled, a crooked lifting of his top lip, showing his sharp canine teeth. "Then why're you going in the principal's office?"

Having regained a small amount of calm as her heart rate slowed, she was able to say, "Is it? I didn't know. I just know I have to pee, and this is a door going into the school."

"Ahhh, Patti," he'd said, shaking his head and looking at her through the greasy, black-dyed hair hanging in his face, "I know you. You've done something big."

Patti had let her fear in the form of irritation burst forth.

"No, dammit! I've got to go pee before I bust open. Now get the hell away from here and leave me alone."

Patti opened the door and went in, shutting it firmly. Addison was waiting, so she forgot about Sid and his accusations. And, this time, like all the ones before, whenever she came to him, James always appeared to be eager and ready for her. He gathered her in his arms and held her close to his rapidly beating heart.

Patti forgot all her troubles, and anything else, when she was with him. She concentrated on pleasing James. For Patti it was not just having sex; it was making love with the man she loved with all her heart.

Chapter Fifteen

Freddie Mueller went about his classes in a bit of a daze, the eager, inquisitive student of BPD, as he called it, and which meant Before Patti Died, no longer in evidence. He now faded in and out of groups of students in the halls and in the boy's restrooms. In the cafeteria and library he sat seemingly deep within his thoughts and appeared to meditate upon the loss of his sister. What Freddie was doing was listening.

His friends knew, of course, about his sister's death, as did his mates on the basketball team.

"Man, that sucks," is one of the more common remarks he received, along with a pat on the shoulder or a pat on the back from young, soon-to-be men who couldn't wrap their minds around his sister's, or God forbid, their sister's, life being extinguished like blowing out a candle. Once vibrant, robust, and full of brightness as it glowed, there was nothing now except total emptiness.

Freddie listened and hoped he would overhear that one conversation, that one comment, that one confided whisper meant not for his ears that would provide a clue of some sort. He needed a lead that would ultimately expose Patti's killer. Perhaps he would never hear it, never unearth the small detail that the detectives could follow up on that would allow them to find the murderer. However, all things are possible, given the right circumstances and the proper tools to do the job. For now Freddie's tools were his ears, and they were always attuned to receive, decipher, discard or keep, the bits of conversation he gathered by being present but unobtrusive.

Freddie and Patti had been very close despite their widely diverse personalities, interests, and behavior. He had often been scandalized when she shared with him some of the stories told and deeds done by one or more of the mostly rough group of teens she hung with. Occasionally, though, he couldn't help but laugh with her as she recounted some act perpetrated on some deserving slacker, like the mailman they saw deliberately slip a bag full of flyers into a Dempsey-dumpster rather than deliver them to the individual mailboxes along the street.

They were incensed! People needed those flyers for sale ads and grocery coupons. So, to get back at him, several of the group scoured the neighborhood for piles of dog shit and dumped it all in the mailman's truck where he would step in it when he swung back in after parking and walking his deliveries along the street. That was hilarious, even to Freddie.

To a store keeper who cursed them, called them scum, and ordered them out of his store with threats to bash in their heads with a shovel kept behind his counter, they formed a boycott with posters and signs saying his produce was bad and that his meat was rotten. People stopped and read their signs, became angry and went inside to confront the man. Livid, he shouted at the customers who then left, vowing never to shop there again. Freddie didn't think this quite as funny, although he was fine with the boycott. After all, the mean storekeeper deserved it.

So, these were some of the activities Patti had been a part of, Freddie mused. But what activity did she participate in that would have led to someone killing her? He couldn't imagine, and so he listened.

One afternoon in the gym before basketball practice, he heard the name Joe Nygaard tossed from one player to another. And Mr. Hoffmann. He heard the teacher's name only once but froze while putting on his practice jersey. He hadn't been on the team long enough to be one of the insiders so he felt he couldn't just ask them what they were talking about. Not wanting to give himself away as an eavesdropper, Freddie couldn't pick up the gist of the conversation. But he did have a name, and when he talked with the detectives again, he would have someone for them to investigate.

While he was driving, Aksel repeatedly glanced at Anja. He couldn't miss seeing how attractive she was. And she smelled so good! She had instantly fallen in love with the Red Door perfume he gave her and wore it every day, just a light spritzing lest she smell like a streetwalker. She told him she'd gone undercover once as a prostitute and liberally drenched herself in a cheap scent so she'd appear, and smell, like all the other working girls. She swore off perfume after that and had not worn it since. Until now.

"What?" Anja peered at him out of the corner of her eye as she attended to the paperwork in her lap. She glanced back at the papers lying atop her dark blue weatherproof pants. "What are you thinking about?"

"Oh, uh, I wasn't thinking about anything." Aksel was quick to reply.

"Sure you were. You wouldn't be looking at me that way if it was nothing," Anja gave a small, nervous laugh.

Aksel stared at the road ahead and looked around at the traffic on either side of them. He did not look at Anja.

I was just thinking. Since you cooked dinner for me on Christmas Eve, perhaps I could cook for you sometime. I make a mean pot of corned beef and cabbage." He turned his head finally and grinned at her which, in turn, made her smile at him.

"At least I used to cook it well. It's been a long time since I prepared a meal for a lady."

"So now I'm a lady, huh? I think this perfume you gave me is going to your head, partner." She said the last word with subtle emphasis.

"Oh, you can be a lady and a partner at the same time." Again the grin from Aksel.

Is this guy flirting with me or is he just being Aksel in a good mood? "Hmmm . . ."

"Huh? Did you say something?"

She raised her voice. "I did enjoy cooking and you eating with me Christmas Eve at my house," she admitted. "I think we established something special that night. We're not just partners. We're friends, too."

Aksel grinned again. "Yep."

Anja waited, but he added nothing further.

Covering the void, she playfully added, "Well, I just happen to love corned beef and cabbage! I graciously accept your offer to cook it for me. So, do I have to wear a dress and heels and do this dinner up right?"

"Of course you do. Do you think I'd go to the trouble for a lady of your caliber to waltz in wearing snow boots and winter gear?"

"But, Aksel, it *is* snowing and it's likely to continue for some time to come."

"How about this? Tomorrow night after our shift, barring any new leads, we'll go to my place. You can bring your fancy duds in a bag which we'll put in the back seat, and then when we get to my house you can take them in and get dressed up for dinner while I attend to it. Sound all right with you?"

Anja smiled helplessly at Aksel. He'd work out their plans and make them fit. Still smiling, she shook her head in mock amazement, rolled her eyes, and said, "Sounds like a plan to me. But you'll have to change clothes, too! If I'm going to dress up for corned beef and cabbage, you have to also."

"No prob. That I can do."

He thought of the freshly laundered trousers and shirts hanging in his closet that he'd just this week gotten back from the cleaners. Yes, he would have something nice to wear. It was worth the effort of gathering up all his soiled laundry, with the exception of underwear and socks, and taking them to the cleaners. It was another effort to find time to pick them up, but now he was relieved that he had done so. The new cobalt blue, light-weight, silk blend sweater his daughter Sisse had given him for Christmas would look great with a pair of khakis and a long- sleeved pale blue dress shirt. *Why, I'm really getting into this dressing up thing!*

"Well," Anja said into the silence, "Turn your heat up and I might get away with a light sweater over my fancy sleeveless cocktail dress." She giggled suddenly, sounding definitely more girlish than he'd yet heard her. "Do you think maybe we're getting a tad carried away by dressing up for corned beef?" She giggled again and added, "I'm casting no aspersions on your cooking, mind you!"

"You may be right, come to think about it. And then there's the problem of how long it takes to cook. We'd be starved to death before we got around to eating." He looked at Anja, who sat waiting for his next suggestion.

"How about me pan searing a couple of steaks in butter? That's more in keeping with a cocktail dress."

"Excellent choice!" Anja said with a huge grin. "Tell you what. I'll spring for a great bottle of red wine, probably a cabernet, to go with it."

"Now, I *am* starving! Too bad we have to wait until tomorrow night."

"By the way, did you know that this fancy, outrageously priced steakhouse in New York City called Peter Luger's cooks their steaks like that?" Anja asked.

"Really? I've heard of that place, but I've never been there."

"Oh, I haven't either," Anja was quick to explain. "I saw it in a student film from USC that my friend's son did for his thesis. And here's the good part . . ." She paused for effect, raised one eyebrow and grinned.

"Well, I'm waiting. What's the good part?"

"The film's setting was World War II and Peter Luger's cooked their steaks the same way back then as they do now."

"Okay, that is interesting! I guess you don't mess with a good thing. Especially a good steak."

"Right. And I was reading a food magazine and it had an article about the chef Bobby Flay, who is all over TV these days. He was showing how to cook a steak at home the way Peter Luger's does. It looked delicious."

Anja stopped and turned more toward Aksel. "But I'll bet yours will be the best of all." There was no smile accompanying these words.

Aksel was serious, too. "Thank you, Anja. I'm sure going to try my best."

The companionable banter between the two partners started up again as they drove to the station. There they found Captain Harjula waiting with news for them.

Without waiting for his two detectives to take a seat in his office, the captain said, "A call came in to me with some interesting news. It seems the Mueller boy has been doing some detective work on his own. He has a name he overheard as maybe having something to do with Jeff Hoffmann's attack. I tell you, I've pondered that phone call since I got it earlier today. I hope it won't land that young man in the hospital like it did Jeff Hoffmann. A basketball player with a broken leg isn't any good to the team. And I'm almost as fanatic a basketball fan as there is! I want to see this kid play, not hobble around on crutches. So, I want you two to check this out."

"And who would that be, sir?" Aksel asked.

"Joe Nygaard."

"Joe Nygaard?" Aksel echoed. "That's the name Jeff gave us. The voice he thought he might have recognized from that night. He's one of his students. We just haven't got to him yet."

"One of his troubled students, he said," Anja added.

"Well, check him out. Since he's a student he should be in school tomorrow. Talk to him then. For tonight, go home and get some rest. See you both tomorrow for a full report." Harjula nodded a dismissal and wearily walked around his desk and out the door.

Aksel watched him go. Then he held out his hand toward the door. "Okay, let's go home and get a good night's rest. We'll need it for each of us to eat a couple of pounds of steak tomorrow night!"

"Why? Is it going to be tough? So tough I have to save all my energy for chewing it?" Anja joked.

"I'll show you, Missy. It'll be so tender I guarantee it will almost melt in your mouth."

"Not in my hand?" Anja pretended to be serious as she looked earnestly at Aksel. Her expression dissolved as she burst out with a girlish giggle.

Aksel laughed, too. *She's flirting with me.*

They looked in each other's eyes and sobered quickly. They buttoned and zipped their coats and opened the door to the increasing wind that greeted them as they headed to the lot where their cars were parked. Their cars were near enough together so they could call their good-nights as they climbed into their SUVs to head home.

Aksel looked around the sparse furnishings of his small one-bedroom apartment. His wife, Barbara, got the house and the kids and most of their possessions. Until now, it really hadn't mattered. Now he wished he had some spots of color or some nice things to make Anja more comfortable when she came tomorrow night so she wouldn't think he was a complete caveman.

Suddenly a brilliant idea formed in his head and he was out the door and locking it before he even had time to consider his actions.

At Target, he found the Housewares Department and stood gawking at the amazing display of colorful accent items all designed to make a drab home look like a show place. A show place his apartment would never be, but he knew he could dress it up with a few well-chosen items.

Aksel, bewildered by the array of home goods available for his choosing, sought the advice of the sixtyish sales associate.

"Ma'am, could you help me, please?"

"Certainly. What is it you need?"

Aksel gave a rueful chuckle. "Just about everything. But I'm afraid I'll have to settle for some accent pieces like pillows and . . ." He paused and looked around at the brightly colored offerings. "...things like that," he finished. *That was lame. She'll think I'm an idiot.*

"Then, let's start with the throw pillows," she directed over her shoulder as she led the way to the next aisle.

Aksel stood before the wall of throw pillows and noticed how some colors went better with others. He thought of his favorite football teams and realized their colors were chosen for a reason. They looked good together.

"Hey, look at this," he said to the saleslady as he put what he thought of as a maroon pillow with a gold one. "It's the Washington Redskins' colors."

Grabbing a green pillow, he held it up with the gold one. "Here's our Green Bay Packers' colors." He put back the green and gold pillows and held up one orange and one of dark blue. "And here's the Broncos'. I think I'm getting the hang of this."

"I should say so," the saleslady said. She laid her hand on his arm for a moment before taking the pillows from him and returning them to the display.

"Just remember your color wheel," she said, "Opposites on the wheel look great together."

"Ma'am, I have no earthly idea about a color wheel," Aksel admitted, suddenly finding the toes of his boots to be very interesting. He looked up just as she opened her mouth to enlighten him.

They spoke together, "What is it?" Aksel asked, as she said, "It's a circle of colors . . ." They both broke into laughter and she continued, "You'd have to see it to understand it, so I'd say your best bet is to forget it."

Still smiling, she said, "Look for me again if you need any more help. I have to check what this page for me is all about." And with that remark she was gone.

Color wheel? What the hell is a color wheel? He thought of the ragged brown afghan his wife had knitted for him so long ago and decided to get rid of it immediately upon returning home. *I'll wad it up and put it in the dumpster out back of the apartment. I should've done it when Barbara told me to get out, even before I moved in to my place.*

Now, he replaced it with a soft, smooth, knitted afghan in cranberry red. The Christmas red, in his opinion, was too feminine for his bachelor pad. To go with it, he picked out two pillows in the same color. *I'll drape the afghan along the back of the blue denim sofa and put a pillow on either end.*

He chose two slightly smaller pillows in a happy yellow color with a nubby texture to place with the cranberry red ones. Into the basket went two smaller pillows in a scarlet and yellow floral design for placing in the armchair. The reds were a close enough match. *I think they'll work just fine.*

Next, he added a 5- by 8-foot area rug in shades of blues and tans with a hint of red thrown in. *Look at me tying my color scheme together. Decorators ain't got nothin' on me! It would be perfect, not only for its beauty, but it would cover some of the stains on his carpet.*

Aksel went next to the dishware and glasses aisle where he chose a complete table place setting for four in a cool sage green color with a darker green swirl in the pattern. Next, he picked out four long stemmed wine glasses and a set of four-footed water goblets. Finally, dish towels in a green and white checked pattern went into the overflowing cart.

"That's enough," he said under his breath, but yet he couldn't stop himself from snagging a bright bouquet of flowers. He'd find something to put them in, he was sure. The next thing he did was to double back and go down the wine aisle where he read the labels carefully and chose a dark ruby red Cabernet Sauvignon and Syrah blend with notes of cherry, chocolate, and black pepper. *God, that has to be good!*

After that he chose two enormous, well-marbled, boneless rib-eye steaks. They were his favorite steaks, which he preferred to filet mignon. He selected two baking potatoes and passed over his usual iceberg lettuce in favor of a mix of greens. *I'll dress them lightly and they'll make a perfect salad. I'll even get some fancy stuff to go in it.*

Dessert. What kind of dessert would go with this meal? He looked at the rich, beautifully decorated cakes in the pastry and cake glass-fronted counter. He considered a good old American apple pie. Maybe she'd prefer a cream pie like perhaps a coconut or chocolate. After much debating, he finally chose a sour cream pound cake baked in its loaf pan, and to go with it a fine vanilla ice cream and a box of fresh strawberries. *I can't go wrong with a simple but delicious dessert such as this.*

Aksel hauled all his purchases out to his SUV and stuffed them in, not thinking of the strawberries until he saw a red stain blossom on the brown paper bag.

"Damn!" he swore. "Now I've squashed the strawberries." He looked up at the sky and shook his head. The yellow glow of the tall parking lot lights cut through the gloom and brightened his mood again.

Once home he quickly divested his purchases of their wrappings. He enjoyed being with Anja, and he anticipated with pleasure the opportunity to spend time with her out of their job environment.

The dishes and glasses he washed, dried, and placed upon the table. Rummaging in a box of unused, miscellaneous items, he unearthed a decorative jar Sisse had painted for him in a school art project years before. It would serve well as a vase for the flowers, so into the jar-vase they went. He added water and they joined the place settings on the table.

Standing in his kitchen, hands hanging by his sides, Aksel looked around at his decorative handiwork and discovered he had a grin spread across his face. It looked good! His place had never looked so inviting. And, well yes, he had to admit it did look pretty. Him? Aksel? Living in a pretty apartment? He'd never thought he'd see the day.

He took one last pleased look, turned off the light, and trekked to his bedroom where he hurried to undress and slide into his bed. He was asleep before the blankets had a chance to warm around his weary body.

In her warm bed with its fresh-smelling sheets and covers, Anja smiled as she thought about dinner tomorrow night with Aksel.

"It'll probably be a fiasco," she said aloud, as if telling it to a BFF. She smiled again in affection for her big, gruff partner. Arranging herself just so, she snuggled deep into her covers, and drifted into sleep.

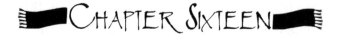

Chapter Sixteen

January 9, 2015

Two things of interest happened that Friday. First, two detectives came to talk to the principal and then went at lunch time to the cafeteria to talk with a student while Jeff had "lunchroom duty". The other? Heather thought she might have a good idea on a lead to the murderer.

Jeff stood near the tray return counter monitoring the kids while they dumped their juice boxes, napkins, anything paper, into the large trash bin. If a teacher didn't monitor the students' actions, some of the goof-offs or troublemakers were likely to throw their entire trays into the trash. It had been done before, and Jeff kept an eagle eye on the kids, determined it wouldn't happen on his watch.

The occasional empty milk carton flew into the bin, always thrown by the athletes, never from the anorexic girls who shunned the fattening stuff. Junk food, somehow approved for school cafeterias, slid through the slot.

The food disappeared down some mysterious machine that Jeff had no idea about, but he heard it grinding away, ridding itself of the unappetizing food. *What happened to good old meat loaf, mashed potatoes and gravy, and green beans like the cafeteria served when I was going to school? Food like my mom cooked.*

The uproarious sounds, the clanging of silverware against plastic plates and trays, the high voices and giggling trills of the girls and the deeper hum of the boys' voices suddenly ceased. Jeff's eyes followed where the kids were looking and saw Detectives Franzen and Frandsen standing in the doorway accompanied by two uniformed police officers. The detectives were in street clothes, so it was Heimerle and Schroeder who got the kids' attention. Jeff didn't know just why they were here, but he knew the two in street clothes were far more worrisome to whomever they came to see than the uniformed ones could ever be.

The mixture of sounds resumed as most of the kids dismissed the police officers. Only a few either eyed them suspiciously or slouched farther into their seats in hopes of becoming invisible.

Jeff's eyes followed the path of Detective Aksel Franzen's. He and his partner were looking at one table only. Three of the students at that table were looking at one of their table mates. And he was looking directly at the detectives and the two officers.

"Joe Nygaard?" Detective Aksel Franzen asked.

"Yeah. Who wants to know?"

"Mr. Nygaard, I'm Detective Aksel Franzen and this is Detective Anja Frandsen."

Joe looked from one to the other. "Married. Cool," he drawled.

"We need you to come down to headquarters with us, Mr. Nygaard. We have some questions for you."

"We think you might be able to help us with a case we're investigating," Detective Anja Frandsen added.

Joe stared at them for a moment, and then in a movement it seemed he was unable to control, he turned his head to look at Jeff. Their eyes locked but there was no expression on either face. Joe turned back to the detectives, with Jeff's eyes following his every move, and addressed Aksel, as if he'd already decided he was the lead cop.

"Sure. That's cool. No problem, man."

He casually rose from his chair and sauntered toward the door with the entourage in tow, his low-hung jeans riding on his hipbones and their frayed cuffs dragging on the linoleum tiles of the cafeteria floor.

Aksel caught Jeff's eye and gave him an almost imperceptible nod.

Jeff took out his cell phone and texted Heather: Joe Nygaard taken in for questioning. Expect detectives to stop by after we get home.

While he waited for Heather's reply, he focused on the look Joe Nygaard had thrown him when Detective Frandsen asked him to come to the headquarters for his help with a case. For a brief moment, it seemed to Jeff that Joe's eyes had been unguarded and almost pleading, as if asking for help, before he narrowed them and looked away.

The detectives escorted Joe to the backseat of the SUV rather than to the police cruiser. He climbed in and assumed a casual pose as the car headed to the station. He lolled against the back of the seat, apparently resting easily, and looked as if he had no worries at all.

At headquarters, the detectives ushered Joe into a brightly lit interview room where he sat alone in the one chair pulled up to the scarred and gouged table. While the detectives watched him through the one-way mirror, Joe seemed to be inspecting the graffiti dug into the table. He smiled when he saw "up yours". Aksel also smiled, but thinking of the pencils used to write confessions, he knew the dangers of a sharp pencil. Sure, they could make an imprint of words in the soft wood of the table, but they could also kill under the right circumstances.

Soon Joe lost interest and began to fidget, rocking his rather rickety chair back on its rear legs and drumming his fingers on the table. The longer he sat there, the more concerned his facial expressions became. The captain and the detectives observed this change in Joe's demeanor as he continued to look more and more afraid.

"I thought he'd lose that cocky attitude if he cooled his heels for a while," Captain Harjula remarked. "You two go in and see what he can tell you. I'll be in my office, so report to me when you find out what he knows."

"Hello, Joe," Anja said with a friendly smile as she and Aksel entered the interview room.

"How much longer do I have to stay here? I've got things to do."

"Tell us what you know about the death of a girl named Patti Mueller," Aksel demanded.

Ah, good cop, bad cop. "I know a girl named Patti Mueller was killed and her body dumped on the pond at The Golf Course. Her brother goes to school with me and is on the basketball team, but I don't know him well. He's just a sophomore."

"Anything else?" Anja asked.

"That's all I know."

"Where were you the afternoon Patti was killed? The afternoon of December twelfth."

"I was in class. I haven't skipped any school this year. At least so far. You can check it out."

"We'll do that, Mr. Nygaard," Anja said. "For now, you are free to go."

Heather sat at her desk and thought of how Principal Addison had gone on and on about Patti's death at the last staff meeting before the Christmas break, even trying to get her to talk about finding the body, and how strangely he'd acted at the funeral. Now thinking about it, it brought back an even more puzzling memory. It was the time she'd left school a bit early for a dental appointment and had driven by the parking area behind the principal's office. She'd looked over just in time to see Patti enter Addison's office from outside. She thought it strange then. She now thought it was another example of what must have been his obsession with Patti. What was Patti doing going into his office like that? She couldn't have gone without him asking her to, she thought.

Having heard the announcement Principal Addison made earlier that morning regarding the staff meeting during the thirty-minute lunch period, she had a sudden thought. With her mind whirring like helicopter blades, she excused herself from her class for a moment to hurry next door to see a fellow teacher. There she rapped on the door and smiled weakly through the glass window that slit the right side near the doorknob.

Lela Magnussen looked at the window to see who was interrupting her class.

"Did you need something, Heather?" Lela asked pleasantly as she opened the door about half way and eased out into the hall. She turned, looked behind her, and admonished, "Please return to your seat, David. I'll only be a moment." With an "Oh, well . . ." and a shrug, she turned back to Heather.

"Are you all right?" Her voice rose in concern and the smile left her lips.

Heather was arranging her face in its best portrayal of pain as she began to explain what she needed. She opened her mouth and the words tumbled out. *Good Heavens, where'd this come from? I hadn't even planned what I was going to say.*

"Ohhh, Lela. I have the worst cramps. Straight from hell. I don't see how I'm going to sit through Principal Addison's meeting. I think I need to just have quiet and a few minutes with a warm towel pressed against my tummy."

She glanced back at her classroom. "Could you keep an ear out for my kids while I run to the teachers' lounge and heat a towel in the microwave? It's almost time for the lunch bell and his meeting, and once the kids have left, I can use the towel."

Seeing the look of empathy on Lela's face, she continued, "I've got to get some relief somehow. These cramps are killing me."

"I'll be glad to listen for anything going on next door, Heather," she said with a glance at her wrist watch. "You'll only take a couple of minutes anyway." Lela pursed her lips in thought and continued, "Perhaps you should just miss the staff meeting and try to get the pain under control." Heather stared into space and slowly nodded her head as if it hadn't occurred to her.

Lela thought for a few seconds and said, "Tell you what—I've got some Tylenol in my purse if you'd like one. And I'll fill you in on what he has to say when I get back. And if he notices and asks where you are, I'll tell him you weren't feeling well and needed some quiet time alone."

"Thank you, thank you, Lela," Heather said with a rush of genuine gratitude. "I've got some Motrin, so I'll take that instead of the Tylenol. Now, I'm going to head to the lounge to warm a dish towel."

The lunch bell rang within a minute of her returning to class, giving her just enough time to thank her students for remaining quiet and exhibiting good behavior while she was out of the room.

She made herself stuff the warm towel inside her wool trousers where it lay against her abdomen spreading warmth throughout her lower body. Then she made herself wait an additional three minutes, counting out the hundred and eighty seconds in slow cadence. Once she reached the end of counting, she cautiously opened her door and peered out. Nothing moved in the halls. Sounding as if coming from far away, she could hear the murmur of voices and the clanging of trays and utensils in the dining hall.

"Now," she said, and trying to look as inconspicuous as possible to anyone who might pass by, she set off down the hall towards the administrative offices.

As requested by the detectives, who paid a visit to him earlier that morning, Principal Addison called his staff together during lunchtime for a very short meeting to apprise them of the situation of perhaps having police officers in the school and the very real possibility they might be questioned. He watched the teachers and office workers file into the conference room.

His attention was diverted by the very thin, almost anorexic, geography teacher. He'd often wondered if she actually had the stamina to travel to the many places with which she regaled her uninterested students. She stopped in front of him with a salad in a clear plastic take-out box in her left hand and asked, "May we eat during the meeting?"

Patting her on her knobby shoulder, he answered by raising his voice over the scraping of chairs and the hubbub of people settling around the table.

"If you have your lunches with you, go ahead and eat. For those of you who want to make a quick dash to the cold sandwich line in the cafeteria, do it now. And hurry back. The meeting will start in five minutes."

To Miss Anorexic he said, "Take a seat and enjoy your lunch," as he sat in one of the wingback chairs, the intent of which was to provide a homey atmosphere to a room meant for discussion and differing ideas.

The hungry staff members trickled in one by one and soon everyone was seated, taking bites of their food, and looking at him expectantly. All accounted for and he could pass on his information. Except one. Where was Heather Forrest?

Heather turned the knob on the door to the main office. Unlocked! She cautiously looked behind her as she entered, expecting someone to materialize at any time and ask her just what did she think she was doing. Slipping inside, she froze, head up and listening intently as she looked around her. Nothing.

She could have sworn she heard something and felt someone behind her. It must be nerves. She crossed the room and hurried around the corner in the little hall, barely giving his secretary's office a glance, and reached to turn the knob on Principal Addison's office door. It opened.

In this office only once before, it was when she'd interviewed for a teaching position. That was when Mr. Aslaksen was the principal, but it looked nothing like the breathtaking grandeur she now saw. She inhaled a deep breath of surprise when she saw the leather chairs and long, inviting sofa coupled with the plaster-of-Paris Greek busts atop their tall Corinthian columns.

"Good Lord," she muttered, totally awe-struck as, on second thought, the busts looked like real marble. Her quick scrutiny of the art pieces made her think they were all the real deal. If they were fake, they were the best reproductions she'd ever seen. They looked just like the busts of important people of the past she had seen in Greece and Italy on a trip with her parents after graduating from high school.

How in the world can Addison possibly afford all these things on a principal's salary?

Heather sat in the chair behind his big desk. In the back of her mind, something screamed that it was not a principal's salary that enabled him to have these things. Did he steal them? Did he have a source of money from somewhere and they were bought legally by him? *Something is seriously wrong here.*

She ran her fingertips over the desk's surface, feeling the ornate bumps, rises, dips and valleys of its trim. The desk's drawers were unlocked, and she frantically searched for . . . What? She had no clue what she was looking for.

Leaving each piece of paper, pamphlet, or folder just as she'd found it, Heather feared she'd find nothing to back up her suspicions. Urgent, she slid her fingers around the opening of the chair well in the desk and discovered there was a drawer just below the desktop in the middle. Easy to miss, it had a generous number of decorative curlicues to protect its presence. Her sensitive fingers continued to search amidst the curlicues. And then she found it. A tiny metal protrusion that when moved to the left popped out the hidden drawer by maybe a quarter of an inch.

Wedging her fingernails inside the small opening, she slowly pulled it out, grinding her teeth at the time flying by. The first thing she saw was a small blue jeweler's box. The second was a thin pile of folded papers. *Could they be important notes? Maybe evidence?*

With shaking hands, she unfolded the one on top and quickly scanned it. It was a page torn from an appointment diary. Heather opened another and began to read. Her heart started hammering as if determined to break through her chest wall.

"Oh, my God!" she gasped. Numerous appointments were listed on the torn sheets but the ones that caused Heather's consternation were the two or three time a week's appointments, written in red pen, for P.M. at 3:00 in the afternoon. *Does the P.M. perhaps stand for Patti Mueller?*

With her whole body now shaking, she struggled to return the papers to look exactly as she'd found them. She closed the drawer and pushed the desk chair to where she hoped was the exact spot it had been.

A noise. Then voices. *Oh, please God, no!* She heard the secretaries talking about the meeting as they entered the outer office. Fear flooded her, filling her with the need to flee. She jerked her head from side to side, desperately seeking a way out without being discovered.

The window. No, no time. She could have cried in fear and frustration. Her eyes returned to the window. Beside it was a door. The window looked at the outside scenery. This door had to lead to the outside. With her thoughts way ahead of her body, she was seeing herself outside and free from detection. She made herself open the door quietly and slip through it when the urge for flight demanded she get out of there pronto.

She was closing the door when she heard Principal Addison say something to his secretary, his voice getting louder as he opened the door to his office. But she had made it. She was outside and taking deep gulps of the cold air. She placed her back against the wall and took three deep calming breaths, courtesy of Ann Forrest's teachings, and then bolted down the cleared sidewalk to re-enter the building's main door. Heather slowed her run to a fast walk as she returned to her classroom. It was still empty, as a few minutes were left before the bell rang, signaling lunch was over and time to go to the next period's class. Too few minutes. She needed some time to calm down.

Picking up her jacket that hung from the back of her desk chair, Heather slipped it around her shoulders, and sat down at her desk. She leaned forward and laid her head on its top and closed her eyes. Her heart and breathing slowed and returned to normal. If her thoughts hadn't been in such turmoil, she thought she might have fallen asleep.

A knock on the door. Oh, yes, that's Lela. Heather opened her eyes to find she was looking into those of Principal Addison. Her heart jumped into her mouth.

She spread her mouth in a small yawn. "Oh! Principal Addison! I'm sorry! I must've fallen asleep. I took a Motrin to stop the pain in my abdomen and put a heated towel against the area, and it does feel some better." She realized she was babbling and talking much too fast and wound down with, "And I apologize for missing your staff meeting."

A twist of his mouth she interpreted to mean missing the meeting was no big deal. However, it seemed her reason for missing interested him greatly.

"I'm curious. What did you say you used that brought you relief?"

Heather backed her chair away from her desk, and before she had too much opportunity to think, she lifted her shirt and sweater, sucked in her stomach, and pulled the dishtowel, still warm from her body, up and out of the waistband of her trousers. She held it up as if it were a flag over surrendered territory.

"This is it," she said, offering it to him in her outstretched hand.

As if stunned, he reared back before reaching for it.

"Why, it's a dishtowel," he said, surprise making his voice rise. "I can't believe how warm it is." Recovering quickly, he added, "That's good to know, so now I can recommend a warm dishtowel when young ladies miss class because of having cramps with their periods."

He dropped the towel on her desk just as the bell rang for the start of the afternoon sessions. "Come by to see me and I'll tell you about the meeting."

"Oh, sir, that won't be necessary. Lela Magnussen volunteered to fill me in."

"Okay. Well, you watch these monthlies. Can't have you going around stuffed with dishcloths and towels, now can we?"

"I suppose not, sir. I'll try to see it doesn't happen again." She gave him her pitiful-face look with turned down lips and drawn together brows.

He scanned her face but didn't comment.

Oh Lord, he doesn't believe me. Now what's going to happen? I know it will be bad, but I don't know what to do to prevent it. Whatever it is.

Students began coming through the classroom door, with curious eyes on their principal. His eyes sought Heather's.

"I'll be going now, but I'll see you around." He turned his back and threaded his way through the students. Those brave enough to raise their eyes to his face saw it cloud over as if a severe thunderstorm was about to begin.

I know she was up to something. She seemed too innocent. Shit, she's really covered her tracks. I'll have to get the boys to take care of her. He smiled at the things he would think up to frighten her off the trail she was pursuing like a bloodhound. *Oh, and I may leave her a little calling card, so to speak.* He struggled to keep a grin off his face and the threatening giggles inside.

By the time he returned to his office, his face was carefully set to neutral. He was uninterested in his secretary Martha's story about the chairman of the school board's call.

"I'll get the particulars later, Martha," he said with a sharp edge to his voice. "If I get any other calls this afternoon, just hold them. I do not wish to be disturbed. At all. Do you understand?"

"Yes sir!" Martha responded sharply, surely wondering what bug was up his butt.

Addison strode around the corner and down the short hall to the door of his office and almost twisted off the doorknob before yanking the door open and thrusting himself inside. His eyes remained steely, but his face softened as he looked around his large, bright sanctuary, the sanctity of which he was certain had now been breached. He was sure the Forrest woman had invaded his space even though she was where she said she had been during his meeting. She would've had to have moved quickly in order to get to his office after the start of the meeting and be back in her classroom before it ended.

His breathing slowed as he scanned the special object d'arts he'd collected. Absorbing their beauty calmed him. Addison was proud of them and even more so of the object de vertus, such as the Faberge egg he'd bought for a horrendous, exaggerated price in St. Petersburg, sitting regally in its blue and gold splendor in a small locked glass display case. The marble bust of Caesar sat tall on its carved marble pedestal, placed just so in order for the sunlight to shine directly upon it. A personal favorite was the large Giclee print of Fernand Cormon's painting of Cain and his family leaving the Garden of Eden after he slew his brother Abel. When in the Musee D'orsay in Paris, he had spent hours standing and studying the huge painting that covered an entire wall. Cain's ice blue eyes were a replica of Addison's own.

He was pleased to share his coveted icons with the few whom he invited into his special place. Having had little choice, he'd invited the police officers inside and even they had been struck by the things they saw, their eyes growing round and wide with wonder as they took in the opulence. And Patti! He'd practically had to hold her hands in his to keep her from touching everything.

At his desk, he sat in the big desk chair and systematically went over every item on it and those in the drawers looking for evidence Heather had been meddling. This time, looking at the exquisite crystal cube with the etching of St. Basil's Cathedral inside Red Square in Moscow gave him little pleasure. He sighed and set it back in its place, noting it appeared as if nothing atop the desk had been disturbed. Even the secret middle drawer where he kept the pages of appointments with Patti that he had torn from his personal appointment diary seemed to be as he left it. The first appointment he made through his secretary. All others he made himself for after the office staff left at three o'clock. But he couldn't rule out the possibility that she had discovered something. To be on the safe side, he'd better have his three teen minions pay her a visit.

Addison managed to do some mundane paperwork while trying to reign in his flying thoughts for the rest of the school day. After the last bell had rung, and the students had gone, he withdrew his cell phone from the pouch on his belt. Without hesitation, he giggled aloud, secure in the knowledge no one could hear him. Oh, it was going to be delicious when the boys got their hands on the snooping bitch. He punched in some numbers, convulsing with laughter as he waited for an answer from the phone on the other end of this call.

Chapter Seventeen

"Hel-lo. It's Joe," he said, responding to his cell phone's fifth ring.

His snappy greeting was designed to be cute, but he forgot all about being cute when the voice on the end of the cell signal barked, "Can you talk?"

Every instinct Joe had screamed at him, "Do not tell him about being taken to police headquarters today and being questioned!" He had spilled nothing to the cops, so they had to let him go. The police cruiser returned him to school. He entered the front door, watched the cruiser pull away, and immediately ran to his old Land Cruiser parked in the student's lot and took off for home. He had a couple of hours yet until his old man got home from work and the shit began.

"Yes, for now," Joe answered. *Thank God my old man isn't home yet.*

"I want you to get the other two and get very creative on Miss Heather Forrest's ass tonight. She's snooping, and it is conceivable that she's found out something. I'm not certain what she knows, but we've got to stop this bitch right now! Do you understand me?"

"Yes. What do you want us to do?"

"Do I have to do everything, dammit? I expect you three to figure out some things on your own. Do something like . . . oh, I don't know . . . send her a note saying somebody wants to meet with her and give her information or something. Just make it happen, you dummy. I pay you enough you should be able to use what little brains you have to get her away from home and come down hard on her. Freaking scare her to death!"

"Yes Sir. We'll get it done," Joe said, and the line went dead after a loud, "You damned well better get it done!"

Joe was troubled and made plenty of wrong choices, but he wasn't dumb. Of the three Principal Addison had hired to do his dirty work, he was by far the smartest. He thought about what the man had said about a note and began to devise a plan. He ran his fingers through his too long hair, pushing it off his forehead, where it seemed to always hang in his eyes and face, and set to work.

He knew the police had questioned Miss Forrest and Patti's family. He knew Patti's brother Freddie from watching him play basketball. Figuring Miss Forrest would buy a note from Freddie to be the real deal, he booted up his computer and sat down to compose a believable story.

Blasting off to the apartment Miss Forrest shared with Mr. Hoffmann at record speed, Joe repeated his checking of the side roads and his rear-view mirror for police presence. All it would take for him to be interrogated again would be if he got arrested for speeding.

The long hairs on the back of Joe's neck rose even before he heard the distinctive sound and saw the lights in his rear-view mirror.

"Shit!" he exclaimed and he slammed his gloved hand hard against the steering wheel. Raging aloud, he slowed the car, preparing to pull over as far as he could without climbing a snow bank.

"Dammit! I knew I was gonna get caught." He came to a full stop and awaited the inevitable.

Joe's jaw dropped and he stared, not believing his good luck, as the police car pulled out from behind, whipped around him, and continued speeding away, lights flashing and siren whooping. He leaned his head against the steering wheel and took a couple of breaths to slow his racing heartbeat.

"Well, I'll be damned," he said, as he started his car and drove off.

He dropped the note, which he had placed in an envelope with "Miss Forrest" written on the front, through the mail slot in her door and hoped she would be the one who retrieved and read it. Mr. Hoffmann usually stayed to exercise in the gym after school, so the likelihood was that she would get to it first. He just had to hope that's how it went down.

Driving marginally slower, he took a different route home and used the time to phone the other two boys and set up their plan for the night. He was so not looking forward to what they had to do. He wished, as he had numerous times already, that he had never let the allure of money overshadow his common sense. *I never should've said yes to the lunatic.*

Having arrived at her apartment, Heather went inside and pulled off her winter wear and picked up the mail from under the slit in the door. She flipped through it and found an envelope with just her name written on it in a sloppy hand. She jerked in surprise when she heard a knock on the door followed by the doorbell ringing.

Heather quickly stuffed the note, which had mysteriously appeared with her mail, into her book bag that sat on the small bench by the door. She smoothed back her hair with the palms of her hands and then ran them down her sweater, smoothing it as well. She realized she was putting off letting them in so she wouldn't have to lie. She squared her shoulders, breathed deeply one time, and opened the door to the detectives.

It was twilight outside and the detectives appeared faceless in the glow of the streetlight that lit up the parking area behind them and revealed shadows in the dips and rises of the banked snow. Their big black SUV sat ticking gently at the curb.

"Miss Forrest, may we come in?" Anja Frandsen asked.

"Oh, yes, of course." Heather managed a small self-deprecating laugh as she backed away and let them enter the warmth of the apartment.

Aksel Franzen was unzipping his heavy coat as he remarked, "Getting mighty cold out there already." He stopped with his coat halfway unzipped and peered closely at Heather. "Are you okay, Miss Forrest?"

Again the small laugh. "Call me Heather," she said automatically. "Why, yes. Why do you ask?" A line developed between her eyes as she concentrated all her attention on Aksel.

"You seem to be distracted. Is there something you can tell us about this day that is bothering you?"

Heather was not ready to talk about her day yet. Instead, she said, "Please come on in and take your coats off. Have a seat and I'll make us some coffee."

"Oh no, don't bother," Anja hurriedly interjected. "We've been drinking coffee all day." She closed her eyes and shook her head. "You know what sounds really good, though? Hot chocolate. Oh, I loved it as a kid and rarely have it now."

Her expression was so much like a little kid asking for her favorite sweet until Heather burst out laughing. “Sure, I’ve got hot chocolate. I like to make it with milk instead of water so that it’s richer tasting. Let me get the milk heating and we’ll have hot chocolate in no time.”

Heather turned toward the kitchen and with a wave of her hand indicated they could sit in the living room if they liked. Aksel caught Anja’s eye and mouthed, “Good job.”

Anja smiled back in response and led the way to the kitchen table. “I’d rather we sit at the table. That way when I spill the hot chocolate, it won’t wind up on your living room rug.”

Putting her conflicted thoughts on the back burner while the hot chocolate was steaming on the front burner of the stove, Heather reached into a top cabinet and got three tall clear glass mugs with handles and poured the rich, fragrant drink into each.

“Here it is. Drink up!” She set the mugs down with a flourish, acting as if she was in a much-improved mood from when the detectives first arrived.

Anja took a sip of her hot chocolate. “Ahhh. Pure heaven.”

“It’s the milk.”

“Yes, it must be.” Anja took another sip and with a quick look at her partner, she forged ahead with the reason they were there.”

“You know, Miss Forrest, we believe Joe Nygaard is one of the men who attacked Mr. Hoffmann on Christmas Eve, right?”

Here we go. Heather nodded and said, “Yes.”

“Well, we picked him up at his school during the lunch period today and questioned him at the station.” She looked to her partner for confirmation.

“And he didn’t admit to anything,” Aksel added.

"However," Anja continued, letting her know that they suspected she knew something, "according to Mr. Hoffmann, you found something of interest today at school that you thought would be helpful to our case. Can you tell us what that was?"

Heather opened her mouth to make a quick reply and then closed it while she thought about just what she did want to tell the detectives. Silence stretched uncomfortably.

Anja started, "Miss Forrest, we really do need . . ." when the front door opened and Jeff stepped into the room.

"Oh," Heather sighed. *I'm so relieved he is home and safe.*

She couldn't seem to help herself. It was as if she needed to physically touch him. As if she could gain strength and resolve from his sturdy body. Rising quickly from her chair, she hurried to him and slipped her arms around his waist, pressing her body close to his and laying her head against his chest. Jeff clasped her even closer as he whispered, "Anything wrong?"

She whispered into his shoulder, "I'm just so glad to see you. It's been a terrible day. And I want to talk to you before I say anything to the detectives. Will you please make them go?"

Still holding Heather close, Jeff looked at the detectives. His face registered sincerity and his tone was serious. "Hey guys, Heather's a little frazzled right now. Can we postpone this until later? I'm pretty undone myself, so I'd appreciate it if we could wait for more questions." His sober gaze moved from one detective's face to the other.

The two detectives eyed each other and silently read the other's impassive face. Anja said, "We do need to talk about this and find out what you know, Miss Forrest."

"That's right," Aksel agreed. "We're working late again this evening for a reason. The sooner we know what we're looking for, the sooner we can solve this case."

"I'm sorry," Heather meekly said. "I'll be more together tomorrow."

Both detectives stood and shrugged into their heavy coats and started for the door. They didn't look pleased. They also exited the apartment without their usual goodbyes.

"Thanks honey," Heather said, turning her face up for a quick kiss. "I just didn't feel like talking with them tonight."

"Did you have anything you could have told them?"

When Heather hesitated in answering, Jeff asked, "What was it you thought you'd found today when you called me?"

Not really understanding why she was hiding the note's existence from Jeff, and deciding to tell him part of the truth, Heather divulged she thought their school principal, Mr. Addison, had some part in it. She really couldn't precisely put her finger on it, but he was acting funny and she had this feeling that he was involved.

"So that's who you suspect. It's not surprising, considering I think he's a complete weirdo." He unzipped his coat and pulled it off and stood holding it in his hands as it trailed unnoticed to the floor. His face was a study in thought.

"You don't think you should've gone ahead and talked to them tonight?"

"Not tonight. I told you I didn't want to talk with them now."

She moved away and picked up her book bag on the bench by the door. "I'm going upstairs to check on some books that need returning. If you want to go ahead and start dinner, I'll be back down shortly to help you." She was eager to read the note. It could be important, but then it might be unimportant altogether. She needed to find out right now.

"Sure," Jeff agreed, and was soon opening a family size frozen pasta entree. Fettuccine Alfredo, one of his personal favorites. It would go in the oven for about thirty minutes and dinner would be ready.

Heather took the book bag into the toilet with her and shut the door. Reaching inside it, she located the note that had been dropped through her mail slot that afternoon. She tried slitting it open with her thumbnail but wound up tearing it instead. Impatiently, she further tore the envelope. "Damn," she whispered.

Heather opened the note, folded so it would fit in a small envelope, and read the contents. It was from Freddie, Patti's brother. He wanted to tell her what he'd found out and asked her to meet him at the high school tonight.

Her quick brain immediately formed a plan. She was all set with how she would handle it and was ready to tell Jeff. But, Dammit, her conscience picked this moment to rise up and hang like a mantel on her shoulders. *Now what am I going to do? I don't want to lie to Jeff. I know we'll have a fight because he won't understand. I know he's loves me and is just trying to protect me.*

"I've got to do this. Oh, I hope it all turns out all right," she again whispered her thoughts.

Jeff was putting the final touches of gorgonzola cheese atop the green salads when Heather returned. He made one of Heather's favorites. Green leaf lettuce with sliced apples and gorgonzola dressed with homemade Italian.

"This looks amazing, Jeff. How soon before we eat?"

"The pasta comes out in a couple of minutes," he said, throwing a quick glance at the stove's timer. "Want to put out the plates and silverware?"

"Okay, and after dinner, I'm going to make a quick trip to the library."

"You are?" Jeff did nothing to hide his surprise. "Why would you want to go out tonight?"

"I've got overdue books from the library and since the weather forecast for tomorrow says it's going to be colder with more snow coming, I'd rather do it tonight than try to brave traffic tomorrow to do it. Come on and let's get that pasta on our plates before it gets any later."

"Heather, it's stupid to go back out tonight. Can't the library books wait?" He opened a drawer and chose a metal spatula from its depths.

"No. I want to return them tonight."

"Well, at least let me go with you in case something goes wrong with the car in the snow."

"No, Jeff," Heather said, her voice rising. "I'll be fine. Now, stop bugging me about it. I'm going and that's final."

Jeff yanked open the oven door and pulled the pasta out fast enough that some spilled over the side of the dish and plopped onto his shoe, and then slid to the floor. "Dammit!" he snarled.

"It's okay. Don't worry about it. I'll finish cleaning it up when I return." She poured herself a large diet coke and took several swallows. "Want any?" she asked Jeff.

"No, Heather, I don't want any." He glared at her. "What I do want is for you to come to your senses and stay home."

"Now it's a matter of principle, Jeff. I'd go even if I didn't want to." Bright red spots glowed on both her cheeks.

Jeff sat down and began to push the pasta around on his plate without tasting it.

Heather hurriedly ate several bites. *I'll say something nice and maybe he won't be so angry.*

She rose from her chair and said in a teasing voice, "You *really* don't mind if I go, do you? I promise not to be gone long, other than to check in a couple of books. I *will* be careful, Jeff."

"Hell yes, I mind. I can't keep you here, but this is a damned ridiculous thing to be arguing about, especially after what we've been through. But if you are determined to go, then be my guest." He gestured toward the door.

Snorting in anger, she muttered under her breath a number of things Jeff probably couldn't make out. She stomped to the closet and withdrew her heavy coat. She flung it to the floor and gathered up her sweater and scarf and all her other layers of clothing she would need and jerked them on.

Last, and just the opposite of how she had been behaving, Heather picked up the coat and donned it with extravagant slowness, and slipped her gloves on her hands, working one finger at a time into them. Her actions dared Jeff to comment. He didn't.

Again, her conscience butted in. *Should I really go meet Freddie? Maybe I'd better not go. I hate fighting with Jeff and, more than that, I hate lying to him. But I really need to know if he's found out anything. Oh, I don't know what to do. Maybe I'll try again with Jeff.*

"Oh, Jeff, I'm sorry. I have to do this. Please don't be this way."

"I'm just trying to be sensible here, Heather. It's ridiculous for you to go back out tonight in this weather. You're just asking for trouble. Why must you act so stupid?"

Heather tried to contain her anger and hurt and her warring emotions. She hung the book bag from her left shoulder by one strap, and quietly said, "Bye, Jeff."

Jeff looked away and said nothing. When she opened the door and turned back to look at him, Jeff again did not respond. He was still sitting at the table, looking down at his plate, and drumming his fingers on the tabletop when she let herself out the door.

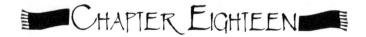

Chapter Eighteen

January 16, 2015

Heather fled from her pursuers, dashing down the hallway faster than she'd ever run. She stayed upright on the slick surface as her winter boots grasped the floor with each long stride. Whoops! She managed a one-legged dance as she strove to retain her balance. Attempting to run, she slid again.

What is that? Looking behind her at the floor, she saw she'd hit a wet spot the custodian had neglected to dry when cleaning the floor earlier. Precious time lost! Sprinting again, she hit the big double doors, blindly reaching for the bar that would open them to the outside. She dared a look back. Three hulking teens blasted into the "T" of the hall she had just left. Their socks slipped and skidded on the highly polished floors. They'd obviously removed their heavy boots so she wouldn't hear them coming. One went down amid shouted curses. Regaining his feet, he rejoined the other two.

She threw open the right side door and bolted out into the frigid air. Wildly she looked around, her head whipping one way and then the other, trying to find some avenue of escape in the deep snow piled beside the iced sidewalks. She heard their angry shouts and curses and a white-hot shot of adrenalin flooded her body, re-igniting her instinct to flee.

Without thinking, Heather started running, dashing along the sidewalk in complete terror. Suddenly her feet slid from under her and she fell heavily on her right knee. The pain was piercing, and she feared she may have cracked a knee cap or torn a supporting tendon.

Dammit! But my knee injury could be insignificant in the face of what those three boys will do if they manage to catch me. She forced herself to rise and seek a hiding place somewhere. Anywhere.

An indistinct shape rose about ten yards in front of her and she quickly limped toward it, the pain from her knee excruciating. *My God, I think I really did sprain it or break something.*

Hobbling, she reached the shape she'd seen. The concrete block wall designed to hide the trash and garbage cans containing the refuse from the cafeteria. *Oh, please don't let them find me.*

She ducked down behind it. She held her breath, and she could hear her heart drumming an erratic beat in her ears. When her lungs could contain her breath no longer and she began to see spots dotting the darkness before her eyes, she exhaled as slowly as she could. Now she fought the urge to expel the air all at once and to gasp for sweet oxygen from the icy wind which blew swirls of snow around her. Almost faint with the need of her hungry lungs, she took shallow gulps as the wind drove its cold breath into her gaping mouth. Her body sagged against the freezing blocks where two walls of the structure came together in an "L." She prayed the ones chasing her wouldn't find her cowering in the corner.

The note! How could I have been so egregiously gullible? Why would I believe what it said? Her mind darted to the words she had been so eager and willing to believe.

> Miss Forrest,
> Please meet me at your school tonight at 8:00. I have some important information for you that I can't tell the detectives myself. I think they suspect me, but I'd never do anything to hurt my sister. Come alone because I don't want anyone to know you got the information from me. I'll meet you in your home classroom.
>
> Freddie Mueller

Thinking she might get the answers she needed to prove who had murdered Patti if she met Patti's brother tonight, she decided to do it. The note seemed so innocent. She realized now that her need to know the identity of the murderer had totally usurped any sense of danger that she should have experienced at once. *Stupid, stupid!*

She hadn't even told Jeff the truth about where she was going on this bone-chilling night in January. Thinking about it now, she wished she'd never said she was making a quick trip to the library, even picking up the armload of library books and putting them in a tote bag. They'd had a huge fight because of her stubbornness. *Oh, why did I lie to him?*

Of course he objected to her going, much less going alone, because the snow was piled deep even though the snowplows worked feverishly to keep the roads clear. Confident then, she'd pooh-poohed his concerns because, after all, they were having the mildest winter so far that had ever been recorded. But other than that, it pissed her off that he didn't just hush and let her do what she wanted. She hadn't wanted to lie to him, but she thought she had to do this alone.

She'd been positively euphoric at the prospect of being the one to see that justice was done. However, instead of Freddie showing up, those three large older teens had skulked up the hall toward her room. Thank God she wasn't in her room when they came. She'd arrived early and wanted to be there when Freddie appeared, but she hadn't considered the large diet coke she'd mostly consumed with her dinner. That is—when she and Jeff weren't yelling at each other. So, she'd had to go to the bathroom and couldn't wait any longer.

After hurrying down the hall to the teacher's bathroom, she fished her key ring from the pocket of her coat and unlocked the door. *What a shame we have to keep everything locked* flitted through her mind as she quickly urinated. She had time only to pull up her wool pants with her gloved hands before she heard a sound. It sounded like someone talking quietly. The nape of her neck prickled, and she shivered the length of her body. She expected it to be Freddie but, just in case, she hit the "off" light switch.

Heather had taken a breath and cracked the door a slit so she could peer down the hall. Her heart clamored in her chest when she saw three tip-toeing figures, obviously trying to both be quiet and to stay upright, as they headed toward her classroom. If they planned to frighten her, it was already working. *My God! Who are they? Are they the same ones who hurt Jeff?*

Her mind sped as she thought of a number of scenarios, all bad, and with serious outcomes. She was poised to flee. But where?

As soon as the trio opened the door to her classroom, Heather began running, slowing only when she slipped, and didn't stop until she hit the bar on the big double doors that opened on one side. She blasted through to the outside with the three hurrying some distance behind her. She knew it was only moments before they found her, but she was completely out of ideas as to what to do next. Beginning to hyperventilate with terror, Heather could do nothing to stop it. She could hear their voices calling to her.

"Miss For-rest? Where are you?" This came to her in a dangerously mocking, sing-song voice.

What chilled her insides was, "We're gonna get you, Bitch!"

A different, calmer voice said, "Miss Forrest, stop running. We just want to talk to you. We know you're right here somewhere, so stop hiding and come on out."

Heather, terrified, stayed pressed against the wall, hoping they wouldn't hear her gasps for air.

"Well, looky here what we found," the first voice said with an overlay of sarcastic glee.

Heather yelped as all three appeared in front of her, filling the space with their large bodies.

"Wh-what do you w-want w-with me?"

The second voice hissed, "We're here to make sure you keep your mouth shut, Bitch!" His ski mask covered his lips so that his message was muffled, but Heather got it. Her heart beat faster as he reached for her. She drew back, pressing herself into the corner of the two walls. Trapped.

He lunged for her arm and dragged her out onto the sidewalk. Her feet slid on the treacherous ice and she fell, landing on the feet of one of her attackers whose widespread stance kept him on his feet, while the one dragging her lost his balance and fell hard atop her.

"Now, ain't this cozy?" He yanked his ski mask aside and ground his mouth into hers before she knew what was happening. Heather wrenched her head to the side, desperately trying to evade his searching mouth. Suddenly, his body was lifted off hers by the other two.

The calm voice, not so calm now, urgently said, “Stop that! That’s not what we’re supposed to do. Rough her up a bit and then let’s get out of here.” He turned his back and looked away.

The first one, the mocker, grabbed her left arm and twisted it behind her back, bending it up high and tight.

“Owww, owww, please stop!” Heather cried. Tears born of pain and fear felt hot on her nearly frozen face. Had she not been clothed in the bulky winter clothing, she feared her shoulder would’ve been broken—and maybe her arm as well.

The mocker said, “Just a little message from someone who can do to you what he did to that girl. He says you’d better stop your snooping and stay out of this.”

The one who had mauled her mouth angrily added, “He says you’d better keep your nose out of the investigation and have nothing more to say to *anybody* about *anything* connected with that girl’s death. This is just a walk in the park compared to what will happen to you next time we come after you.” When he drew his foot back and kicked her in the left thigh, Heather knew he was still pissed by not getting more than a half-assed attempt at kissing her and he wanted to hurt her.

“Owww,” Heather wailed. It did hurt, but not nearly as much had he had his boots on and not just the socks that they wore when chasing her down the hall. She could have laughed, had the situation not been so serious, as he jumped back, hobbling on his other foot, holding his hurting foot in front of him and looking to see if he’d broken his toes.

“Dammit to hell!” he hollered. “That hurt!”

The one who spoke with some sanity said while in turns rubbing each foot against the back of his opposite calf,

"My feet are freezing. We've got to get back and get our boots on."

He looked down at Heather. "You stay right there until we're outta here. And you'd better not call the cops! You don't know who we are, so don't even think of trying to identify us. Don't think about it. Don't guess. And . . ." He paused as if he wanted to say more. He finished with, "Just don't make us come back." Then he and the other two hurried along the sidewalk and disappeared back inside the building.

Heather lay with her heart beating wildly, and her thoughts flying in every direction. She tried to rein them in by sheer will. *But I can't stop thinking about what that last guy said. Damn them!* Her thigh throbbed. Her arm ached and her shoulder felt wrenched out of its socket, but she figured she'd be in a lot more pain if anything was broken. She tried sitting up. It was a struggle since she could only use one hand to balance herself. Finally, she got her feet under her and stood unsteadily, favoring her left leg and smarting thigh.

She thought about calling the detectives who were working Patti Mueller's case, but she was so afraid of what the three boys might do to her next time if she told on them. She couldn't do anything now, anyway, like alert Security, because everything appeared to be dark inside. The boys must have made it back in the building before Security armed all the doors to lock from outside. If you were inside the building you could get out once the doors were locked, but not back in again. Everyone who had been in the meeting in the auditorium in the south wing left shortly after she arrived. Her mind continually seized on one thought and then jumped to another in the few minutes since they had left her there.

Limping and hurting, Heather made it to her car without falling. She was pathetically grateful it wasn't her right arm that had been injured. At least she could do most things using her right arm and hand. She had left the car door unlocked and was thankful she did. It was precarious footing and just as she grabbed the door handle with her gloved fingers, wiggling them into the well, she changed position just enough to lose her balance. She slid and landed hard on her already sore right knee.

"Ohhh. Dammit!" she shrieked. She wasn't worried about her involuntary outcry because right then she didn't care if the boys came back and hit or kicked her again.

Heather felt a twinge in her right shoulder and realized she'd also wrenched it slightly. Her padded hand had remained fast inside the car handle well when she fell. Holding on to it, she pulled herself up and rotated her shoulder a few times. It only hurt a little now.

"So, now my whole left side is a mess and my right knee hurts like hell," she muttered angrily, "but I can drive. At least I think I can. Now, if my right shoulder isn't damaged . . ." Her voice trailed away unable to complete her thought. It was just too overwhelming to think about.

She opened the door and awkwardly slid behind the steering wheel, started the car, and pulled out of the school's parking lot. "Thank you, Lord," she whispered when she encountered only light traffic on the familiar roads, which tonight had a layer of blowing snow across them. She experienced no problem with her right leg and the accelerator. It was a little more difficult with braking, but she managed to do what she needed to in order to return to the safety of her home.

The windshield wipers battled the lightly falling snow all the way to her parking spot at the apartment. She slowly climbed the couple of steps and reached to open the front door. *I hope it's not locked. I just want to get safely inside my home.*

Jeff paced the small living room, as he'd been doing for an hour. Again, he went to the window to look out. His face softened and his shoulders sagged as he saw her return from wherever it was she had gone. He turned away from the window as Heather climbed the steps. Although relieved, his anger flared like a firework.

Relief and anger combined into an ugly look on Jeff's face. He threw open the door as she put her hand on the knob, grabbed her arm and pulled her inside before she had the chance to warn him to be careful.

"Where the hell have you been and why the hell did you have your cell phone turned off?" he demanded. His voice grew angrier and louder with each word until he was shouting.

Heather winced as he held her at arm's length by each shoulder. He continued without her answer. "Just tell me! I've been worried sick. I called the library and they said they hadn't seen you."

"Jeff, you're hurting my shoulder." She tried to step back from him. "I'll tell you everything, but you need to stop yelling at me and help me out of my clothes."

Jeff looked into her face, his brows drawn together over his glasses. "Are you okay, Heather?"

"I don't know yet. We need to get my clothes off so we can find out."

"Well, Dammit, Heather! What happened?"

"I know you're going to be upset with me, but I thought I was going to meet Freddie Mueller, and his note said not to tell anyone." She stopped and hung her head, not meeting his eyes. "So, I didn't."

"You couldn't even tell me?" His voice held a distinct edge.

"No," she mumbled.

"Heather, we're in this together!" he raged. His voice, while loud and angry, was also tinged with worry. "You've got to keep me in the loop. We can't hide things from each other." Jeff tilted her chin up, forcing her to look up. She still didn't meet his eyes.

"Hmmmph," he breathed, and took the ends of her indigo scarf and unwrapped it from around her neck, and then unzipped her coat. Silently, he reached in, gathered her hair, and freed it to fall down her back. He began to remove her coat from the injured shoulder, slipping it down her arm. She flinched and pulled away.

"Just wait a minute. Let me do that, Jeff." She pulled the glove from her right hand and then gingerly pulled the one from her left, forcing her to move her sore arm. She tossed them toward the sofa where one fell short and dropped to the floor.

As she gently started to remove the coat, she threw her head up and looked straight into his eyes. "Oh Jeff, I don't want to tell you this," she started, her voice ragged.

"What?" Jeff's voice was deadly calm.

Heather's face was drawn with pain as slid the coat off her other arm and then slipped it down the injured one. She dropped the coat on the floor. Instead of answering, she asked, "Will you help me with my sweater?"

Silently, Jeff reached for the hem of the winter-white knit sweater and began to lift it over her head. He saw how she was favoring her left arm and shoulder and was a little gentler while removing the sweater and unbuttoning and pulling off her pale blue shirt. The tight line of his lips had to tell Heather he was angry as hell, but she also had to recognize he was making an effort to calm down.

Neither said anything as he slipped the wool trousers down her thighs and indicated with a nod of his head that she should sit on the sofa so he could remove her boots. This he did, pulling them free from her feet and stripping off her heavy socks. Next, he pulled the fine wool pants that matched her indigo scarf from each leg and reached to remove her warm tights.

"I'll take them off," Heather said, rising from the sofa. She hooked her fingers in the waistband and carefully rolled them down her legs, frowning at the pain in her left shoulder. As she went on removing the tights, Jeff could see her injured thigh.

"Good Lord, Heather! What in the name of God happened to you?" Jeff threw his arms wide and dipped his head, needing an answer.

Impassively, she continued rolling down the tights which allowed him to see the bruise forming on her right knee.

"And what is that? Did someone do that, too?"

With eyes down again, she muttered, "No, I did that one to myself." Then she lifted her head and brushed her hair from her eyes. Now looking at Jeff, she spoke quietly, seeming to have run out of defiance, "Please help me pull off my bra and put on my nightgown and robe, and then I'll tell you. Could we go upstairs to do it and then get in the bed? I'm so cold."

"Okay. We'll get you warm, but you're going to have to tell me what's happened, Heather. And I'm not waiting all night."

She nodded. "I don't want to talk about it, but I will tell you, Jeff."

Jeff leaned down and slid his right arm behind her knees and leaned her back into his left arm. He lifted her into his arms and climbed the stairs as if she weighed nothing. "I hope once you're settled and warm, Heather, you'll stop all this subterfuge," he said, sounding only marginally calmer.

He stood Heather upright at the door to the closet where she reached in and retrieved her night wear. Jeff turned the covers and sheet back on their big queen bed and then helped Heather pull off her bra, gently sliding the straps down her arms. Then he quickly helped her into her gown and fluffy robe for added warmth.

She gingerly settled into the bed and Jeff pulled the covers up and tucked them around her. He walked around to the other side of the bed and turned back his own.

Standing on first one foot and then the other, he removed his boots and shed his clothes down to his undershirt and tighty-whities. Usually tidy, Jeff neither looked to see, nor seemed to care in the least, where his clothes landed as he threw them in the direction of the open closet door.

He slid under the covers and moved to the middle of the bed near Heather. Reaching for her, he slipped his left arm under her neck, and held her against his shoulder, being overtly careful not to hurt her injured one.

"All right, Heather, are you okay now? Are you ready to tell me what happened?"

"Oh, Jeff, I was so scared." She stopped and sniffed hard. Her nose started to run from the warmth after being in the cold for so long. A part of it could be due to threatening tears as she remembered what happened to her.

"It wasn't Freddie Mueller who sent me a note to meet him. It was three big guys." She paused and swallowed hard. "And they attacked me."

Heather raised her head from his shoulder and looked directly into his flinty eyes. "They wrenched my arm behind my back and almost broke it. They kicked me in the thigh. And they warned me to quit snooping around trying to find Patti's murderer."

"They didn't try to sexually abuse you or rape you, did they?" His eyes were wild, boring into hers with his blazing blues.

"No. Nothing like that." She didn't mention the kiss.

"I guess we can be grateful for that, at least."

Heather said nothing in reply. Jeff lay still while supporting her head on his chest, his body thrumming with anger.

"Damn them!" Jeff at last ground out through clenched teeth. "This whole thing just makes me so goddamned mad I can't stand it!" He turned on his left side and looked down at Heather as she pushed her pillow under her head.

"But you're sure they didn't hurt your knee?"

"No, I fell on the ice, and then again when I was getting into the car."

Jeff continued thinking. His brow furrowed and he stared off into space as if he was seeing something materializing out of thin air.

"They must've been the same three who attacked me, the bastards," Jeff burst out, physically warming as more rage suffused his body.

"I may not be able to do anything about what they did to you, but I sure as hell know who can, Heather. We've got to let the detectives know about this. And it's time for you to tell them what you told me about discovering who you think killed Patti."

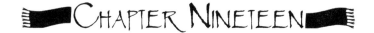

Chapter Nineteen

Entering Aksel's tiny ceramic tiled foyer, Anja could see into his dim living room, and beyond that, a dining area and kitchen.

"What a lovely apartment, Aksel!" *I wonder if the lights are low because he's planning for this to be a real date?*

They removed their winter boots and Aksel placed them in the corner of the foyer, setting hers right next to the heating vent on the floor so they would heat up and stay warm.

"Here, give me your coat and I'll hang it up for you." Taking hers, he placed them both on the rack by the door. "Now, come on in."

Anja pulled a bottle of wine from her bag and handed it to Aksel.

"Take this with you to the kitchen. It should greatly improve our mood for the evening." *I hope it does wonders. We need a break.*

She'd paid more for this French Cabernet-Merlot than she'd ever paid for a single 750 ml bottle of any kind of wine. Any wine's name beginning with Chateau sounded special. It'd just felt right to her when she saw its label and read the accompanying article from *Wine Spectator*.

"Thanks. This must be the special wine you promised." He chuckled. "I've got wine, too. We'll really let our hair down on this Friday night and enjoy our steaks with a couple of bottles like this."

As Anja rezipped her bag, she caught Aksel staring inside it. He raised his eyebrows and she knew he'd glimpsed the black lacy panties lying on top of the other clothing she'd packed for this special night. *I should be embarrassed, but really, I'm not.*

They moved from the foyer into the living area. Anja gasped and abruptly stopped.

"Aksel, I had no idea that you had a way with decorating. The colors are wonderful!" She picked up one of the red and yellow flowered pillows and examined it. She put it back in the chair and ran her hand over the nubby textured yellow pillow lying with the cranberry red one at the end of the sofa.

"Very nice." *Wow, I'll bet he did this just for me. He told me he's had a man's "no colors" apartment ever since his divorce. This is anything but no colors!*

"Thanks, partner." Aksel showed most of his teeth in a huge smile. "If you want to change clothes, my bedroom is just down the hall on the right. The bathroom is directly across from it. Take your pick. I'll be in the kitchen getting the steaks seasoned and to room temp."

"What about you changing clothes? If I do, you do."

"I'll do that after you."

She looked up at Aksel with eyes twinkling and a teasing smile. "I didn't know you had it in you, partner. You—an interior decorator! Who knew?"

Shrugging her shoulders and turning her palms up as if she was asking someone an important question, her smile turned into a laugh. "What other surprises do you have in store for me tonight?"

"You never know."

In Aksel's bedroom, her eyes flicked from the beige bedspread to the beige curtains to the beige carpet. *I wonder what happened in here. Or rather, what didn't happen in here.* The room was neat but had no color or warmth. She figured if this evening turned into anything other than partners enjoying each other's company, it would soon be a hotbed of warm colors.

She removed her shirt, slacks, and socks. She paused to think a moment and decided she did want to be fresh, so she stepped out of her white cotton panties and into the black lacy ones. Thinking she was being quite daring, she slipped on a black spaghetti-strapped cocktail dress, the skirt falling just above the knee, and the neckline plunging between her breasts. A pearl necklace, nearly a choker, adorned her neck and pearl drop earrings dangled toward her shoulders. *May as well go the whole nine yards.*

Opening the bedroom door, Anja looked up the hall to make sure Aksel wasn't lounging against the wall waiting for her. *Good. He's not in sight.*

On three-inch heels, she scooted across the hall to the bathroom where she applied her makeup, dabbed perfume in her cleavage, and tousled her short dark hair. She added a spritz of hairspray in hopes it wouldn't immediately fall back into its normal straight shape. *I want it different this evening.*

"Ta-Da!" she said, feeling a bit nervous and, well, *sexy*, to tell the truth.

Aksel came from the kitchen with a dishtowel stuffed in the front band of his trousers, a make-shift apron as it dangled toward his knees, and another towel in his hands. He stopped in his tracks and stared.

"Well, I'll be damned. You do clean up well." He came to her and took both hands in his big rough ones. "I'll never be able to match you, but I'm gonna try to at least be presentable." He let go of her hands and motioned to the sofa.

"Sit. Have a glass of wine." He winked at her. "Be back in a flash." Anja saw him shake his head and grin as he spied the black high-heeled sandals she wore. She knew he'd never seen her in anything but boots in the winter and sensible flats in the summer. *I do believe he likes me dressed like this.*

Anja wandered into the kitchen. She found an opened bottle of cabernet on the counter and two wine glasses beside it, their facets gleaming. She poured a glass and took a sip. "Pure bliss," she whispered. Taking another sip, she let the wine roll to the back of her tongue, savoring its tart sweetness.

She set the glass down on the dining table, which was hardly bigger than in a bistro, and was set with silverware and pretty green plates that in the dim light appeared to be sage with a hunter green swirl. *I wonder if he knows green is my favorite color.*

In the middle of the table in an unusual decorated vase was an arrangement of fresh flowers: Blue and white Hydrangeas, white calla lilies, and pink and white peonies. She bent to smell them. The peonies boasted a light spicy fragrance. *How could he possibly know I think these three are the most beautiful of all flowers?*

"We're more alike than I could've ever guessed," she mused aloud.

Looking around, she spotted salad greens lying on the counter. She opened a cabinet searching for a salad bowl and found a simple glass one. She began to tear the lettuce into it.

Aksel appeared wearing a royal blue sweater and khaki trousers. It was a good choice. The sweater turned his eyes dark blue.

Anja filled the other sparkling glass and handed it to Aksel, picked hers up and touched it to his. "Sante."

"Sante." His eyes fastened on hers and something seemed to lurk in their blue depths. Merriment? Happiness? Mystery? Assessment? Anja wasn't sure what she saw there.

"To a great evening . . ." they said together, glasses raised in front of them. Both laughed and sipped the cabernet. Over the rims of their glasses their eyes held.

Aksel set his glass on the counter. "Well, let me get these steaks going." He ducked his head and looked away. Tension filled the air, so thick until Anja felt she could part it with her hands. It was something Anja had not felt before. She was sure Aksel felt it, too.

While Aksel busily put the steaks in the smoking hot iron skillet for a quick sear, Anja resumed making the salad. She found a few special food items he'd left on the counter with the lettuce. She thought it must be his intent to add them to the salad, so onto the torn green leaf lettuce went crumbled blue cheese, candied ginger strips, and artichoke hearts. She looked in the refrigerator and found a carafe of dressing made with oil and balsamic vinegar. *Must be Good Seasons Italian Dressing mix. My favorite.*

They sipped their wine as they continued to prepare the meal, each one glancing at the other and smiling. Anja finished the salad and took it to the table.

"This is a fabulous salad. The kind you get in a fancy restaurant."

"Great! That's just what I hoped. I thought you could turn those things into a salad fit for kings." Taking his eyes off Anja, he looked at the finished salad. "And it looks like you did."

Anja smiled and wrinkled her nose at him.

The potatoes went into the microwave for six minutes and then Aksel slid them into the toaster oven on high heat to finish baking and to crisp the oiled skins. He opened the bottle of Chateau Cabernet-Merlot and set it and fresh wine glasses on the table.

The steaks were perfect. Seared on the outside and dark juicy pink on the inside. The aroma filled Anja's senses and she realized just how hungry she was. Aksel slit open the potatoes and she saw they were crusty outside and mealy within. Butter and sour cream oozed from them as he set them on the new green plates beside the steaks.

They sat across from each other at the table and Aksel poured the Cabernet-Merlot into the fresh goblets.

"Thanks, Aksel." She pointed a finger at the table setting. "The plates are lovely. You know, green is my favorite color."

"Oh, really? I didn't know that. I like green, too." They smiled at each other and started on their steaks.

"Mmmm." Anja closed her eyes as she chewed, savoring the burst of flavor in her mouth. "This steak is to die for."

"Glad you like it. I tried to cook it the way Luger's Steakhouse does."

"I don't know what theirs tastes like, but this is heavenly."

"Thank you, ma'am." He took a sip of wine and cleared his throat. "What do you think is going to happen next with the case?"

Anja looked down at her plate and was slow to answer. "I truly don't know, Aksel." She looked up at him, eyes searching his face. "I really don't even want to think about it. Let's make a pact. Why don't we not talk about the case tonight and just enjoy this great meal. Deal?"

"Deal." Aksel chuckled low in his throat and gazed at his partner with undisguised affection that Anja could read on his face and in his eyes. Anja's laugh tinkled, joining Aksel's.

Aksel took a bite of the salad and smiled around the greens. "Yep. Fit for a king."

They ate their dinners while the conversation wound down and the feeling between them grew. Soon they simply searched each other's face, eyes large and dark with emotion.

"Dessert!" Aksel leapt from his chair to pull the cake and strawberries from the fridge.

"Oh, lovely." Anja leaned her head to the right and looked up at the big man as he prepared the delectable looking sweet, clearly approving his choice.

Finished with slicing the cake and placing it on clear glass dessert plates, he spooned the berries over it. Then he took a half gallon of vanilla bean ice cream from the freezer and scooped out a serving for each plate. Anja thought he acted as if he was the first man to ever serve such to a woman as he placed hers in front of her.

"It looks yummy, Aksel." She lifted a spoonful to her tongue, savoring it before she swallowed. "Mmmm, it *is* good. I think I'll hire you to be my cook if everything you prepare is like tonight's meal."

"Then we'd be together all the time, not just at work," Aksel softly said as he peered deep into Anja's dark eyes.

Neither seemed to notice they were leaning toward each other until, just as their lips touched, Aksel's pocket rang.

"Shit!" he spat as he punched the phone's answer button. "Who the hell is calling now?"

His angry face softened as he listened. He mouthed "Forrest" to Anja. There ensued another few moments of listening while Anja could only guess at the message.

"We'll be right there." He thumbed off the cell phone.

"We need to get dressed again. Heather Forrest has been attacked."

Jeff Hoffmann opened the door. "Come in detectives. Heather has quite a tale to tell." He was bristling with emotions, his face a thundercloud, and his body was as tense as a tight rope.

"It's a wonder his jaw doesn't break," Anja whispered to Aksel from the side of her mouth as Jeff's jaw muscles bunched. They continued to bulge as he gritted his teeth.

He wore the popular draw-string lounging pants with a long-sleeved tee that could substitute for pajamas. Heather shivered in pajamas and robe. Anja glanced meaningfully at Aksel. *Anger? Cold? Pain? Or fear?*

Jeff returned to Heather's side on the sofa and pulled a moss green afghan from its back and draped it around her shoulders. The detectives took the two matching stuffed chairs facing them.

"Okay, Miss Forrest, tell us what happened. Leave out nothing, no matter how inconsequential it may seem," Aksel said.

"I assure you, nothing is inconsequential about what happened to me tonight!" Heather rubbed her hands over her thighs.

Could be due to agitation. Or maybe it's just to warm them. "Then please let us help you, Heather." Anja stood and took Heather's cold hands in hers.

"All right, I'll try." Still breathing heavily, Heather withdrew her hands and brushed back her hair, smoothing it down on both sides. "There were three of them."

She explained about the note, supposedly from Freddie Mueller, as the reason she had gone to the school. She told about her fear and hiding from them. Looking directly at Anja, her details of the attack spilled out, including the kiss.

Jeff sat straight up on the sofa. “What? You didn’t tell me that!”

“And you can see why,” Heather exclaimed.

“Let her finish, Mr. Hoffmann,” Aksel said sternly. Jeff sank back into his seat.

Heather continued describing her ordeal and how utterly defenseless she was in preventing any of her injuries, including the falls she took on the ice.

“I’m so sorry I didn’t tell you, Jeff,” she admitted as she looked down at her hands where they pleated her robe into accordion folds. “I truly thought I could discover the truth after what I found at school today. And the note *said* not to tell anybody!” Her voice broke on the last sentence and she peered through the unruly hair that again obscured her view, beseeching Jeff to understand. “I *am* sorry, Jeff,” she repeated in a strangled voice.

Aksel shoved his hands into his trouser pockets. “Then what happened, Miss Forrest?” He stood and paced the length of the small living room and back again.

Heather looked down and took a deep breath. It seemed she was thinking about what to reveal and remained silent as she sorted through it.

Anja said, “Heather, why don’t you tell us what you found at school today? I would imagine we’ll have something there to go on.”

“Right.” Heather took another deep breath.

“After Principal Addison announced all the staff members were to gather in the conference room for a short meeting during our lunch break, I decided I wouldn’t go and would instead see if I could get into his office and see what I could find. I pretended to have bad cramps as my excuse for missing the meeting.”

With eyes narrowed and fixed on the wall above Aksel’s head, Heather talked of the events that happened next. What she had seen and done. What she suspected. She then spoke of Addison coming to her room in search of her, and said she was sure he didn't believe she'd been at her desk suffering from cramps, even after showing him the warm cloth she'd placed against her abdomen. She stood and mimicked pulling the cloth from her waistband as she had done with Addison.

"I can't prove it, of course, but I'm certain he is the one who got those boys to attack both Jeff and me. They attacked me because I was supposedly *snooping.*" She sat down again and put her head in her hands.

Suddenly she looked up again. "I don't think one of the boys wanted to be there because he tried to keep order and not let the other two hurt me too badly. He just told me not to try to guess who they were because I didn't know them. But they sure knew who I was."

"That sounds like something Joe Nygaard may have said." Jeff spoke slowly. "I think he likes me. I really don't think he would want to hurt either one of us."

"Then why'd he *do* it?" Heather demanded.

Jeff shot back, "How the hell should I know?" They glared at each other until Heather looked away.

The detectives looked at each other. Anja gave a tiny shrug, noticeable only to her partner.

Aksel said, defusing the awkward situation, "Then I think we need to bring Joe Nygaard in again and lean on him hard. Maybe fabricate some stuff and pretend we have proof."

"Yes," Anja agreed. "Make him spill what he knows because he'll think we already know it."

He must have paid the boys a lot of money," Heather thought aloud. "I think Principal Addison is rich—really rich." She rose and paced the small area in her living room.

"You wouldn't believe the phenomenal amount of art he has in his office. It may be fake, replicas of the real thing. But, the bust looks like real marble. And the small pieces look real, too. Like the egg, for instance. It certainly looks like a fine replica of an original Faberge. I've seen photos of those eggs in art books and they cost a fortune. I'd say he has plenty of money to pay those boys." Heather took in breath and heaved a long sigh. She sat again on the sofa.

Anja nodded. "You know, I did notice a lot of artsy stuff when we were there this morning. I thought he was just being pretentious and showing off."

Aksel said with a mischievous grin, "I thought he was a collector of fake art and got his kicks from everyone admiring the stuff."

"What I'm saying is I believe it's real and that he has the money to do anything he wants." Heather wrung her hands but didn't seem to notice she was doing it.

Anja again thought, Cold? Or agitation? Probably both.

"Okay, let's find out what we can get out of Joe Nygaard and we'll pay Mr. Addison a little visit, too. We'll find out what he has stashed in his own home, as well."

"Right, let's go get Joe now," Anja said.

"Do you have to have a warrant?" Jeff asked.

Anja shook her head, the remainder of the tousled hair falling back into shape. "No, not for questioning."

Aksel opened the door. "We'll get back with you."

Jeff and Heather sat where they were, neither one moving for the moment.

Jeff suddenly shot a look at Heather. Then leaping to his feet, he yelled, "God Dammit, Heather. I took a beating for you. They almost broke my fucking leg. And you're still keeping things from me?" He stood looking down at Heather and breathing hard. He continued through clenched teeth, "And who was it that accused me of keeping things from her, huh? The one who demanded we always tell each other everything? Could that have been you, Heather?" His voice dripped sarcasm.

Heather looked down at the floor and didn't answer.

"Say something, Heather," Jeff demanded, bending down his long frame so he could see her face.

"What do you want me to say, Jeff?" she shouted, jumping up from the sofa. "Nothing has gone the way I expected it to. I'm sorry you were injured, but I'm injured, too!"

She turned away from Jeff and stalked into the kitchen. "Do you think I meant for all this to happen? Do you think I planned it? Hell no, Jeff. I thought I was doing the right thing. And I tried not to involve you. That's why I didn't tell you what I was doing and where I was going."

Jeff snapped, "Oh, so you were trying to protect me, huh?"

"Yes," Heather shot right back, "and if you can't see that, then you can kiss my ass!"

"That does it." Jeff threw his hands into the air. "I'm outta here. I'll be spending the night at Mom and Dad's."

Yanking open the closet door, he pulled a heavy coat from its depths, drew it on and zipped it. He jammed his sock-clad feet into his boots, and without bending to secure the Velcro, he turned his back to Heather and strode to the door.

"That's right, Jeff. Run away instead of talking. Act just like what you're accusing me of!" Heather stood with her hands on her hips, fuming, as he slammed the door behind him.

"Damnation!" she howled, fury replacing all other emotions. She climbed the stairs to the bedroom, stripped off her robe and got back in the bed she and Jeff vacated when the detectives came. She was too angry to sleep. She was too angry to cry. She was mad as hell.

Jeff's face still bore a mutinous look as his dad opened the door. "Don't ask, Dad. Just get me a pillow and a blanket and I'll sleep right here on the sofa. And for God's sake, keep Mom out of here. I can't talk about it right now."

"But, son . . ."

"I'll talk about it later, Dad. Just not now, please." He shut his eyes and took a deep breath as he clenched his hands tightly into fists, unclenched them, then clenched them again.

"Okay, Jeff. Whatever it is, it will get better, I promise." He turned and headed for the linen closet located in the hall. He returned with a pillow and two blankets. "Can I help you make up your bed?"

"No, thanks, Dad," Jeff said in a loud and dismissive whisper.

As he made his bed on the sofa, he continued to think about what his dad said. *Will it get better?*

Chapter Twenty

January 17, 2015

The killer returned early that Saturday morning before the sun rose and parked about fifty yards up the street from the Fox Towers. Disguised all in black with a loose-fitting black jacket that was perfect for hiding a 9mm G43 Glock with a silencer, he hid behind some tall evergreen bushes at the entrance to the parking garage. A posted sign told him the barred gate wasn't accessible before eight o'clock in the mornings. Since he didn't possess a resident's fob to open the gate, he needed to wait until someone came along to open it for him.

These stupid, trusting idiots. They should know not to plant trees and shrubbery that anyone can hide behind and follow a car in. Someone like me. That set him off in a fit of giggles. He forcefully restrained himself from guffawing with laughter. Stop it, dammit, he told himself, as he swallowed the laughter threatening to bubble up again.

He followed a car inside the garage driven by a little gnome of a man who stretched his neck to peer over the steering wheel. Addison ducked down behind the car, figuring there was little chance he would be seen because, as with so many of the elderly, it was doubtful the man could turn his head.

Locating Jeff's car, he squatted down on the other side of the vehicle beside it. Anticipating his victim would come from the elevator, which was in the opposite direction, he was secure in his hiding spot. He just hoped it wouldn't be long and that no other enterprising soul would be out and about this early.

In the end, he waited longer than he would've liked. He went from kneeling on one knee to the other. He duck-walked to the back of the car and peeked around the tail lights to see the elevator. He was risking being discovered by Security. But he wasn't worried. *My luck will hold. It always does, doesn't it?*

Several people entered their cars and drove away. *Okay, everything's good. No, wait!* A young boy, perhaps four or five and holding the hand of an elderly man, looked right at him. He placed his finger to his lips in the "Shhh" sign and winked at the boy, offering him a slight smile. The boy returned neither, just looked back over his shoulder, keeping eye contact, as he was led farther away.

The elevator doors opened again, and he watched the tall young man exit and walk to his car. He was ready when Jeff Hoffmann inserted his key in the car's door lock.

A single shot was all it took. The silencer he'd attached did its job and the shot went unnoticed as Jeff Hoffmann took the full force of the bullet in his chest. He crumpled to the cold floor of the parking garage, staining the concrete red as his life spilled from him.

The killer held back his laughter as he tucked the gun inside his jacket and retraced his route. *Walk naturally. Don't hurry and no one will even notice.* He raised his head and looked around the parking garage. The noise he'd heard was a car engine. *Oh, shit!*

Another elderly resident pulled in and parked in a row of cars near the exit. Now he was heading toward him, shuffling along one slow, unsteady step at a time. Addison quickly bent down on his left knee and tried to disappear as he "fumbled" with the Velcro strap on his right boot. The old guy passed him without a greeting and continued on his way toward the elevator. *Shit, that was too close of a call.* His mercurial mind then told him: *I knew it. No way was I going to be caught.* He rose and slipped unnoticed out of the now open garage entrance.

He saw two dogs, trotting with noses to the ground, as he walked to his car. *Hungry strays. Somebody's lost their golden retrievers.* They made him think of police bloodhounds chasing a scent. *There's no way anyone would think I did this, but maybe I'd better be a little more careful. They might bring out bloodhounds to get a scent. Better make sure there's nothing for them to smell.* With that bothersome thought, he drove home in the weak, struggling sunshine and parked in his garage.

Jeff's killer stripped off his outer clothes and wrapped the Glock inside the black jacket. He would dispose of them in a place where they wouldn't be found. His thoughts flew back to Paris and how he disposed of the girl's clothes. *Nope. Better not start thinking about that now.*

Anja rang the doorbell of the small wood-framed house. With its white wooden siding and red shutters with red trim around the door, the house showed signs of age and the red was no longer bright. Sitting on a street with similar homes, its once cheery red paint set it off from the others. Leaning her head back, she drew in a lungful of the cold, fresh-smelling air through her nose. She exhaled slowly through her lips, admiring the frosty puffs as they dissipated, each on the heels of the gust before.

"Yeah, whaddaya want? Can't a man have some peace in his own home on a Saturday?" A scowling man in a dark indigo bathrobe and brown slippers mashed down in the heels opened the door and stood in the doorway. He smelled like he'd been on a bender, the whiskey fumes seeming to emanate from his pores. The puffy red eyes and foul breath added to the impression.

Aksel stepped forward. "Mr. Nygaard?"

A guarded "Yeah?" came from the unshaved face.

The detectives showed him their badges and Aksel spoke again. "Detectives Franzen and Frandsen. Is Joe Nygaard your son?"

Mr. Nygaard nodded his head—a quick couple of jerks that set his fleshy jowls wobbling.

"We need to speak with your son. Is he home now?"

The bloodshot blue eyes narrowed as he assessed them. He pursed his lips in thought and just when Aksel was sure he was working up a lie, he said, "All right. Come on in. I'll get him."

As they entered the cold house, its chilliness abetted by the bare linoleum floors, Mr. Nygaard bellowed, "Joe, get your ass in here. There's some detectives out here to see you."

"What's the matter, Dad? What do they want with Joe?" The timid voice came from the hallway. The detectives looked to its source and saw a young girl of ten or so standing in a partly open doorway that was maybe her bedroom. The child had her fingers in her mouth, the nails bitten to the quick.

"None of your damned business, Miss Nosey. Now get back in your room."

The child ducked her head as if ashamed, her dark blonde hair hiding her red face. She faded back into the small bedroom and softly closed the grimy door that bore the dirty prints of hands and fingers around its handle.

Although the house was too cold for comfort, it was still too warm for their winter gear. Both detectives took the opportunity to unzip their coats while waiting for Joe to appear.

In his room at the end of the hall, Joe Nygaard lay on his back, propped up on his pillows. After shoveling the front stoop and the driveway in the dark—obeying his father's orders to get out of bed and get it done, of course— he crawled back under the covers and pulled the quilt close around his shoulders. He was leafing through the latest *Thor* Marvel Comic Book when he heard his father's bellow. The slick paper book slipped from his suddenly paralyzed fingers and fell to his chest. It lay there a moment and slid to the floor. There was nothing to stop it. Not Joe, who felt his heart stop and then restart with a rapid pounding.

"Dammit, I freakin' *knew* they would be back for me. What the fuck am I going to do now?" He whipped the covers down and threw them aside. Sitting up, he felt the jolt when his bare feet touched the almost freezing floor. He spied his socks on the floor near the boots he had worn when shoveling the snow. He rose and, snatching them up, he again sat on the edge of the bed and yanked them on. The socks provided a modest barrier between his cold feet and the colder linoleum. Joe knew better than to go completely barefoot in this house during winter.

Okay, Joe. Get a hold of yourself.

He tried to calm his violent heartbeat, now exacerbated by anger wedded to his fear. *That Addison maniac is who they should be talking to, not me.* His shoulders slumped in defeat. He could figure no way in which he could divulge the horrible things Addison had made him and the other boys do. If he did talk about it, the crazy bastard might well hire another set of desperate teens who badly needed the cash and have them do some serious harm to him. His heart skipped another beat or two as he thought it could be much worse than simply harming him. He could be killed.

"Joe? What're you drag-assing for? Do I have to come back there and get you?"

His father's voice cut through the horror going on in his head and Joe knew he had to get out there and face whatever the detectives had found out.

"Coming, Dad," he called.

I've got to look like I'm not worried about anything at all and that I don't know a thing about Patti Mueller or Miss Forrest. I really am sorry about Mr. Hoffmann because I like him. Joe's mind was working double-time as these thoughts accompanied him from his room to the living room to face the detectives and their questions. *But, I gotta stay cool.*

Only a little fear showed in Joe's eyes as he asked, "What's up, detectives? I believe I told you all I know yesterday, but I'll be glad to help if I can."

"Whaddaya mean? Yesterday?" Mr. Nygaard looked from Joe to the detectives. His head swung back to Joe. "Answer me, boy. Did these two . . ." He indicated Aksel and Anja with a jerk of his head. ". . . question you yesterday?"

Joe quickly lost his bravado and nodded his head, while switching his gaze from Aksel to Anja and back again.

"Without my permission?" His chin jutted forward and his voice went up an octave. "He's still a high school student!"

Anja stepped closer to Joe and got in his face. "Joe? Look at me. Listen to me carefully." She swiveled her head and eyed his father. "You, too, Mr. Nygaard."

When she had their attention, as well as Aksel's, and the little sister who peeked through the slit of the opened door, she spoke.

"How old are you, Joe?"

"Eighteen," Joe mumbled.

"Eighteen," she repeated. She looked directly into Joe's hazel eyes. "Are you aware that in the state of Wisconsin, even though you are still attending high school, that you are no longer a minor and you do not have to have a parent present when being questioned by an officer of the law?"

Again Joe's mumble: "I guess so. I think they told us that in Civics class."

"Is that why you offered no resistance to helping us out with the questions we asked you yesterday?"

Joe raised his eyes and looked into his father's face. "That's right."

"All right, Dammit. Somebody better tell me what this is about, and damned quick," Mr. Nygaard sputtered.

Aksel came to stand beside Mr. Nygaard. "We have reason to believe your son knows more than he said he does about the person responsible for the death of a young teen girl . . ." He was interrupted by a loud gasp from the young girl now standing openly outside her door and listening intently.

Her father glared at her. "Did anybody tell you to come out of your room?"

She picked at her nails and her eyes drifted down and to the side. "No sir."

"Then get back in it and stay there," he roared, the tendons in his neck swollen and standing out.

Aksel picked up where he'd stopped when interrupted by the exchange between Mr. Nygaard and his daughter. ". . . and we need to take him back to the station and this time we'll keep him there until we are satisfied he's telling us everything he knows about the death of the teen girl and the beatings administered to teachers Jeff Hoffmann and Heather Forrest."

What?" Mr. Nygaard exploded. "Joe, you sure as hell better not be mixed up in anything like this. Why, I'll kick your butt into next week, I'll . . ."

"That's enough, Mr. Nygaard," Aksel told him. Surprised, Nygaard clamped his mouth shut and looked away from Aksel to Anja, whose dark eyes burned as if she could bore holes in him.

Turning back to Joe, she said, "You aren't under arrest, Joe. Not yet. But you will be if you don't willingly accompany us to Headquarters for questioning."

Without a word, Joe returned to his room and emerged carrying his boots and heavy hooded parka. He sat on the edge of a kitchen chair and shoved his feet into the boots, securing them with the Velcro straps. He stood and shrugged into his coat. No one said a word while this was happening. Mr. Nygaard's face turned from red to a violent purple but he remained silent. When Joe was ready, he headed out the door with the detectives following him.

At the door, Aksel paused and tapped his fist against his chin, obviously thinking of what he wanted to say. He took his fist down and turned around to face Joe's father. "What I see here borders on child abuse. You've threatened your children in front of police officers. Child abuse is illegal. If you don't want to be arrested, I'd advise you to watch your temper and leave your kids alone. Try being a parent instead of a bully." He nodded curtly to the big man who stood with his mouth open and chin heading toward his chest, and drew the door shut behind him. He joined Joe and Anja and the three got in the SUV for the drive to the station.

"Would you like a cup of coffee, Joe? Maybe a soda?" Aksel smiled as he propped his right shoulder against the wall, casually leaning on it. Joe sat on the side of the scarred interview table nearest the wall. He faced Aksel who remained leaning against the facing wall, one leg stretched out in front of him. In the small room, he was the perfect picture of comfortable confidence. He also seemed to ooze authority.

They'd escorted Joe into the station and down the dim inside hall to the brightly-lit interview room. Its extra lighting helped prevent seeing out of the one-way mirrored window, but it allowed those outside to see the activity inside the room. For this time on a Saturday morning, the station was busy. Calls came in from dispatch, officers brought in people for questioning, and the aroma of freshly-brewed coffee permeated the air.

"Uh, yeah, I'll take a cup of coffee with cream and two sugars. Thanks."

Aksel eased away from the wall. "You got it." He opened the door and asked someone in the hall to bring Joe's coffee. Returning to stand across the table from Joe, his demeanor changed.

"Okay, Joe, this is what we know." He paused, watching Joe's face and body for reaction.

Joe sat slouched in his chair, butt slid forward with his spine against the wooden slats of the chair's back. At Aksel's steady gaze, he sat up.

"Yeah, what's that? What do you know?"

When Aksel pursed his lips and looked at Anja with eyebrows raised, as if asking her if it was time to tell him what they knew, Joe hurried to add, "I ain't done nothing, man."

"So . . . you haven't done anything, huh, Joe?" Anja walked to the desk and leaned down in front of him, daring him to deny it. "That's not what we heard."

"Yeah, Joe," Aksel said, picking up the thread. "We heard you were head of the bunch of thugs who attacked your teacher, Jeff Hoffmann, on Christmas Eve."

"And led the guys who beat Hoffmann's girlfriend, Heather Forrest, *last* night," Anja added. "You know, Joe, we're hearing all kinds of things that put you right in the middle of these attacks."

"And in the middle of Patti Mueller's death," Aksel added.

"No! No way," he exploded, jumping up from his chair, sending it crashing into the wall behind it. "You're not going to pin *that* on me. I may have been in on the other stuff, but I sure as hell did *not* have anything to do with killing Patti Mueller!"

Aksel barked, "Pick up that chair and sit back down."

Joe righted the chair and sat again with eyes big and looking as if he realized he was in deep shit.

"So, you do admit to being a part of the attacks on the two teachers?" Aksel asked.

Cornered, Joe backpedaled. "I didn't say that."

"You think there's something wrong with my hearing, Joe?"

"No, I don't mean that, either . . ." he began. He stopped and looked around the small, gray-walled room as if looking for inspiration. Finding none, he blurted, "Oh, hell, I don't know what I mean."

Anja said, "Okay, Joe, you've implicated yourself in the attacks. You know what happens now."

"Am I under arrest?"

"You will be."

Joe threw himself down into his seat and sat slumped over the table with his face pressed into his palms. "Oh, Jesus Christ, what am I going to do now?"

Anja stood beside him and looked down at his bent head, his brown curly hair still a mess from the hat he'd worn when shoveling snow.

Aksel looked up from his study of Joe Nygaard with his head cocked, listening. There it was again, a discreet knock on the door. He lifted his shoulders in a "Beats me" shrug and tipped his head to Anja.

"I'll get it," Anja said. She opened the door and stepped out into the corridor.

The captain stood with his hands clasped behind him. "Jeff Hoffmann's been shot." He swung his head from side to side as if puzzled. "This case just keeps getting worse."

"Is he dead?"

"Oh, yes. I'm afraid so."

"Dammit all to hell! They were mad and sniping at each other when Aksel and I left them last night." Anja stopped as a thought hit her. "Heather Forrest does know, doesn't she?"

"No. At least I've not been told so. I want you and Aksel to go tell her. You also need to question her because she's a suspect, too, until we can rule her out."

"Of course. When did it happen? And where?"

"We just got the call. He was shot in the underground parking lot at The Fox Towers. You know that retirement high rise apartment building that sits right on the Fox River?"

"Yes, Sir. That's where Hoffmann's parents live. He must've been visiting them."

She pushed back the left sleeve of her plaid blazer to expose her watch. "It's just now nine twenty. With it being this early, he may have spent the night there."

She ran her hand through her short hair and her eyes were unfocused as she stared at nothing, perhaps recalling the events of the night before. "Unless I'm mistaken, I'll bet he did spend the night with his parents. He probably wanted to get away from the fight with Heather."

"Well, get to the bottom of this as fast as you can. You and Aksel get over there pronto. I'll see that Joe Nygaard is taken care of until you can get back to him." Captain Harjula gestured to the one-way mirror where they could see Joe sitting slouched in his chair. Aksel leaned forward with both hands on the table, talking to an unresponsive Joe.

The captain shook his head. "We'll put him in a cell and then we'll see how long it takes him to talk. He hasn't lawyered up, has he?"

"Not unless he did it while I've been out here." She put her hand on the doorknob of the interrogation room and turned again to the captain. "Who's there at Fox Towers?"

"One of the residents called 911 and Chuck and Diana answered the call."

"I just hope the Hoffmanns haven't found out yet." She opened the door a crack and motioned for Aksel to join her.

Anja replaced her blazer with her winter gear and climbed into the driver's seat of the SUV. She filled in her partner about Jeff Hoffmann's murder as she drove to the Fox Towers apartments. She took her eyes off the road ahead, clear now due to the snowplows, and looked sideways at Aksel. "I imagine Maggie Greene will be pissed to get Jeff's body, especially with the connection to Patti Mueller. Pardon me, the *alleged* connection. She's really hot about this one. This senseless murder of a teen girl has her angrier than I've seen her in a long time. She seems to take it personal. Besides, she's so good at her job, you know."

"Well, maybe not entirely senseless. Remember, she *was* pregnant," Aksel reminded her.

"True." Wondering aloud, Heather added, "I don't know how she does it all. I mean be the coroner, the forensic specialist, *and* the medical examiner all at the same time."

From the corner of her eye, she again glanced at Aksel. He was silently staring out the windshield at the dreary day surrounding them.

Normally not a chatty Kathy, Anja added what she'd said to the captain: She hoped no one had told the Hoffmanns yet because the two of them needed to not only inform them, but Heather Forrest, as well.

Aksel remained quiet with eyes narrowed and a double line of wrinkles on his forehead. He looked as if he was assessing every piece of the puzzle that faced them as Anja finished the preliminaries of what she knew.

He spoke at last, "He's ramping it up, Anja. Heather's in real danger and he'll come after her next. And soon, I would think. We need to hurry and check everything out and talk to the Hoffmanns, even if someone else has already told them. Then we need to get over to Heather's apartment."

"I think we better send a car to keep an eye on the place until we can get there," Anja replied.

"Good idea."

Aksel placed the call. Captain Harjula listened and assured him he would place a patrol car in the parking lot so the officer could see Heather's front door. Plus, he would assign a partner to be on foot, should there be a reason to check out any suspicious person seen hanging around.

"Okay, I think we've got it covered for now," Aksel told Anja, as she brought the SUV to a stop outside the garage entrance of the retirement apartments.

They ducked under the yellow crime scene tape and quickly scanned the area.

Camera," Anja said, pointing to the security camera attached to a ceiling beam between the entrance and the elevator. "Gotta get that footage checked. Maybe it captured something. But it sure is attached at a strange angle."

Two uniformed police stood with an older couple. Aksel muttered, "Seems like his parents already know."

"Hello, Diana," Anja greeted the officers. "Good morning, Chuck. I'd like you two to get the security tape and secure it for us to look at later."

"Detectives," Diana acknowledged. Beside her a sobbing woman with dark hair going gray was supported by a tall gray-haired man whose own tears swam in his glassy eyes. "This is John and Eva Hoffmann."

"We're sorry for your loss, Mr. and Mrs. Hoffmann," Anja said, her voice low and sincere. "Have you had a chance to tell Heather Forrest of Jeff's death?"

Eva Hoffmann, looking as if she could spit fire, responded they had not, nor were they going to.

"She was fighting with my Jeff last night and that's why he was here in the first place. If she'd been a good girlfriend, or whatever she was to him, he would've been safe at home, instead of here where some lunatic could murder him. He was so upset last night until he didn't even want to talk to his mother." She wound down amid a freshet of tears.

"Mr. Hoffmann, can you add anything?" Aksel asked, as his critical eye assessed Jeff's dad.

"Just that Jeff wouldn't talk about it at all last night. He was too pissed off." He heaved a sigh and told them, "The last thing I said to him was things would get better." He looked at Aksel. "Great fatherly wisdom, huh?"

"We *will* get who is responsible for this, sir," Aksel said.

Anja asked the uniforms, Diana and Chuck, to escort the Hoffmanns to their apartment and make sure they were all right. Aksel watched them escort the older couple onto the elevator. His eyes returned to Anja to immediately flick away to the murder scene.

"Let's do it."

Jeff's Pathfinder and the other cars in its row faced the front wall of the garage. The elevator was located in the middle of the row behind them, five parking spots to the right of the back end of the Pathfinder. The detectives knelt down on the concrete beside Jeff's body, careful not to disturb the wide-spread blood stain that had started to thicken.

Jeff lay on his right side with his legs bent at the knee. It looked like the force of the bullet slammed his body against the car parked beside his and he'd slid down to the floor as his legs buckled. He tilted to the right and had come to rest with his face and chest turned toward the floor. It was here where his chest had poured out his blood and it had turned into the sticky residue it was now.

The police photographer stood nearby with his camera. "Ready for me now?"

"Yes, Jerry. Take pictures of everything here and then we'll have a look at them." Aksel drew on his rubber gloves as the photographer put down a number marker. The flash gave a quick burst of light as he took the first picture. He then took several more from different angles, each photo identified in sequence by the numbers he placed.

When the photographer was finished, Aksel gently lifted Jeff's left arm, which had fallen across his chest, to look for the source of the blood and the entry point.

"It's here, Anja. It looks like the son-of-a-bitch shot him right in the heart. See?" He pointed to the neat hole in the navy jacket, dark now and surrounded by thick blood which was losing its bright red color.

"That's why there's so much blood."

"Right. Now I'm going to turn the body slightly," he paused and looked to the photographer. "Here, get pictures of this, too."

He turned the body farther onto the stomach so they could look for an exit wound.

"Doesn't look like there is an exit wound. The round must still be inside the body."

The photographer took more pictures as Anja said, "We need to find that shell casing."

Both detectives lay face down on the garage floor, avoiding the blood stain and Jeff's body, and looked under the cars on either side. Aksel pushed his head and outstretched arm under the Nissan Altima that Jeff had come to rest against, having slid down its side. He looked behind the left front tire, slid further under, painfully scraping his upper back in the process, and reached as far as he could toward the other side.

Meanwhile, Anja searched with her gloved fingers around the driver's front wheel of Jeff's Pathfinder. Her sensitive fingers found an elliptical pebble, but no shell casing. *Crap. Where is it? It's got to be here somewhere. I don't think the shooter would've taken the time to search for it.*

"I don't see anything under here," Aksel said, carefully backing out from under the Nissan. "I think the shot would've come from the other side of the Pathfinder." He rose to his feet and, picking his way, he tip-toed around behind Jeff's car where Anja still lay on the garage floor.

"See anything at all?"

"Aksel!" Anja said, her voice sounding like a little girl who's just received a pony for her birthday. "I think I may see something. Back there. Back under the car by the passenger side rear wheel."

Aksel again dropped to his stomach just behind the SUV's rear wheel to peer under it in search of the shell casing. He slowly ran his fingers around the inside edge of the tire where it rested against the floor.

"Yes!" he said.

Anja looked into the aisle between the rows and called, "Jerry, take a picture of the shell casing before Aksel brings it out." Jerry lay down at the back end of the SUV and took several pictures, turning his camera to capture every angle.

When he'd finished, Aksel reached his hand to the spot with the casing and then withdrew it. The shell casing was between his thumb and forefinger. "Got it!"

He stood and called to Officer Chuck, who was helping Diana with crowd control. Several residents of Fox River Towers watched the police, moving about the perimeter of the crime scene.

"Chuck, come over here and try to insert your car key in the door lock of the Pathfinder. Be careful not to step in the blood or to step on Detective Frandsen. I want to look at the probable trajectory of the bullet."

Anja stood up and moved out of Chuck's way.

Aksel came to stand at the driver's door and looked around and down at the lock as he determined the best spot for aiming at Chuck.

"Okay; I think I've got it." He eased around the back end of the Pathfinder and aimed an imaginary handgun at Chuck's chest, sighting down his finger barrel.

"This is it. I think this is where he was when he shot him. I can see Chuck's shoulders and chest above the top of Jeff's car. And because he's tall like Jeff, I could shoot him right in the chest with no problem. And if the coroner can excise the bullet without harming it, and it wasn't flattened too badly by hitting the ribs, we'll find that bastard's gun and match the slug to it. We'll get the blood spatter and trajectory team to make sure that's the right direction when they get here. And," Aksel continued, "the casing would fall right where you saw it, because the gun ejects spent casings to the right, and this one had a slight hill to roll down because the concrete is uneven here."

"Well, thank God Maggie Greene *is* the area's best coroner and leading forensics specialist. She'll find all the ways to prove who Jeff's murderer is."

"And Patti Mueller's," Aksel added, as he dropped the photographed shell casing into a clear evidence bag. "Now we've gotta go," he told the officers. "The coroner is on her way."

They started out the entrance just as Maggie Greene ducked under the yellow tape. Looking each one directly in the eye, she said, "Detectives, get that bastard. I've had quite enough of his handiwork in my morgue."

"You got it, Maggie," Aksel declared. "Now, we've gotta get back to the station.

Anja murmured to Aksel, "I wish we had more time here. There's so much more to do."

"Yeah, me, too. I'd also like to see what's on the camera footage. And talk to the man who found Jeff's body and called it in. However, we've got to get back to Joe Nygaard. I've got a feeling that we'll get quite a bit of incriminating evidence from what he'll tell us when we film and record his statement."

"Let's hope you're right."

The detectives, with Aksel at the wheel, began the drive back to the station as fast as the icy roads permitted. They had one petrifying moment as a late-model blue Mustang, driven by a teen male at a higher speed than the conditions warranted, was unable to stop at the light at the intersection they were approaching. The young driver must have realized he was going too fast to stop for the light to turn, for he applied the brakes just as the detectives' SUV entered the intersection.

Aksel yelled, "Look out, Anja!" and pressed the gas pedal. The SUV shot forward and the blue Mustang swerved into the intersection behind them, missing them by inches, and performed an awkward dance as it fishtailed from one side of the road to the other. It came to a halt as it took a nose-dive into a plowed snow bank beside the main thoroughfare.

"Good God! We're lucky that kid didn't hit us," Anja gasped. "Boy, am I glad you were driving, Aksel!"

Peering in the rearview mirror, and then turning to look over his shoulder out the back of their SUV, Aksel watched the teen slowly open the Mustang's door and emerge into the cold. He kicked aside the packed snow that allowed his car door to open only partially. He threw his arms above his head and kicked the front tire still embedded in the snow.

"Should we see about this, Aksel?" Anja asked, her face set in a worried frown.

"Nah, he's all right. We can call it in as a one car accident. But, right now, we need to get back to Joe Nygaard."

"Yes. You're right. I hope he's not just sitting there trying to come up with a plausible lie that he hopes will get him off." Anja looked out the window at the lowering sky.

"Well, let's go in and tell him we know he's guilty and see how long it takes for him to start telling the truth."

"Okay. It's likely to work with Joe if I act the sympathetic one, because that boy needs someone to act like they care about him. It's a crying shame it has to be a police officer trying to get a confession."

"Yep," Aksel agreed. "This day is proving to be almost an 'out of body' experience."

"Yeah, I know what you mean. For me, it's like I'm watching a movie and the two of us are trying to catch some one and we're actually just chasing our tails, going around in circles."

Neither had any idea what the rest of this day would bring them.

Chapter Twenty-One

A guard escorted Joe Nygaard back to the interview room he had been in earlier that morning. He sat at the table and picked at his nails, reveling in the freedom to do so. He had not as yet been arrested nor put in handcuffs. The detectives had said nothing of what was so important that they had to leave. They had just dumped him in lock-up.

Joe jerked and his head shot up as the door burst open and Detective Franzen charged in. His partner entered behind him and shut the door.

"Right now, Joe. You'd better tell me everything you know about the Patti Mueller case right this minute." The male detective's face was vibrant red, as if he had just gotten a sunburn, and he delivered this demand in a dangerous voice.

"I'm tired of you giving us the run-around. I want to know everything you know about this whole thing. From start to finish. From Patti Mueller to today. And I want it *now*!"

Joe raised both hands in front of his face like he feared the detective would hit him. "What makes you think *I* know anything?" he got out, his voice shaking.

Anja calmly answered, "Tell us what you know, Joe. This case has gotten a lot worse. You've already admitted to being involved, so you better try to clear yourself before you get charged with murder."

"I'm not all *that* involved." He looked to the side and then dropped his eyes to the floor. Anja had been taught that was a sure indication of a lie. But then he raised his head and met her eyes as he made a vehement denial. "I sure didn't have anything to do with any murder!"

Aksel looked at Joe for about half a minute, stern expression still in place. "Tell you what we're gonna do. We're going to ask . . .," he paused and walked around behind Joe, leaned down near his ear, and said in a loud whisper, ". . . and you're going to tell."

Joe dropped his eyes to his hands and picked at the dry skin around his left thumbnail. He set his jaw and his lips formed a tight straight line in his flushed face.

Anja sat in the chair nearest Joe, folded her hands, and laid them on her thigh. She and Aksel had planned their questioning routine on the way back to the station. At that time, she'd commented to Aksel that she hoped either his masculine anger or her female understanding would get Joe to talk. Something had to.

Now she was looking at Joe's bent head. His too long hair was still a nest of curls from the watch cap he had worn while shoveling snow and then again on the ride in. "Joe, let's wrap up this case and get justice served for Patti Mueller."

Joe looked up, perhaps to see what she would say next.

She supplied it. "And justice for your teacher, Jeff Hoffmann."

"Yeah, Joe, just tell it to us like it happened. Whatever your involvement, we'll take into account your cooperation with us." Aksel's voice was now low and earnest.

"I don't know what to say," Joe whined.

"Yes, you do, Joe. You know what to say," Anja said softly, her voice mild and seductively coaxing. "The truth."

Joe watched the detective. Then he dropped his face into his hands. Uncontrollably, it seemed, he began to beat his hands against his head, muttering to himself through closed teeth, too low for Anja to hear.

"God, I *can't* tell them. I have to say I didn't do anything. Oh, why did I ever get mixed up with that crazy man?"

He stopped bashing his head with his hands. "I'll do what you asked," Joe blurted, his eyes shifting around the room and not looking at either detective. "I'll tell you everything I know, but it's not much because I didn't do anything."

"Well, now, that's what we wanted to hear." Aksel smiled at Joe, a big tooth-filled grin, and turned to Anja. "He says he'll tell us all. Isn't that terrific?" He turned away, opened the door and went out into the hall, closing the door behind him. He didn't return for a few minutes. He took his time outside at the one-way mirror turning on the recording system.

While he was gone, Anja remained seated near Joe and gazed at him. She didn't speak.

Joe sat straighter in his chair with dread registered in the set of his mouth and in his hooded eyes as Aksel returned and stood with his hands on his hips. He looked at Joe and nodded his head as if he'd come to a conclusion about something. Next, he opened his interrogation with a zinger.

"We know you were party to killing Patti Mueller. You helped put her body on the pond at the golf course."

Joe's mouth fell open so quickly it was almost comical. "I did not!" he yelled, his eyes wild and roving as if looking for escape.

"We have ways of proving this, Joe. You did that just like you helped beat Jeff Hoffmann on Christmas Eve."

"No, I didn't."

"Yes, you did. Hoffmann recognized your voice. Why do you think he's avoided you since then?"

"I don't know."

"You worked with several others. Wanta tell us who was the mastermind? We've got some pretty serious proof of who it is, but it'll help your case if you give us the name."

Joe squirmed in his seat and rubbed his hands on his thighs. He said nothing.

Anja asked, "Could I get you something to drink, Joe? Perhaps a cup of coffee? Or maybe something cold, like a Coke?"

"Uh, a Coke would be good."

Anja spoke to Aksel as she moved her seat closer to Joe. "Detective Franzen, would you mind asking for a Coke for Mr. Nygaard?" She added with a smile, "In fact, I'll join him. Would you get one for me, too?"

In the interrogation process, it was important to establish rapport with the suspect. Anja had long ago been taught the Reid Method that dated to the 1940s, which, among other guidelines, involved the "good cop/bad cop" routine. She and Aksel were to act as if they already had proof and knew most of the answers. They were to be tough. They were to be kind. They were to be whatever they needed to be in order to get a confession.

The Cokes arrived and were set in the middle of the table. Everyone, including Aksel, reached for a can, popped the top, and took a few swallows of the cold, sweet drink.

Continuing, Anja said, "So, Joe, we know you didn't dream up these horrible things." She leaned forward in her chair so she had to look up at him with her head turned to the side and toward him. It was a non-threatening position, one meant to encourage confidences.

Reaching out with her right hand, she almost touched him, but stopped short. The act of one wanting to help another was established.

"Someone approached you and asked for your help. Tell me how it all started."

It looked like Joe was going to respond as he sighed, opened his mouth to talk, and then closed it again.

Play on his sense of honor and duty. "You'll be doing the right thing," Anja said. "Think how painful this has been for the Mueller family. They need to know why their daughter was killed. I know you'd hate for this to happen in your family." *That'll make him think of protecting his little sister.*

Joe dared a glance at Detective Franzen.

Aksel gave several slow nods, indicating his agreement with Anja.

Joe brought his fist to his mouth; a classic thinking pose. Without taking it down, he hesitantly began to talk, bouncing it against his chin.

"Let's see . . ." Joe looked up and blinked his eyes, thinking. "It started on the Friday before Christmas, the last day of school. This guy was waiting by my car when school was dismissed. He told me he knew who I was and he knew all about my family. And somehow he knew that we didn't, uh, have a lot of money."

Joe stopped and dropped both his hand and his eyes as his face turned red.

"That makes sense, Joe. Those kind always know a vulnerable spot and take advantage of it," Anja said, her warm brown eyes looking up at him.

"He offered me a thousand dollars." He ducked his head and shrugged. "What was I supposed to do? I needed the money."

"And . . .?" Aksel asked.

"And two hundred-fifty each for two other guys. But I had to find them for him."

Aksel jabbed Joe's file with his pen. "Okay, you were the leader. The other two had to have been pissed that you got so much more money than they did. That had to cause a problem among you."

"I, ah, I actually didn't tell them."

Aksel raised his eyebrows and nodded. "No, I guess you didn't. They wouldn't have done the work." He turned his back to Joe. Quickly he whirled back to face him. "So, did they, Joe?"

"Yes, of course!" Joe shot back.

Anja rejoined the questioning. "The three of you attacked Jeff Hoffmann and almost broke his leg. We know. We took him to the hospital. And the man who hired you told you to do that."

"Yeah, he did. We were to hurt him real bad and tell him to stop snooping in Patti's death. Mr. Hoffmann is my favorite teacher. I didn't want to hurt him, but we had to in order to get paid. And I needed that money!" Joe flung his head up, defiant eyes blazing. "We were told not to kill him, though, which I would never do."

Seeing the looks exchanged between the detectives, Joe exclaimed, "You gotta believe me. I'd never do that!"

Aksel now stood behind Anja with his arms crossed. He cradled his right elbow with his left hand and commented in a mild voice, "That's interesting, Joe. You're saying you understood that Jeff Hoffmann wasn't to be killed." He stopped and dropped his arms to his sides. Raising his right hand, he tapped his temple, as if trying to figure out something. Fiercely, he announced, "But yet, he *was* killed this very morning."

"Mr. Hoffmann's dead?" Joe's voice was barely a squeak, like that of a frightened kitten, and his face drained of color. He swayed as if he might pass out.

"Yes, Joe," Aksel snarled. "He certainly is."

"Oh, my God," Joe said, sliding down in his seat. He leaned forward and put his face in his hands. "That bastard!"

Suddenly, Joe surged erect, and with eyes gleaming and mouth twisting, the words poured out of him. "The crazy man's name is James Addison and he's the principal at my high school. That's where Mr. Hoffmann and Miss Forrest teach."

Joe stopped again and swallowed hard. With eyes unfocused, he stared into space for a moment, seemingly gathering his thoughts.

"Okay, Joe. What did this Addison guy first ask you to do?" Aksel asked, stepping closer to him.

Joe shrank into his seat but continued with his story. "Christmas Eve, Mr. Hoffmann went out shopping and I called the other two I got to help me. Rocky Westberg and Bobby Helgason. When he left a shop, Bobby grabbed him and Rocky slammed him in the knee with a baseball bat."

"You were there. So, you helped," Aksel said.

"Well, I didn't hurt him, but I helped put him in the car." Joe looked at Anja, pleading now. "That wasn't so bad, was it?"

"Just go on and tell us what happened, Joe. The more you volunteer to us, the better things will be for you." She nodded, encouraging him to go on.

He sighed, a big intake of breath, and breathed it out slowly. Then he continued with a rush, and as he warmed to his story, Joe's voice grew more eager, the words tumbling out. He often looked to Anja as if for approval. She rewarded him with a nod or a smile each time.

"Addison also threatened to hurt my little sister and to send Rocky back to Juvie if we didn't do what he wanted."

"And what he wanted was for you three to attack Miss Forrest." There was sympathy for his situation in Detective Anja Frandsen's voice.

"Yes, he called, mad as hell, and said for us to beat up Miss Forrest and tell her to stop snooping. Just like Mr. Hoffmann." He winced as he said Jeff's name. "I wrote her a note and pretended to be Freddie Mueller and told her to meet me in her homeroom last night. But she heard us and ran outside."

"What did you do then, Joe? We know the truth, so tell us what you did," Anja said, as she leaned close, beseeching him to confide in her as, again, her hand reached toward him without quite touching him.

"Joe acknowledged her reaching out to him by looking at her hand and then into her eyes. He ducked his head and mumbled, "We found her and Rocky got a little crazy after she fell down. He tried to kiss her but she wouldn't let him so he kicked her a couple of times. We left her out there by the garbage cans and then we all went home. I felt bad about doing that to her, but what was I going to do?"

"What did you decide to do then, Joe?" Aksel asked.

Joe shrugged his shoulders. Then rushing his words, he said, "Mr. Addison said he'd find a way to pin Patti Mueller's murder on us and said everyone would believe him over us because he was an adult and in a position of respect while we're worthless trash. He called us hoodlums and scum. So, I had to do what he wanted."

Joe pondered that for a moment before continuing. And this time he addressed his remarks to Aksel. "What about him? He's the worst man I've ever known." His facial features all pinched together as if he smelled a bad odor and he gave a short, involuntary shiver. He hung his head and said no more.

Aksel asked, "Are you finished? Anything else you want to tell us?"

"No," Joe answered, sounding depressed and defeated. His limp body seemed to melt into the chair like a wet rag doll.

Aksel turned and left the room again to turn off the Martel LX Police Interview Recording System the captain had requisitioned for their use earlier last fall to the tune of almost eight thousand dollars. It had a camera installed inside an operating thermostat located on the wall and one in a round bulb-like thing in the ceiling. The microphones were inside innocent looking wires that appeared to operate a computer and a radio.

The door knob turned and the door opened to admit Aksel.

"Oh, hell," Joe declared, as if having an epiphany. He looked first at Anja and then at Aksel. "I don't need a lawyer, do I?"

Aksel carefully replied, "Not unless you think you need one. And then you'd still have to ask for one."

Anja added, before Joe could think it over, "You've already told us everything, Joe."

Joe, looking thoughtful, nodded his head. "Yeah, you're right. I guess I have."

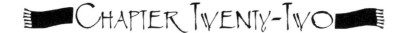

Chapter Twenty-Two

"I hope to hell she hasn't heard anything on the news yet," Aksel said, as he navigated the big SUV through Saturday traffic.

"I suppose she hasn't, or otherwise, I believe she would've tried to reach us. If she was thinking straight, that is."

Aksel parked the SUV in the spot reserved for Jeff Hoffmann. It was a sobering thought to realize Jeff would never park there again.

Anja rang the doorbell at Heather's apartment.

Heather Forrest lay in bed in her upstairs bedroom. She was in a state between dreaming and wakefulness. Somewhere within the realm of her consciousness she heard the doorbell and its Merry Christmas ditty that neither she nor Jeff had gotten around to changing. It would only take a couple of seconds, a matter of pushing a tiny switch was all there was to it. But they hadn't. It would take effort to do it. It seemed everything took a huge effort to do these days. She'd ask Jeff to do it.

She stretched out her hand to him and discovered he wasn't in bed with her. His side was still made up, the duvet tucked about his pillow. *Where is he?* And then she remembered. She remembered the fight they'd had and Jeff being so angry he'd left to go stay the night at his parents' apartment.

A swift glance at the bedside clock. *Good Lord! It's 11:15.*

Thinking about the night before, she recalled everything as it all flooded back to her. *But it took me forever to get to sleep last night. I cried for hours. And I not only was furious with Jeff, but my whole body ached from falling on the ice and from those three boys hurting me. Damn 'em to hell, anyway!*

The bright, tinkling notes of "We Wish You a Merry Christmas" ascended the stairs to her as the doorbell rang again. Although she wanted to ignore it and just remain in bed doing nothing, Heather threw aside her warm covers and got up. She couldn't imagine who it could be, unless it was Franzen and Frandsen with an update. *Wouldn't it be fabulous if they've caught those boys?*

She reached for her robe and slipped it on, then fished her slippers from under the edge of the bed and slid her feet into them. A quick glimpse in the bathroom mirror brought dismay. Her hair was a disheveled mess and her eyes were red and swollen. There was nothing she could do about her eyes, but she ran a brush through her tangles and heaved a sigh. *Whoever it is can take me or leave me. I really don't care.*

Heather unlocked and opened the heavy storm door which during the winter months replaced the wooden front door. She squinted into the sunlight, recognizing the detective duo immediately.

"I thought it might be you. Come in and I'll put on some coffee." She turned and headed toward the kitchen.

Aksel threw Anja a questioning look. "WTF?" he mouthed.

Anja shrugged her shoulders and whispered back, "Don't know."

Heather spooned coffee into the coffee maker and poured in the water from the sink's tap. On tiptoes, she reached into a tall cabinet and brought out a grocery bakery box filled with assorted cookies. She set them on the table and while placing some paper napkins beside them, she said. "I had Jeff put them up high so I'd stay out of them."

She smiled and chuckled. "I proved I could get them anyway."

Reaching again, but not as high, Heather opened the cabinet above the coffee maker and brought out three coffee mugs. She seemed to concentrate for a moment, then reached for another cup and set it with the others.

This time Anja shot Aksel a questioning glance as she indicated the fourth cup with a nod of her head. Aksel raised his eyebrows in return.

"Oh, go ahead and sit at the table. I'll pour the coffee. It seems like I'm brain-dead this morning because I got very little sleep last night." Heather looked at the detectives and pursed her lips. She tightened them and then opened them to say, "Jeff and I had a big fight after y'all left and he took off to spend the night with his mom and dad." She produced an unladylike snort. "Hnnh, just look at me."

She pointed to her swollen eyes. "I cried most of the night. I'm so sorry we had such a bad fight. Especially one that would send him over to his parents. How in the world will I ever face them after this?"

Anja made a non-committal sound. It must have satisfied Heather's rhetorical question because she lifted the carafe and poured coffee into three cups and returned the glass container to the coffee maker. She joined the other two at the table.

It was time to tell her, as it appeared Heather had no idea Jeff was dead. Either that, or she was playing a good game of hiding it. Taking the lead, Anja rose from her chair, brushed her hair back with her hand and plunged in. "That's what we want to talk to you about, Heather."

She moved to stand at Heather's side and put her hand on her shoulder. "We need to tell you some bad news. Aksel and I are so, so sorry, but we have to let you know Jeff was shot and killed this morning."

Heather stiffened and wailed, "Oh, my God, no!" Then her body folded in on itself and she collapsed. Aksel leapt up and caught her as she tumbled sideways from her chair.

"Oh, shit! She's fainted!" Anja exclaimed.

"Dammit," Aksel spat. He lifted Heather into his arms and took the several steps to the living room sofa. He laid her down while Anja hurried to the bathroom and wet a washcloth with cold water. Bending over her, Anja briskly rubbed the coldness into Heather's face while Aksel shook her shoulder.

Urgently, he called out, "Heather! Miss Forrest!" He continued to shake her shoulder.

Their actions finally roused Heather. She opened her eyes to see Anja bending over her and wiping her face with a washcloth. Again, she remembered something too horrible to contemplate. "Jeff's dead?"

Anja took her hand in hers and nodded. "Yes, Heather. Aksel and I verified it."

"But how? Where? What happened? I can't believe he's dead. Oh, dear God, it can't be!" Heather shook her head wildly as the words were torn from her.

Aksel related the story as they knew it. Throughout his short recitation of the events of Jeff's death, Heather continued to sob, but appeared to understand the situation as described. She wanted to know two additional things.

"Do Jeff's parents know?"

"Yes."

"Why didn't they call me?"

Aksel explained Mr. and Mrs. Hoffmann had only learned of it a short while ago and were dealing with their own grief.

Looking skeptical, Heather said, "I guess." Then she asked her second question. "It was Principal Addison, wasn't it?"

Anja answered slowly, shaking her head with sympathy, "We truly don't know for sure yet. But we are going to find out, Heather. We're not stopping until we get him behind bars."

Anja encouraged Heather to get a girlfriend or someone close to stay with her for a little while so she could have someone to talk with. At least until she'd wrapped her head around it and had let some of the shock dissipate.

Heather declined, saying she was immediately calling her mom and dad in Florida and they'd certainly be here by tomorrow sometime. She would make it through the night alone. She knew she had to call Jeff's folks, too, and she'd gather up the courage somehow to do that. She felt she would be all right for the one night alone. She had lots to think about as she wanted to offer anything she could to help the investigation.

"What more can you tell us about James Addison?" Anja asked. The captain had to be filled in on what Heather knew. And they needed it to have a viable investigation.

"I don't know any more than what I found in Principal Addison's desk. Except how he looked and acted when he came to see me after I got back from his office."

"And how did he act?" Anja pressed.

Heather got up and went to the kitchen. She opened the refrigerator door, leaned down and looked in the vegetable bin. What she'd intended to do wasn't evident for she closed the door and returned to the seating area. Perhaps it was a delaying tactic.

She took a seat and replied, “Well, nothing overt. Just suspicious. Even so, I’m certain he was behind both Patti’s and Jeff’s murder.” She looked away, blinking her eyes and clearing the tears. “His actions are too suspect not to bring him in for questioning.”

“I assure you we are going to do just that. As soon as we get something substantial with which to hold him, that is. Bringing him in just to play cat and mouse, where he would most likely be the cat, would not be productive.”

“Right,” Aksel said. “We can’t overplay our hand and alert him to what we do know. And, Heather, you’ve got to be careful in everything you do.”

The doorbell played “Joy to the World” and Heather jerked, her eyes flying to the door. Aksel opened it to find the two police officers who had been assigned by Captain Harjula to keep an eye on things, particularly Heather Forrest, lest the maniacal killer should come after her.

“Come in, fellows. Miss Forrest is right here.”

The officers introduced themselves to Heather and reported they’d seen nothing suspicious at all in their first rounds of the buildings and parking lots of the apartment complex.

“We’ll take turns being outside, so one of us will spend time in the cruiser, both to warm up and to be a deterrent to prospective crime as an active police presence,” the young blonde Officer Morganstern said.

Officer Johansson added, “We’ll have a shift change, but another couple of officers will replace us. You’ll be well protected, ma’am.”

“Yes ma’am, Miss Forrest. We’ll be on the lookout for anything at all,” Morganstern vowed.

“Heather, you be aware of everything. Pay attention to every sound, every little creak or shuffle or anything that sounds different from what you usually hear. Keep the TV and radio low. Better yet, keep 'em off," Aksel warned again.

"There would be no talking to him, because he's totally unreasonable," Aksel continued, as he lifted aside the front window curtains and checked the window locks. "I don't think he can get past these officers to get to you, but so far he's gotten away from two murders without being seen. So you must be watchful and aware at all times."

"We think you're going to be okay." Anja added. "But we want all of us to take every precaution to make it so." She gave Heather a little shake of the shoulder and said, "Go make that phone call to your folks. I hope they can get here soon. Maybe even sometime tonight, if we're lucky."

Heather had lots of acquaintances, women to whom she was friendly and who returned that friendliness, teachers from her school, a few neighbors, regulars at her gym, but none were close friends. She supposed Lela Magnusson came the closest to a real girlfriend, but she'd never needed one until now. Jeff had been all she needed or wanted. How ironic that it was he that she needed now.

Meanwhile, James Addison was in a fantastic mood. He'd gotten rid of that nuisance, Jeff Hoffmann, and now was planning a return engagement with Hoffmann's nosy little bitch girlfriend. It was such fun to terrorize her. Hurting her boyfriend Jeff was great. That really hurt her. Killing him was even better. That certainly did more than hurt her. He hoped it devastated her. Oh, more than that, he hoped it incapacitated her. He wanted her to badly, horribly hurt. To hurt so badly until she could hardly bear to live. Then he'd see that she didn't. Killing her would be deliriously exciting fun. Just the thought started him giggling.

But first, a call to Joe Nygaard, directing him to gather up the other two morons, and as the line from the movie *Pulp Fiction* goes, "Get Medieval on her ass." He hadn't yet even heard about last night's visit paid to her at the school. He was eager to find out just what they did to her so he could vicariously share in it. He tapped Joe's number on his cell phone.

"Dammit, Joe! You worthless piece of shit. Where are you?" Exasperated, Addison raged aloud and threw his cell phone aside and didn't give a damn that it slid from the sofa to the floor. He was pissed that he'd called Joe several times and Joe had repeatedly ignored his calls.

Fuming, he yelled into the silence of his library, "If you don't hurry up and answer, I'll have to start planning an outing to visit Miss Heather Forrest myself."

At the other end of his connection, Joe Nygaard's cell phone buzzed and danced across the surface of the small bedside table in Joe's bedroom.

It was a lonely dance. No one was there to see or hear it.

Neither of the detectives had eaten a substantial breakfast that morning and both were hungry. Aksel said, "I'm starving. We haven't even had time for a cup of coffee. How about us picking up a couple of subs from Jimmie John's?"

"Sounds delicious. Of course I'd eat a leather shoe sole right now. But, whatever it is, it can't possibly be as good as our steak last night. Now, that was good!"

Aksel grinned at her and headed for the sandwich shop on Main Street.

They ate their Italian subs as Aksel drove back to the station. Between mouthfuls, they talked about the

Hoffmann murder and the homicidal suspect. Would he attempt to get to Heather? If so, perhaps they could catch him in the act before he could harm her. They hoped to be able to pick him up and get him to the station for questioning before he had the chance to try to find Heather.

"That reminds me, we didn't caution her to stay inside. She'll want to go to the airport to pick up her parents." Anja pulled out her phone and dialed Heather's number.

"No answer." Anja slowly shook her head from side to side. "Why isn't she answering her phone?"

"It could be as simple as her being in the shower."

"Yeah, it might be that." Anja left a message telling her to have her parents take a taxi from the airport and for her to not go out of the apartment until she heard from them saying it was okay. She then called the captain and briefed him on the meeting with Heather Forrest. Yes, they were on their way back to the station right now.

The killer still sat stewing at home in his library, getting angrier and more vengeful.

"Well, hell," he said, as he kicked the hassock that matched his oxblood leather chair, sending it tumbling across the carpet until it rolled to a stop. Addison jammed his cell phone back into the holder he wore on his belt. As if addressing it, he said aloud, "He's never going to answer his damned phone."

Spinning on his heel, he headed to the library's door, slamming his right fist into it, knocking it open. He glanced at his knuckles and threw his smarting hand into the air.

"Joe, you useless slug, I guess I'm going to have to do this myself." He continued to speak aloud as if he had an audience. "All right, I need to find out what's going on at the fair Lady Forrest's house."

He thought for a few seconds. “That’ll work. I’ll say “wrong number” and hang up if she answers. Then, at least I’ll know where she is.”

From his phone contacts he retrieved Heather Forrest’s home number and dialed it. There was no answer.

“Dammit, where are you, Miss Snoop?” That made him think of the tall, thin, black rapper, one of whose names was Snoop Dog. He giggled crazily while imagining Heather Forrest married to the rapper and going by the name of Mrs. Snoop Dog.

He dialed again. It rang four times and Heather was on the line.

“Hello?” She sounded stuffy as if she’d been crying.

As planned, he said, “Wrong number,” and pushed the disconnect button. Now, it was time to develop the rest of his plan and put it in motion.

Ann and Jack Forrest were hurrying to board a plane in Gainesville, Florida at that very moment. Upon hearing the news of Jeff’s murder from their distraught daughter, Ann screamed for Jack, telling him the sorrowful story between sobs.

They each threw some clothes into suitcases and included their black dress clothes suitable for Jeff’s funeral. Jack loaded them in the car and they set out for the airport.

Using the Google search engine on her phone, Ann looked for flights that would take them to Green Bay. They were prepared to remain at the airport until there was a flight that would get them there, no matter how circuitous the route.

Delta had one flight leaving at 4:50 P.M. getting to Green Bay at 8:12 that evening. Ann called Delta and booked two tickets. Although a small plane, the first leg to Atlanta had plenty of seats available, but the leg from Atlanta to Green Bay was almost full. No two seats were together, so both were assigned middle seats six rows apart.

Once at the airport, they parked in the long-term lot, which at the small airport meant a very short shuttle ride to check in. They pounded down the corridor to their gate, and completely out of breath, found everyone had just boarded. Ann was sure her heart had stopped beating. *Oh, God. What do we do now?*

Jack hammered on the counter with his knuckles and jumped as if spooked when the phone began to ring. The counter agent was right outside the door and came in to answer it. On a day when the Forrest family needed a break, this was it. The call was from the ticket agent asking that they hold the plane so the Forrests could board.

Settling into the close confines of her seat, Ann remembered Heather saying to take a taxi from the airport because she'd been told to stay inside the safety of her apartment behind locked doors. *This sounds really bad. It has to be dangerous. What are we blindly walking in to?*

Chapter Twenty-Three

Agitated and bereft all day since learning of his son's murder, John Hoffmann had more to deal with than a lot of normal men could handle. Eva was inconsolable, and he'd tried to be supportive of her and her grief over the death of their son. Because of the enormous amount of attention and coddling that she required, he'd had no time to deal with his own grief.

Sorrow and pain weighed on him heavily because he'd lost both a son and a best friend. While Eva adored her son and loved him almost inordinately, it was his father to whom Jeff told of his deepest thoughts, secrets, and desires. Thus, John knew how Jeff felt about Heather Forrest. He knew Jeff had planned to marry her and raise their family right here in Green Bay, at least for the first few years of their marriage.

Heather was an only child, as Jeff was, so her parents would need to have her family close to them at some point. Jeff had spent hours discussing with John the logistics of how to make everything work out with him and Heather and both families so that everyone would be happy. This very thing, plus their getting involved in a murder investigation with harm done to both of them, made Jeff wait. He had to be careful in choosing the appropriate time to officially ask Heather to marry him and to present her with an engagement ring.

Then, too, there was the matter of Eva's indifference, bordering on dislike, of Heather. No woman would ever be good enough for Jeff, particularly a southern girl with that outlandish accent and parents who lived so far away until they'd never be friends. According to Eva, in-laws should take turns every Sunday having huge dinners where all the combined family came together. Jeff needed a nice, local girl, German like they were. But that was all in the past now.

Or was it? John had been unable to get Eva to agree to call Heather to talk about Jeff's death and to offer what comfort they could. He imagined Heather was hurting as badly as they were.

Heather pulled up the covers on her bed, deciding it was so late in the day until there was no need to make it up. The sheets needed changing since she changed them every Saturday and they'd been on the bed for a week. Even if her mom slept with her and her dad slept on the sofa downstairs, she couldn't bring herself to put fresh sheets on because she couldn't stand the thought of washing away Jeff's smell. She went to his side of the bed and plucked his pillow from beneath the duvet. Holding it to her nose, she breathed in its own special scent. Yes, there were the notes of his after shave and cologne, the aromas she associated most with Jeff. It felt like a small part of him could still be with her as long as she could smell him. She replaced the pillow under the duvet and tucked the cover around it. With determination, she walked away from the bed, wondering how long the smell of him would last.

Downstairs, she went to the fridge and stood staring into its bright depths in hopes this time something would appeal to her. Again, she closed the door without discovering anything remotely appetizing.

Opening the door to the linen closet, she searched the shelves for the queen-sized sheets for the pull-out sofa. There they were, hiding behind an electric blanket. She took out the sheets, the electric blanket, and a duvet she found rather more wadded than folded on the bottom shelf. These would go on the sofa when she found the energy to make it up. Next, she found two towels and matching washcloths for her mom and dad to use.

Heather went to the front window on the right side of the door, pulled the heavy drapes aside, which she'd yet to open that day, and peered out into the gloom. The parking lot was lit by a yellow pole lamp, lovely to look at but providing very little light. She looked for the policeman assigned to patrol the area in front of her apartment. She didn't see him. Or his partner. Then she saw movement in the police cruiser parked in Jeff's spot. It looked like a hand was raised in a wave. She waved back and let the curtain fall back in place. She turned around and looked at her small living room. *What can I do now? I'm going out of my mind just waiting around for something to happen. Maybe I'll clean the bathroom. That's easier than making up the bed.*

Instead, she turned back to the console table placed in front of the other front window located on the other side of the door. It was a twin to the first.

She picked up the 8 by 10 picture of Jeff and her in its silver frame. The picture was taken by a freelance photographer in a park this past year at the beginning of the summer break. They were enjoying the warmth of the sun and had clasped hands facing each other, laughing at the antics of a child swinging high on the swing set. Both were still laughing when the photographer said, “Hey, look!” They turned their faces to him and he snapped the picture. He showed them the digital picture in which he captured their obvious happiness. Sold! He promised to have the photo to them within three days. And so he did. They shopped for the perfect frame, silver with little X’s and O’s dotting the edges.

Heather kissed Jeff’s face in the photo, hugged the picture to her heart, and set it down after looking longingly at something that would never again be. *Will I ever be that happy again?*

And then it hit her. She knew what she would do. She’d call Jeff’s folks. *I should have already done it. Of course, they could have called me, and should have, especially considering the potential for danger I’m in.*

“Oh, I hope Mr. Hoffmann answers,” she murmured as she dialed the number.

She counted five rings before John Hoffmann picked up.

“I’m sorry, but I told you press people earlier that I have nothing to contribute to your news story. I’m afraid you know more than I do.”

“Mr. Hoffmann,” Heather tried breaking in on his speech. He didn’t hear her as he continued his angry, but controlled, rant.

“You’ve been down there watching the forensic squad do their thing and you’ve asked a million questions of everybody who went to the garage at any time today. Surely you have enough to make a good story for tomorrow’s paper. Now, I’m asking you to leave us alone, please.”

Heather listened to John Hoffmann and heard the weariness and pain in his voice. Afraid he’d hang up at any second, as soon as he said “please” she jumped in.

“Mr. Hoffmann, it’s me, Heather!”

“Ohhh, it’s you, Heather...”

The tell-tale relief in his voice as it trailed off washed over her. *He's glad to hear from me. Oh, thank you, Lord.*

"Yes sir, I wanted to call and find out how you and Mrs. Hoffmann are doing. I know it must be terribly hard being right there where . . ." Her voice faltered. She tried again. ". . . where it all happened."

"Oh, Heather, I'm so glad you called. I've been thinking about you and that *I* needed to call and check on *you*." He stopped and cleared his throat, giving Heather time to ask about them.

"And how is Mrs. Hoffmann? I'm sure this devastated both of you—like it did me."

"Eva's really not handling it well at all. She's cried all day and there seems to be nothing I can do to help."

"I imagine you are hurting just as bad. I know how close you and Jeff are. Were. I mean were. Oh Lord, I still can't believe he's gone." Heather dissolved into hiccupping sobs and stammered, "I'm so s- sorry. I d-didn't mean to do that."

"It's okay, Heather. You're right. We're all hurting and it's good to talk with you because you understand that." He paused and seemed to struggle with what he wanted to say next. Eventually he said, "Heather, when Jeff came last night he wouldn't talk about why. He just said he couldn't talk about it right then, but he was really upset. He didn't even want to see his mother. I just have to know what happened." He stopped for another deep pause. "If you will tell me."

The tears flooded back and Heather said through sobs that shook her whole body, "No one can p-possibly know how very sorry I am that we had a fight. It was my f-fault because I was stubborn and went by myself early last night to find out w-what I thought was information about the Patti Mueller case." She paused and emitted a shuddering breath. Continuing, she said, "Instead, I got beaten up pretty bad by the same teens who almost broke Jeff's leg." She wiped her streaming eyes and blew her nose. "And I will always b-blame myself for Jeff leaving and going to your house. But what I've realized is that m-madman would have found a way to kill him here last night, if he had been here. He's d-determined to kill us both." She cleared her throat, making a most unladylike sound, reminding her of when Jeff, she, and the detectives had laughed at her less than feminine nose-blowing honk.

Absolute horror registered in John Hoffmann's voice as he asked, "Are you by yourself now?"

Sniffing hard and clearing her throat again, Heather took a deep breath, letting it out slowly. Doing these actions allowed her to get her crying under control. "I'm by myself right now, but my mom and dad are on their way. They're already in the air and should be here by a little after nine. And there are two policemen outside guarding the apartment."

"That's good. You don't need to be alone." He was quiet for a few moments as he thought.

"Heather, I had no idea all this was happening. I'm so sorry. I know you're scared."

"Yes sir, I certainly am. But I think I'll be okay. The police are on to . . ." Her words broke and she noisily cleared her throat, taking a moment to regain her voice. "They're on to Jeff's killer by now, I'm sure."

"Well then, on a slightly different topic: We could certainly use your help tomorrow in making plans for a funeral service. You have as much say in this as Eva and I, and I hope you will go with us to make all the arrangements."

Heather withdrew a Kleenex from her jeans pocket and wiped her eyes and then blew her nose. "Thank you, Mr. Hoffmann. I'd very much like to be with y'all to do that. I hope Mrs. Hoffmann will let me."

"The truth is she is very angry with you right now, but I think when I tell her what's happening, she'll relent. Anyway, we'll talk tomorrow and make plans. Eva's calling me, so I have to go. Goodnight sweetheart."

Heather almost came undone over John Hoffmann innocently calling her sweetheart, which was Jeff's favorite name for her. Tears instantly welled up again as she laid down the phone and then collapsed on the sofa. She wrapped her arms around herself and cried heart-brokenly for the loss of the man she'd truly loved.

Chapter Twenty-Four

In the small interrogation room in which Rocky was held, Anja acted the ingénue police officer and Rocky bought it. Belligerent at first, he denied any involvement. "Joe Nygaard's full of crap. There ain't no way I'd get mixed up in something like this."

"But I would've thought you'd be just the guy he would want to help him. You'd be good at watching his back and keeping him safe."

"Nah, he can look out for his self. I ain't his keeper."

"Oh, Rocky, you're so big and strong. Aren't you Joe's friend? I'm sure you couldn't deny him help if he needed you." She knit her brow and gazed at him so earnestly until Rocky had to take the credit she must believe was his due.

"Yeah, well, he *did* need me. He asked me to help him out with that Addison guy. I didn't want to do it, but what'cha gonna do? You know?"

"So, you did go with him when Mr. Hoffmann and then Miss Forrest were attacked? You were a part of it?"

"Sure. He needed me to protect him if anything happened."

"Did you participate? I imagine you walloped them both pretty well."

Rocky grinned, "I sure did."

Soon he not only corroborated Joe's story down to dotting I's and crossing T's, but he swelled with the attention she gave him and began to tell her how he would handle the investigation.

The gist of his story was Principal Addison led them on with the promise of big money if they would beat up a couple of people for him. But he only gave them $250 for Mr. Hoffmann and he hadn't even paid them for last night's work with Miss Forrest. The cheapskate jerk needed to be put in jail for that, even if he didn't kill Patti Mueller and Mr. Hoffmann.

"But I'm sure he did. He's just that kind of man," Rocky declared. "Why else would he want us to shut them up? He didn't want to get hurt, or have somebody bash in his girly face, or he'd probably have done it himself."

Aksel's session with Bobby went about the same, except Bobby in no way tried to impress the detective with his skills in solving crimes. Aksel asked him lots of questions and after sulking and denial didn't stop the big cop's repeated accusations, Bobby broke and admitted to being a part of it. He spoke in monosyllabic answers. Once expanded by Aksel's insistent probing, his answers were replicas of Joe Nygaard's. The three teens told the same story about James Addison: he was one crazy, scary dude, and he'd hired them so he couldn't be caught and held responsible. Nobody was supposed to find out he was behind the beatings.

"There ain't no telling what Principal Addison will do to me, Rocky, and Joe if he ever gets to us again. I didn't want to be a part of it after I heard what he wanted us to do. But, two hundred and fifty dollars – twice! That would've been five hundred dollars to spend how I wanted. I guess we won't ever get the other two hundred and fifty. I tell you, that man is crazy!"

"Well, Bobby, I don't think you need worry about that. He'll be going to jail for the rest of his life."

"No parole?"

"Nope. No parole for killers like him."

All three teens implicated themselves in the crime of assault and battery. Along with Joe, Rocky and Bobby were placed under arrest and taken to a cell. They were each allowed one phone call and, of course, each called a parent with the expectation of being bailed out. Rocky's and Bobby's fathers came for them later in the evening when all the paperwork had been completed.

It was not so with Joe. His belligerent father had already said, "Hell no. I ain't gonna spend one red cent to get you out of jail. You can stay there until you learn to behave."

Joe likely figured he was better off where he was.

The killer made his plans, and all was ready. His attire was all black, which included a black ski mask that he would don at the appropriate time. Now, he had to wait until the Forrest bitch went to bed. Maybe he could use the time to create an alibi should he need one.

He quickly put on a dark charcoal gray sports coat that went well with the black twill trousers he would continue to wear for later. Over this he donned his black London Fog trench coat. Black leather gloves and black boots completed the picture of a successful young businessman out to enjoy dinner at one of Green Bay's finer restaurants. His heavy black winter jacket would remain in the rear of his SUV with the ski mask and other important items necessary for the fun and games that would occur later that evening.

Making a reservation was key. That way he'd have a computer and phone trail plus a paper trail showing he was there. He used Google's search engine to find the reservations number for Chefusion, a fine dining restaurant located downtown on Broadway. He reserved a table for one in the main dining room for 8:00 P.M. The staff should remember such a handsome man as he dining alone. Even more so if he created some memorable incidents. He looked at himself in the mirror over his desk. *Am I brilliant, or what?*

Addison began making plans for just how obnoxious he could be, the ruckus he could cause, the attention he could draw to himself. He smiled as he considered the fun things he could do. He'd have to drink a couple of glasses of wine so they'd think he became intoxicated. They'd think, too, that a man in his condition certainly could not carry out a well-planned murder, for what he had planned for Miss Heather Forrest would require clear sobriety. And soon, as it always was with him, his self-assurance led him into maniacal giggling as he pictured embarrassing everyone around him.

I'll make damned sure they don't forget me being there.

Works of art. That's what the menu items looked like at Chefusion. He thought the chef must be proud of offering a menu unlike any other in Green Bay. His entrees were particularly creative.

James Addison ordered for an appetizer the Prince Edward Island mussels in their fragrant tomato and wine broth. He made loud and effusive praise about them. He stood from his chair and bowed to the server when his entrée appeared. He had the crab stuffed oven-roasted trout. The smell was heavenly, the taste sumptuous, and the accompanying saffron rice was perfection itself. This he jovially told to an adjacent couple who ever since being seated had avoided the boisterous man by turning away from him and complaining to the waiter about the noise. That didn't deter him from his loud comments.

A young waiter dressed in neat serving attire, puffed up with importance that he was a part of the fine dining experience of the establishment, approached the noisy diner with purpose.

"Sir, I must ask you to lower your voice. Our other diners would like to enjoy their meals in a quiet and calm atmosphere."

"Is that so?" Addison boomed. "What are you going to do about it, little boy? When you have as much money as I do, then you can order me around. Until then, get out of my freaking face!" The waiter turned on his heel, face flaming, and went to report to his senior captain.

Fortunately, for the other diners, Addison ate in silence for a while, chewing his food thoughtfully as he drew pictures in his head of what he would like to do to Heather Forrest. Dessert was to come with his prix fixe meal so when he finished his entrée he loudly called, "Waiter? My dessert, please!"

The server captain came to take his order, discreetly whispering descriptions of the selections as Addison asked him a question or two about every dessert offering. He also loudly asked him to speak up so he could hear him. He ordered the lemon butter cake. As the number one waiter made his way to the kitchen, Addison stood and noisily called him back.

"You! Yes, you. Come on back here," he said as the waiter turned, astonishment dropping his jaw. Addison continued, "No, I don't want that lemon cake. I've changed my mind. Tell me the dessert specials again." He finally chose the bread pudding, the chef's own recipe. Figuring he had created enough memories for every diner there, he ate his dessert quietly, paid with a credit card, and left the restaurant with the loud promise to return soon so they could all dine together again. Delighted, he wondered how many customers his performance tonight had cost the restaurant.

He climbed into his SUV and let his giggles burst out. He'd hardly been able to contain them in the restaurant. Imagine that little shit trying to tell him to be quiet! He checked his watch and his excitement and his giggles grew. It was almost time to pay Heather Forrest a visit.

Captain Harjula called his detectives into his office for a briefing on the day's extraordinary events. After apprising him of where they were with the three teens, they told him the last thing they would do tonight was to go by Heather Forrest's place and check on her. They would also get reports from the two policemen who were guarding her.

"Good job, detectives. I feel like we may wrap up this case soon. It looks like leads are pointing to James Addison as our man."

"Yes sir. It looks that way. We need to catch him doing something so we can arrest him. He'll play his hand soon, I'm sure," Aksel stated.

"Well, check it out. You two need to get some dinner and then go over there so you can see what he's doing tonight. If he's doing nothing except sitting at home, bring him in for questioning."

"Thank you, sir. We plan to do just that." Anja, by now slap-happy, couldn't help but add in an over-the-top southern accent, "After all, tomorrow's a brand new day, Miss Scarlett."

The familiar line spoken by Scarlett O'Hara in *Gone With the Wind* brought a nostalgic smile to the captain's stern countenance. "Okay. Tomorrow. Maybe it'll all come together then. But now, have something to eat, and then see if you can find Addison. Go on, get out of here."

Leaving the station after a busy day that was both physically and emotionally exhausting, the detectives stopped at a local Italian restaurant and, ravenous, they each ordered enormous meals with extra garlic bread.

They ate quickly, and fortified with renewed energy, left to see what was happening with Heather Forrest. They couldn't rule out James Addison trying to get to her. Once they had the three teen's confessions, he needed to be picked up for questioning. However, they hoped to catch him trying to do harm to Heather. If they were lucky, they'd get to him in time to prevent that actually happening.

They went to his house, rang the bell and rapped loudly on the door, but still there was no answer after several minutes of repeated rings and knocks.

"Man, this is one fancy place," Anja said, taking a break from the ringing and knocking to glance around the opulent home's front.

"Right. It matches the fancy things we saw in his office. I still wonder where he got the money for all this," Aksel said, shaking his head in wonder.

Back in the SUV, they waited for Addison to show up for most of an hour. Time that was precious to them. Time they could be investigating Jeff Hoffmann's death with Maggie Greene at the morgue.

Anja called Captain Harjula and asked for two uniforms to come there to watch the house for Addison's return. "Aksel and I think we could be more useful somewhere else, doing something besides sitting. It's after nine already."

The captain agreed. The plan was for them to immediately return should the policemen report an Addison sighting.

Aksel put the car in gear, and as he executed a u-turn, the tires crunched through the snow piled along the side of the cleared road. Even so, Anja heard his worried "God, I hope he comes home soon."

"And that he hasn't messed with Heather. You know, Aksel, I understand that we officers of the law are not to get attached to the victims we work with, but I've got a special feeling for our Heather." Anja's concerned frown said even more than her words.

"I know what you mean. I feel it, too. And I felt it for Jeff." He smacked his thigh and then shot his hand out in front of Anja's face, palm up.

"I'm asking you, was it right? They innocently stumbled into this and now they're paying for it. Jeff paid with his life. And if that crazy son-of-a-bitch gets the chance, Heather will, too."

"I know. So, we've got to stop him, Aksel."

Chapter Twenty-Five

The Forrest's plane arrived five minutes early. They found their luggage made it on the plane in Gainesville and arrived for them on the luggage carousel. However, their good luck seemed to end at the taxi stand. The line was longer than one would think for an early evening arrival.

"This line is moving slower than molasses," Ann remarked as she threw down her soft carry-on bag. It landed beside her large suitcase. "Will they ever get to us?"

When it was finally their turn and the next taxi stopped in front of them, Ann let out a huge breath of relief, threw her hands in the air, and said to the unlucky driver, "It's about time. I have very little patience left."

Jack slung their bags in the trunk, not waiting for the driver to do so.

"Please hurry," he said, as he gave him the address. The driver's teeth gleamed through a dark beard and mustache as he grinned at him.

"No problem, man. I get you there very quick."

They were on the way to Heather's apartment by 9:45 p.m.—not the 9:30 they'd hoped for. But they *were* on the way as the driver peeled out of the line and sped off.

Jack said he hoped he wouldn't get a ticket because they'd asked him to hurry.

"Me too," Ann agreed as she took her cell phone from her purse and called Heather to say they would be there soon.

"Oh, Mom, I'm so glad you and Dad are here. I'll be waiting for you. Knock on the door and I'll let you in. I love you. Please hurry."

"She really does sound better than she did earlier, Jack. I think us being with her will help a lot. She has to be beside herself with worry."

"I'm glad she sounds better, honey. I know I'll be glad to see for myself that she's okay."

As Aksel parked the SUV in the apartment lot, he noticed the police car was parked in Jeff's spot. The moment they appeared at Heather's door, the uniformed policeman on patrol asked them their business there. The detectives identified themselves and Aksel told him to tell his partner the two of them could take a break. "Go get a cup of coffee or grab a burger because we'll be here for thirty minutes or so."

Anja rang the doorbell and Heather looked through the peephole to verify it was them. No matter that their faces were distorted, she could still tell it was the detectives by looking at each one in turn. She unlocked the door and let them enter.

"Good girl," Anja murmured.

"How are you, Heather?" Aksel laid his hand companionably on Heather's shoulder.

"Well, some better since I talked to Mr. Hoffmann." She turned her reddened eyes to them. "At least *he* isn't mad at me. I guess Mrs. Hoffmann will hate me forever."

"Give her time. She should come around." Anya looked around at the bed linens lying on the sofa waiting to be put on. There was no smell of welcoming coffee. And Heather looked like hell.

"Meanwhile, Aksel and I are going to help you get things ready for your folks." She looked at her partner and nodded her head toward the sofa. "Perhaps Aksel can make out the sofa bed and I'll start some coffee. I think all of us could use a cup, and I imagine your parents would appreciate something hot after encountering this cold weather."

She put both hands on Heather's shoulders. "I also think you'd feel better if you washed your face and combed your hair." She turned her in the direction of the bathroom and gave her a little nudge.

"You're right, Anja. I do need to clean up a bit. And thanks to both of you for your help. Coffee sounds great. Now why didn't I think of that?" She shook her head and walked to the bathroom door but stopped with her hand on the knob. "Truthfully, all I can think of is Jeff. And how afraid I am." She swept her hand down her body. "Look at me. I'm a mess. This is consuming me and I'm not thinking about anything else." She went in the bathroom and closed the door.

"You know, on second thought, I think we should leave the sofa as it is for now." Anja picked up the sheets and towels and laid them on the back of the sofa. "Her parents will need somewhere to sit until time for bed. I imagine they'll want to talk with Heather for at least a while before turning in."

"Right." Aksel looked at his watch. "They should be here any time now. Let's get that coffee going. And I'll look for some cookies or something to go with it. It's doubtful Heather has eaten anything all day."

"Yes, and I'd better see if there's any decaf. Everybody needs to sleep tonight." Anja began looking in the cabinets to find the coffee. She paused, faced her partner, and quietly called, "Aksel?"

"What?"

"You're sure it's okay, professionally I mean, for us to do this for Heather?"

"I guess. But, isn't it just doing our job?"

"You know it's not. I think these two, Heather *and* Jeff, got under our skin. We got close to them. We cared about them."

"And now we're going the extra mile. Is that what you're saying?"

"Yeah. Is that being professional, or are we playing favorites?"

"Whatever. Call it what you will. But we're going to protect this girl and get that S.O.B. and I don't care if it looks like favoritism. Hell, we *like* her. We don't want her to be killed like Jeff." His eyes blazed. "And that's what matters."

James Addison pulled into the apartment complex parking lot located around to the side of Heather's building. From there he could see the front of her apartment and anyone coming or going. He'd been there not more than five minutes when a taxi stopped directly at her door. An older couple got out and the driver opened the trunk and pulled forth two large suitcases. He carried them to Heather's door. Money was exchanged and he got back in the car and drove away.

Addison sat there with his mouth open as he watched this happen. *What the devil is this? Who the hell are these people? It must be that bitch's parents.* He closed his mouth, his thoughts whirling. *Doesn't make any difference; I'll kill the whole damned bunch. I just have to figure this out and bide my time. But I will do it. And I'm going to do it tonight.*

Reaching a decision on what to do, Addison slid between the two front seats and slithered over the back seat to crouch in the space in the back of the SUV. It was empty except for the black clothing he'd brought so that he might blend with the night. He removed the dress clothes he'd worn to Chefusion, except for the black trousers, and began to garb himself anew.

Three very different elements converged on Heather Forrest's apartment at approximately the same time. The first was the appearance of the detectives, who were admitted inside. The second was James Addison, who initially stayed in his car and changed into his dark clothes. The third was the arrival by taxi of Heather's parents who also were let in the apartment. The detectives knew about Ann and Jack Forrest's arrival. James Addison knew about the Forrests, but he didn't know about the detectives. The Forrests knew about the detectives. But no one knew about James Addison. He was the wild card.

Jack Forrest rang the doorbell and Aksel looked through the peephole. Seeing a man and woman outside the door, and taking no chances, he motioned for Heather to come peek and see if it was her parents.

Heather looked through it and reacted without thinking. Immediately she began to unlock the door, her hands shaking as she flipped the deadbolt.

"No, Heather!" Aksel grabbed and held her hands. "You must verify they are alone out there. Never just assume."

He looked through the peephole again, and as far into the surrounding area as he could. He saw no one.

To be safe he had Heather ask her parents through the door if they saw anyone at all in the parking lot. They replied no, so Aksel opened the door and Jack wrestled their bags inside.

Heather restrained herself until her mom and dad were inside and Aksel had relocked the door. Then she was hugging both parents and she and her mom were crying, with arms around each other.

Jack turned to the big guy who opened the door. Aksel offered his hand and said, "Detective Aksel Franzen. I'm part of the team trying to apprehend the person responsible for the murders."

He indicated Anja with an outstretched hand as she walked the few steps from the kitchen where the coffee had finished brewing. "This is my partner, Detective Anja Frandsen."

Anja smiled and shook Jack's hand. "Pleased to meet you, sir."

Jack looked from one to the other and asked Anja, "Are you his sister or his wife?"

"Neither. We just have similar last names. Can I help you with anything, sir? Perhaps you and Mrs. Forrest would like a cup of hot coffee. It's just finished brewing."

"That'd be great."

Aksel went to the kitchen and took from the cabinet five flowered coffee mugs. Yellow and red roses with lots of green stems and leaves. A bit of color on a dark night. He'd earlier unearthed a package of oatmeal raisin cookies and took them out of the package to sit in the plastic container in the middle of the table. He added to the cookies some teaspoons, paper napkins, the sugar dish and a quart of milk.

Anja was attempting to get everyone to the kitchen table so she and Aksel could tell them what had transpired that day. "Have you eaten anything, Heather?"

"I don't think so."

She turned to Ann and then to Jack. "Did you get any dinner tonight?"

"No," Ann said, and Jack shook his head.

Anja put an arm around Heather's shoulder and squeezed. Heather's eyes held the first gleam of light she'd seen yet today.

"Come with me, Heather, and let's find something in the cabinet to heat up. I bet you've got chicken noodle or tomato soup. You three need to have some warm food in you so you can go to bed and sleep well."

"Will I ever sleep again?" Heather wondered aloud.

Anja had no answer, only a shrug, a pat to Heather's shoulder, and eyes filled with sympathy.

The detectives needed to warn the Forrests about the danger they were in but had to be certain that they didn't panic and do something to endanger them further. For the three to sit around the table and talk about the day while eating something nourishing was a positive sign that her parents were indeed a help to Heather. But there was still doubt that the killer would refrain from making a move because there were two others in the house.

While Heather was explaining to her parents about Jeff being shot by a complete madman, she divulged all the information she had found out from the detectives. Her tears welled up, but she didn't have the gut-wrenching sobs of earlier. She did not, however, talk about the fight that made Jeff mad enough to leave her last night and go sleep at his parents' house.

Aksel caught Anja's eye and jerked his chin toward the sofa. "Anja, why don't you and I make up the bed while Heather talks to her mom and dad?"

As Anja helped him arrange the pull-out, she whispered, "What's up?"

"I don't feel good about this. I think we better stay right here tonight. I don't think Addison knows we're here, or the guys watching the place would've known he was around when we came. So, I think he may still try something, thinking she's either alone, or if he saw the Forrests come in, that it's just her and two elderly people. That bastard, with his ego, would think he could handle three inferior people with no problem."

"I think you're right. We'd better stay."

Anja and Aksel had the bed made up in just a few minutes. They approached the table where the soup bowls were empty and the coffee cups full. The cookies were disappearing quickly. Aksel reached in and snagged one. But before he ate it, they needed to share their plans.

Aksel took the lead and briefly explained about Patti Mueller's death, Jeff's attack, Heather's attack of last evening, and why James Addison was their number one suspect. Anja related they would be staying the night with them in case Addison should think himself invincible enough to try something. If he did, she and Aksel would get him before he could do any harm.

They related their plan. Ann would sleep upstairs with Heather. Jack would take the sofa bed. Anja and Aksel would take turns remaining awake, sitting upright in a kitchen chair so as not to be too comfortable. The partner would curl up in one of the big chairs. Maybe even push the two chair seats together, essentially making a perfectly acceptable lounging bed. It was now after eleven o'clock, so everyone needed to go to bed and rest whether they slept or not. Aksel would take the first watch.

In Heather's bedroom, Ann and Heather shed their clothes and donned nightgowns. Her luggage still downstairs, Ann wore one of Heather's, having kept her figure these forty-nine years. She drew back the covers and started to get in on the side that looked to be Jeff's. A Swiss Army knife, some coins and a book about basketball were on the nightstand.

Heather put her hand on her mom's arm. "Take my side, Mom. I want to sleep on this one. I can at least smell Jeff's scent until I have to wash the sheets." Her voice broke and she slumped into her mother's arms.

"Come on, darling. Let's get in bed and we'll talk."

They threw back the covers and slid in, automatically meeting in the middle with Heather's head on her mom's shoulder.

"Now, tell me about what happened last night. I know it's tough to talk about, but it will do you good. Okay?" Ann turned her head and dropped a kiss atop Heather's thick curls.

Amid hitching sobs, Heather related the events of the previous evening that put Jeff at his parent's apartment. "I'll always regret not sharing everything with him. And to my dying day, I'll remember that the last time I saw him he was storming out the door mad as he could be at me," she ended.

"Shhh," Ann said, hugging Heather close to her. "Think of the good times with Jeff. Eventually the bad times will fade and the happy times will be all you remember."

Heather snuggled into her mother. The comfort she found there and knowing the detectives were downstairs keeping them safe enabled her to fall asleep. Ann quickly followed.

Chapter Twenty-Six

From his hiding spot, stretched out on the floor in the back of his SUV, Addison was sure he was safe from being seen by those two idiots that were undoubtedly supposed to be guarding the silly twit. He had already parked and changed clothes when he saw the cruiser pull in and park. One clown got out and began to walk around. The other one stayed in the car.

Dammit, now I have to do something about them. I should've thought about this. He slapped himself hard on the side of his head. The next second he was smiling. *I can't think of everything, now can I? It'd take someone far smarter than I to cover every little possibility.* He giggled aloud. *And where would we find someone like that?*

He mulled over the problem created by the patrolmen and soon had his answer.

Addison saw the lights go out on the first floor, and then a few minutes later, the second floor of Heather's apartment went dark. He'd give her time to get to sleep and then it was "Goodbye, you snooping bitch." He giggled crazily at the pun he'd made earlier when he thought of her as Mrs. Snoop Dog, and now she was a snooping bitch. *Hah! It's incredible how smart I am.*

He raised his head and watched the policeman on patrol. When he went behind the building on the other side, Addison opened the backseat door of his SUV and slid without noise to the pavement. Circling behind the parked cars in his black clothing, he was almost invisible. He came up to the driver's side of the police cruiser from the back. A double rap on the window got the policeman's attention and he rolled it down a few inches. Addison affected broken English and pointed to himself, to the cruiser, and then back behind him, indicating car trouble.

The young policeman opened the door and placed one foot on the pavement. While he rose, Addison stabbed him in the chest with a sharp filleting knife. The officer slumped forward. Addison caught him, shoved him back into the car and carefully closed the door. He had to stifle his laughter as the thrill of the kill enveloped him.

Now for the other one.

His dispatch of the second officer occurred with not quite the same ease. As the policeman came around the corner of the building on the other side, after checking out everything behind it, James Addison was waiting for him. He jumped out in front of him with knife raised and aimed for his throat. The officer reacted with alarming speed, knocking aside James' arm, causing him to drop the knife. He had time to yank his pistol from its holster, but James Addison had recovered from his surprise and knew he was fighting for his life. He grabbed the hand holding the gun and twisted it up. Years of conditioning made him unusually strong in all parts of his body. He swiftly brought down the arm holding the gun and smashed it against his bent knee while his fingers frantically searched for the policeman's wrist nerve. Just as he smashed the gun hand into his knee, his fingers found the nerve and the officer's hand dropped the gun. Addison kicked it away, reached down and scooped up his knife. In one fluid movement he slit his opponent's throat. He choked back his laughter.

Glad I didn't have to shoot him with his own gun. That'd be way too noisy.

Blood soaked the policeman's jacket and pooled in the snow beneath him where he'd fallen in a heap. His killer bent over the body and secured both arms, crossing them on the blood-soaked jacket. He lifted the man in his arms and dropped his body behind the hedge that bordered the building.

Dammit! What am I going to do about this blood? If I leave it here, someone is sure to find the body right away. Some asshole with his dog out for a shit will find it and call in an alarm before I get to that Forrest bitch.

James' eyes searched the parking lot and didn't see a soul. Even though it was Saturday, it seemed no one else was out this late on such a cold winter night. He wiped the knife on his trousers and put it inside his jacket. Being careful not to impale himself on the knife, he began scooping handfuls of the reddened snow and throwing it behind the hedge. When he'd scooped until there was no more bloodied snow, he filled in the indentation in the surface with fresher snow he found under the edges of the hedge. It would have to do.

Following his plan, James melted into the shadows at the corner and waited to give Heather time to be fast asleep. As close to the brick wall as he could get, he leaned against it for an additional twenty minutes. It seemed like hours.

Eager, but telling himself to take his time, the killer crept to the left front window. He took from his deep pocket a Silberschnitt Pro ten-inch-diameter circle glass cutter. He'd paid almost a hundred dollars for it. Its companion, the Lexan handled ten-inch vacuum-lifting circle cost much the same. *Definitely worth it. Here goes.*

The window screen was no problem at all. He pulled from his pocket a ten-inch screw driver and inserted the tip along the side of the screen's frame. He pried the frame away from the window's side in three places. With the last pry, he stuck the screwdriver in about five or six inches and flipped out the screen. *First hurdle conquered.*

It was a double hung window sash with thermal pane glass. The bottom window was locked at the top so it couldn't be raised.

He applied the vacuum lifter to the pane and used the glass cutter to make a perfectly round hole. The vacuum lifter quietly removed the first pane of glass. He repeated his actions with the second thermal pane, gaining access to the lock. Reaching through, he flipped it. *Yes!*

Inside the darkened house, Aksel had slid down in his straight-backed kitchen chair and his chin rested on his chest. He tried hard to stay awake but kept catching himself nodding off and coming to with a jerk. However, his detective senses were still intact, and he awakened completely when the soft grating sounds began at the window.

Jack Forrest lay on his side facing away from the window. Against odds, he'd fallen asleep within minutes of crawling under the covers. Anja dozed fitfully in the makeshift bed made of the two stuffed chairs pushed together. Aksel stood up, causing his chair to slide back with a scraping sound. He froze, listening hard. Nobody inside moved and the small noises continued at the window. *God, it sounded like a cannon to me.* Cautiously, he tapped Anja on the shoulder. Her reaction was expected. She jumped as she woke and focused her eyes on her partner. He placed his finger to his pursed lips.

Anja mouthed, "What?"

Aksel could barely read her lips in the gloom, but he pointed to the window where small sounds still emitted. Aksel pulled out his gun and nodded to Anja's, which lay on her stomach within easy reach. Motioning with his gun toward the stairs, Anja got the message. She pushed away the chair in front of her so she could get up. On the carpet, it made no noise. She ran to the stairs and took two at a time. At the top, she stopped, turned and braced against the wall with her gun trained on the window.

James Addison fought the heavy drapes out of his way and stepped through them into Heather Forrest's living room. Directly in front of him stood a big man with a gun pointed straight at him. Aksel's .40 caliber Glock 22 looked as big as a canon as James stared down its barrel.

Tearing his eyes from the gun, they swept to his right. *Someone lying in a bed.* He followed his instincts and threw himself sideways, landing in the bed by the sleeping man. In one move, he thrust his arm under the person's neck and jerked the head to him. With his left hand, he pulled his own Glock from his left pocket. He pointed it at his captive's head.

"What the . . .?" Jack Forrest managed before Addison cut off his speech by tightening his hold on his neck. Jack began to struggle. He grabbed his attacker's arm and tried to pry it away from his throat.

Calmly Addison told him, "Be still. And be quiet. Not one word or I'll kill you now."

Jack must have believed that too calm voice and went limp in surrender.

Addison didn't once take his eyes off Aksel's, gauging what he would do.

Aksel's eyes drilled into the killer's in return, as if assessing his options.

At the top of the stairs, Anja listened for sounds coming from Heather's bedroom. There were none. Perhaps they

had not awakened. She sighted her Glock on the shoulder and arm wrapped around Jack Forrest's neck. If she took the shot, she might hit Mr. Forrest in the neck or head and kill him instantly. His body was in front of the killer, thus she couldn't chance a shot to the body. It had to be either his head or the arm. That's all she could see. She squinted her eyes, hoping for a better view. It didn't happen.
She had to do something and do it now. Not only Jack Forrest's life, but Aksel's life depended on it, too.

Downstairs, the hairs on the back of Aksel's neck raised. Thoughts flew like wildfire through his head. He could shoot Addison. But if he should kill him, he'd not get the proof he needed to close the Patti Mueller case.

Come on, Anja. Do it. Shoot him in the shoulder, not the head. Shoot the son-of-a-bitch!

She did. Taking the most careful aim she had ever done in her life, she aimed the Glock at Addison's shoulder and squeezed the trigger.

Addison flew back against the back of the sofa, his shoulder shattered, causing his arm to fly up and away from Jack's neck. The Glock fell from his hand.

"Dammit, you shot me," he screamed, as he tried to scramble off the bed to get his gun.

"Stop right there," Aksel ordered. He pointed his gun at Addison's head and bellowed, "Anja!"

"I'm here, Aksel." She had her Glock in her right hand and handcuffs dangled from her left. She glanced for a micro-second to where Jack Forrest half stood and half slumped against the bed, his face pasty white.

Heather and Ann stood at the top of the stairs wild-eyed and trembling.

Anja calmly said, "Heather, call 911. I think your father is having a heart attack."

Ann gasped and started down the stairs.

Aksel moved in closer. He held his gun mere inches from Addison's head as Anja pulled the killer's injured and bleeding arm behind his back and snapped the handcuff on it. She grabbed his good arm with its hand clenched in obvious rage and pain and clicked the cuff in place.

Heather rushed down the stairs, almost beating Ann to Jack. "The ambulance is on its way, Dad. Hang in there."

Ann helped Heather ease Jack back onto the sofa bed. "You're going to be okay, Jack. You've got to be. We've all had enough for one day."

Aksel put his hand through Addison's elbow on his injured arm and dragged him to a kitchen chair. "Sit down, damn you. You're under arrest." He turned to Anja. "Do you want to Mirandize him, or shall I?"

"Oh, you go right ahead, Detective Franzen. I'm just going to delight in hearing those words applied to him."

With his gun still pointed at the killer's head, Aksel began, "You have the right to remain silent. Anything you say can . . ."

The door banged open and the paramedic team attempted to enter the small living area which seemed to be filled with people.

"Stop there," Anja yelled.

Aksel had not even paused in conveying the Miranda rights. He continued to the end and then said, "Come on in. The patient's over there." He nodded toward Jack, who now sat on the side of the sofa-bed.

The paramedics looked at the guy in handcuffs with the bleeding shoulder and then moved to the older man who was pale and lethargic. They took Jack's blood pressure and assessed him.

"I don't think he's in imminent danger, but we're going to take him to the hospital and let them check him out." They loaded him onto the stretcher and into the ambulance.

"Ann, I'll be all right. Please don't worry. Stay here with Heather. She needs you more than I do right now. Besides, neither of you can go because you're both running around in just your nightgowns. So stay. Now get out of this ambulance. I'll call you to come get me tomorrow."

Ann leaned down and kissed him. "Come back to me," she whispered. "I love you."

With that, the paramedics helped the two ladies out of the ambulance and drove away with red light flashing atop the ambulance. But no siren. That had to be a good sign.

"Okay, ladies. Go back to bed and try to rest, even if you don't sleep," Aksel advised. We're taking this man in for booking."

"The first thing I want to do is call Mr. Hoffmann and tell them we've got Jeff's killer," Heather said. She put her arms around Anja and hugged her. "Thank you for sticking with me through all this. I know I was a pain at times."

She moved to Aksel and reached up to hug him. It reminded her of hugging Jeff because he was as tall. Only Jeff wasn't as thickly muscular. Oh, Jeff... The pain came in a huge, rolling wave. She bit back the words that flooded her, begging her to say them to Jeff's murderer.

At that moment the murderer spoke up, "When are you idiots taking *me* to the hospital? Somebody has to see about my arm where you shot me, you ignorant bitch."

Aksel grinned, a feral lifting of his lips. "You'll get there some time before daylight. Maybe. But first, we're going to book your ass for two counts of first-degree murder."

"Only two? Think again, smart guy. You might be surprised what you find outside." He broke into a fit of high, crazed giggles.

Aksel yanked him out of the chair and dragged him, stumbling, to the SUV. He opened the door and thrust him inside. He turned to Anja. "Call the station, and if the captain is gone, call him at home. We need a search team to check out this slimeball's brag that there are more bodies."

Then it hit him. *Where are the patrolmen*? He broke into a run on the way to the police cruiser. He opened the door and the young officer tumbled out.

"Good God, he *is* dead! Anja, go ahead and make that call. We need that search team out here right now."

She made the call and came to stand by Aksel.

He said, "It's almost over, Anja," and put his arm around her shoulder, drawing her close to his side. "We sure gave it our all."

Addison yelled and flailed around in the back seat. "Come on, you morons. I need to see a doctor. Get in here. Pay attention to me. Right now, you useless shit bags."

They tuned him out.

"I don't care if the bastard bleeds to death," Aksel admitted.

"Unfortunately, that isn't likely to happen." Anja ruefully shook her head.

Anja stood close and looked up into Aksel's face. The moonlight gleamed in her eyes. Soon it was blocked by Aksel's head as he brought his lips to hers for a long kiss.

Aksel lifted his head and then leaned his forehead against hers. "You are going with me in the morning to tell the Muellers we got the bastard, right?"

"Yes. I wouldn't miss it. Just to see Freddie's face when we tell them will make my day."

"After we book this piece of slime, do you want to go to your house or mine?"

Anja smiled up into his face. "Mine."

Chapter Twenty-Seven

February 17, 2015

Heather arrived early at the high school and found the entrance was already unlocked for the day. Dust motes danced in the weak sunlight dribbling through the tall windows on both sides of the large doors. Relieved to know at least the janitorial staff was there and she wasn't alone in the sprawling building, she shuddered as her memory darted back to similar doors she'd dashed through a month ago when running for her life. This was the first time since that horrible night that she had been back. Pulling her camel hair coat tightly together, she set off down the halls to her classroom.

Her low wedge heels struck the floor, clicking like a tap dancer, as she passed one familiar room after another. Pausing at the door to the science lab, she peeked through the frosted glass, recognizing nothing of the blurred images inside. Marveling at having never noticed that this classroom alone had an opaque window in its door, she felt a chill travel across her shoulders and raise the fine hairs on the back of her neck. *More secrets*. Heaving a sigh, she again gathered her coat tightly around her and continued toward her classroom.

It was her first day back since Friday, January sixteen. She had taken an emergency leave of absence after the happenings of January seventeen, the horrific day that Jeff was murdered, and but for the bravery of detectives Aksel Franzen and Anja Frandsen, she, too, would've been killed. Most likely her parents, as well. "Thank God," she thought. Gratitude and relief fought with fear and anger to win that small spot in the corner of her heart located by the larger chamber reserved for Jeff.

Tap, tap, tap. As her steps rang out in the empty hallway, she thought of Jeff's funeral where it seemed most of Green Bay turned out to celebrate his too short life. His funeral service was held at King of Kings Lutheran Church, as Patti's was. The same pastor performed both services. Afterward, Heather had several counseling appointments at home in Gainesville with Pastor Robert where she confronted her anger and grief with questions and tears. The pastor was calm and reassuring and Heather released some of the guilt that lay heavy as a boulder upon her shoulders.

She had accompanied Jeff's parents to make all the funeral arrangements. She thought John must have worked hard to bring Eva around. John told her when he shared with Eva the things Jeff had told him about his love for Heather, Eva found it in her heart to forgive her.

Thinking back, she was glad she'd taken the month off from teaching after everyone assured her she should. It was a month when she'd assessed and reassessed her life and what she would do now and, perhaps, in the future. Her parents wanted her to leave this frozen land and return with them to the warmth of Florida indefinitely. It was tempting. She had many friends back home. She could easily get a job in Gainesville or one of the small surrounding towns. She'd done her internship at the small high school in Bronson and had so loved the little town and its people. If there was an opening, she'd certainly be hired there. Perhaps the biggest plus was she'd have the constant love and support of her parents.

She said out loud, "I'm not a quitter. I went after that vile bastard to expose him as Patti's killer. And to keep him from killing someone else. And I failed with Jeff's death." Her nose prickled and she swallowed hard and blinked her eyes to keep the tears from forming. "But I won't let this crazy case make me afraid to help someone if I can." Her words echoed in the empty corridor.

Deep in thought, she turned the corner into the same hallway she'd fled down the last time she was in this building. The night the three teen boys chased her, found her cowering in fear, and then beat her. *If I don't continue to do what I can, that maniac will still be the winner* played in her brain as if a recording was implanted there.

She passed Lela Magnussen's classroom, and then reaching hers, hesitated at the door. A deep sigh accompanied her inside. Her nose immediately picked up the scent of chalk. She smiled. *Nothing says "classroom" quite like the smell of chalk dust.* Looking from the rows of desks to the top of her own, she found the young substitute teacher had left the room neat for her. She'd also left her a note. Heather picked up the note written on personal note paper lying in the middle of the table. Written in large looping letters, it read:

> Dear Miss Forrest,
> It's been a pleasure teaching your students while you were away. They couldn't say enough great things about you. I hope you will find they are just like you left them.

I have to tell you that you are an inspiration for me, both by your teaching and your values. I don't know that I could have been as strong or as tenacious as you or show the courage that you demonstrated in getting the murderer arrested.

I'm so very sorry about the loss of Mr. Hoffmann, which is perhaps the saddest story I've ever heard. You are incredibly brave. You're my hero and I am so glad you are returning. I think you'll like the new principal. She seems to be a no-nonsense administrator, but also seems to have a fun side with a great personality. From what I hear about you, the two of you will make a fantastic team.

Sincerely,
Mary-Beth Allen

Heather put the note in her desk. *Oh, how I wish I could share this with Jeff.* She dabbed at an escaping tear with a Kleenex from the box Mary-Beth left on her desk.

She's going to be a good teacher. Even though they are my kids, and I have to admit to being jealous that they had another teacher, I'm glad things went well for her.

She heard the talk and laughter of kids in the hall and knew her first period students would be coming in at any moment. They'd be full of questions and she was prepared to answer every one of them as honestly as she could at this point.

The students streamed through the door. Amid cries of "Miss Forrest, you're back!" and "We missed you!" came the questions she'd waited for, including "Are you going to stay here?"

"Good morning, class," she said. "Do take your seats and I'll answer your questions."

Calling on one student after another, she answered them honestly, deferring the answer to whether or not she was remaining until after the last question was answered.

"Now, let's talk about my plans," she said, as lightly as she could.

"I'm not leaving again before the end of this school year." Heather paused and looked around the room at the open, expectant faces of her students. "However, I'm considering not returning to teaching next year."

A cacophony of sound erupted as the students all talked at once, directing their comments to their teacher and to each other.

"What are you going to do then?" was the most often asked and the one that came to her the clearest. She visibly tensed, even though she'd known she would have to answer the question.

She cleared her throat, buying time. Hesitantly, she began. "I've thought of a lot of things I could do and a lot of places I could move to." Pausing, she looked into the eyes of her students. She'd come to care about them in the four months they had been in her class.

"I've wrestled with a lot of issues," Heather confided. "My roots are in Florida, but I've kind of gotten used to Green Bay's winters. You know, we never have a real winter in Florida." She smiled and the class, embracing her lessening of tension, laughed. "So, I've been thinking of going back to school and taking some criminal justice classes." She paused while the students gave her their full attention.

She resumed. "I'm considering becoming a private investigator right here in Green Bay."

This prompted more questions fired at her from all around the room.

In the second row, where Heather had moved him from the back of the room for his lack of class participation, Conner hesitantly began to raise his hand. He looked around at his classmates and found he was met with only quizzical looks, so he shot his hand high and waited to be called on.

Heather set her eyes on a number of the chattering students, giving them her raised eyebrow warning before taking the question.

As the noise abated, she asked, “Yes, Conner?”

“What are *we* going to do now, Miss Forrest?”

Heather smiled, pleased with both Conner and the question. She was happy to move on to talking about Senior English and class work, quite relieved to talk of something other than her.

“We’ll look at writing short stories and introducing current events into them.”

“Can we write about your story, you know, what you’ve been through?”

Heather took a moment as all the students watched her. She gazed at the wall in the back of the room, looking over her students’ heads, gathering her thoughts. When she was ready, she answered Conner.

“Yes. That would be a good example of a current event.”

THE END

About Lyla F. Ellzey

LYLA FAIRCLOTH ELLZEY is in love with the world around her. Her hobbies are legend, but she especially enjoys taking nature photos, particularly of varieties of mushrooms and colorful blooms. Her mountain of scrapbooks continues to grow as new photos are added. Adventurous, she and her husband travel extensively and have visited five of the seven continents. She is a prolific writer and a month spent in England recently doing research on her ancestors will produce an historical fiction novel.

A member of the Tallahassee Writers Association for a dozen years, she has served on their board, and as chair of committees, and has co-chaired two annual conferences. She has self-published three books, *Loosing the Lightning,* fiction about innocence lost, betrayal and redemption, *She is Woman,* a short-story book about 24 very different women, and *Peregrination,* a slim volume of poetry about journeys both of distance and of the heart.

A Florida native, Lyla is a graduate of USF in Tampa with a double major in English-Speech and she has a Master's Degree in English Education from UF in Gainesville. This education has greatly aided her in her career.

Now retired, she returned to Florida and lives with her husband, Frank, in Westminster Oaks retirement village where she participates in acting, card playing, and volunteer opportunities.

Anticipation of Evil will soon be followed by a novel about DID, better known as Multiple Personalities. Titled *Losing Herself,* it is Susie's story. As a young teen, she is made responsible for her older sister Emma and must confront several different alters living within her much-loved sister and best friend, literally losing herself in the process. Watch for it from DocUmeant Publishing.

Now that you've enjoyed *Anticipation of Evil,* you'll want to stay in touch with Lyla to be among the first to learn about new releases and events where you can visit with her in person.

Visit her website at https://www.lylafairclothellzey.com/ and join her on your favorite social media platform.

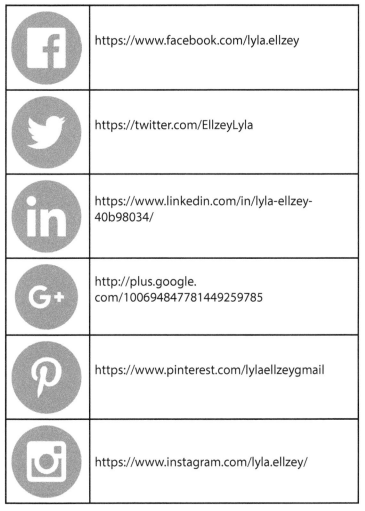

	https://www.facebook.com/lyla.ellzey
	https://twitter.com/EllzeyLyla
	https://www.linkedin.com/in/lyla-ellzey-40b98034/
	http://plus.google.com/100694847781449259785
	https://www.pinterest.com/lylaellzeygmail
	https://www.instagram.com/lyla.ellzey/

Don't forget to leave your review on your favorite bookstore's page.

Other Works by Lyla Faircloth Ellzey

Lyla writes in several genres. In addition to this book, *Anticipation of Evil,* a second book is debuting at approximately the same time. *Losing Herself* is a tale of two sisters, both of whom are intensely affected by the older teen's Dissociative Identity Disorder, known as Multiple Personalities. The younger sister loses herself along the way as she must constantly watch for instances where her beloved sister and best friend becomes someone else. Then she must execute damage control over whatever the alternative part in Emma's body has done.

Loosing the Lightning is a fiction novel whose beginnings are set in the south of the 1940s. Imagine innocence lost. Think of the horror of sexual abuse of a five-year-old child. In this book the reader meets Lily, who frequently endures this abuse until she gains the courage and strength to confront her abuser. She protects her beloved mama with her silence and carries her shameful secret throughout her life. The abuse dictates her choices and she is fearful of a relationship, but when she marries the man of her dreams, he is revealed to be a spousal sexual abuser. Betrayed by him many times, the last is the most devastating of all and Lily is left to survive on her own. Eventually, she meets a man who changes everything. Will Lily finally find the elusive happiness that has evaded her since she was a loved and carefree child of five?

ISBN: 978-1481260114 | $17.50 (includes shipping and handling)

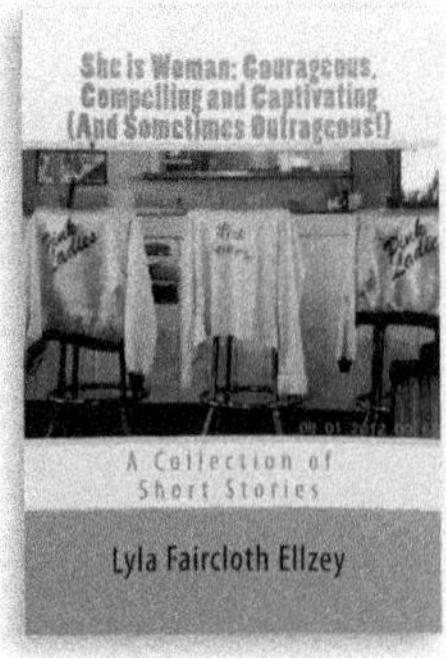

She is Woman: Courageous, Compelling, and Captivating (And sometimes Outrageous!) is a book of 24 short stories about 24 very different women. The reader will laugh, cry, sympathize, empathize, and go through a whole range of emotions as these stories unfold. Imagine Ginger's horror as she watches snow build up on the white sugar sand outside her beachfront home on Florida's Gulf Coast. Think of Irene's fear after her lover shoots and kills her husband. Laugh with, and at, Polly as she pouts about Valentine's Day flowers. Plan with Annette the next adventure for the Pink Ladies. Travel these and the other roads with the ladies of this novel . . . but be prepared for a, sometimes, bumpy ride.

ISBN: 9781481908740 | $16.50 (includes shipping and handling)

Peregrination: The Poetry of Journeying is a slim volume of poetry about both actual travel journeys and the journeys of the heart. Walk with Lyla as she views some of the most magnificent sites and sights our world offers—from the Great Wall of China to the Great Pyramids of Giza in Egypt to the Greek mountain where the Oracle of Delphi spoke to the cave on Patmos where John, in exile, wrote the book of Revelations—and other places. Then join Lyla as she embraces the poetry of love gained, love lost, and true love that endures.

ISBN: 978-1492967361 | $10.50 (includes shipping and handling)

All titles available at https://www.lylafairclothellzey.com

CPSIA information can be obtained
at www.ICGtesting.com
Printed in the USA
FFHW021800030419
51400557-56879FF

9 781950 075003